Our Road to Trust

INTERLOCKING SHORT STORIES OF FAITH

MARY GRACE VAN DER KROEF

Our Road to Trust

INTERLOCKING SHORT STORIES OF FAITH

Cover Design: Mary Grace van der Kroef

Edited by: H.A. Pruitt

Proofread by: Joan Alley (Manna Media Services)

Paperback ISBN: 978-1-7777211-5-2

Ebook ISBN: 978-1-7777211-4-5

Hardcover ISBN: 978-1-7777211-6-9

First Edition

Books by Mary

Fiction:

Our Road to Trust: Interlocking Stories of Faith

How We Love Them: A Hope is Here Novel *(forthcoming)*

Poetry:

The Branch That I Am

Words of Weight

Branches in Bloom

You can find all of Mary's books at www.marygracewriting.ca

Contents

Epigraph — XI

1. Abigail's Prayers: One — 1

2. Words That Pierce — 2

    One

    Two

    Three

    Four

3. The Letter — 30

    One

    Two

    Three

    Four

4. Abigail's Prayers: Two — 65

5. Power Off — 66

One

Two

Three

Four

6. Apology   102

One

Two

Three

Four

7. Broken China   127

One

Two

Three

Four

8. Abigails Prayers: Three   158

9. Just Forget It   159

One

Two

Three

Four

10. The Pill Cabinet   180

One

Two

Three

          Four

11. Abigail's Prayers: Four   209

12. Her Choice   210

     One

     Two

     Three

     Four

     Five

13. Abigail's Prayers: Five   254

14. Scary Things   255

     One

     Two

     Three

     Four

15. Prayers and Pencil Crayons   289

     One

     Two

     Three

     Four

     Five

Time Line   338

About the Author   341

Thank you   343

"Bear one another's burdens,
and so fulfill the law of Christ."
- Galatians 6:2 ESV -

Abigail's Prayers: One

Dear Heavenly Father,

I feel adrift.

I feel a lack of connection.

I feel lonely.

I look into the eyes of my sisters all around me, and I see it there as well.

What has happened?

This loneliness in the midst of a crowd, the gathering of your children. It's not right.

Have I done something wrong?

Can I fix it?

I am just a little woman.

Please show me how to connect with them again.

Amen

Words That Pierce

Mary

One

THE KNIFE STABBED. IT found its mark and slid in between my generous rolls of flesh. This blade had no tangible form, but it cut deep.

"If you really tried, really put your mind to it, I know you could lose weight," Tina said to me.

Her gentle pat on my arm told me she thought her honesty was the cure I needed. She didn't know the damage it left. There was no hint of the life force that now flowed out of me and spattered all over the ground under my chair.

I grasped my mug until the fingers curled around it were white and smiled a little brighter.

"We could all improve ourselves if we tried harder, couldn't we?" I twisted the invisible blade a bit more myself. It hurt, but the deflection worked.

"How is Paul doing?" she asked, her attention now directed towards Debora's eager face across the table. The question was met with exuberant chitchat.

I drank the dregs of my lukewarm coffee and held a smile while glancing at the wall clock that hung above the church's coffee room entrance. Ten more minutes. Not long. But my life force was seeping out onto the ground, and I didn't know if I would make it.

"Excuse me, ladies. Coffee goes right through me."

They all chuckled as I grabbed my bag from under the table.

"See you next week?" Tina asked as she tucked a stray strand of dark glossy black hair behind an ear and pivoted sharp shoulders towards me.

I slid my Bible into my open bag and waved nonchalantly. "God willing!"

I said this goodbye as I used my large hip to shove the chair back under the table. If I hurried, I'd make it.

I passed through the hall doors and into the carpeted foyer and thanked God there was no line at the women's bathroom. Once in the ladies' room, I chose the small corner stall even though I had to lean over the toilet to shut the door behind me. I locked it, then closed the toilet lid, and sank onto the porcelain throne. The tears poured, and I kicked my bag, spilling its contents across the ground while holding my guts with my hands. The invisible waves of shame wouldn't stop as I leaned forward until my forehead touched the cold metal stall door.

I knew the bathroom would soon become a popular place. Mix a group of women (many who are mothers) with a large pot of coffee, and it's inevitable. I didn't have long to bind up my bleeding soul.

I closed my eyes, my belly still trembling.

She didn't mean to hurt you.

She doesn't understand what being big is like.

She meant it as encouragement.

You're being overly sensitive.

She doesn't know your health issues.

People have said a lot worse. Suck it up. Get over it.

I said all these things to myself in a split second.

If she knew she hurt you so badly, she'd be sorry.

Really, was that true? If it was, then I should tell her. But I could never do that. She didn't deserve it. I didn't trust her. I didn't trust any of them. They might be my family, my sisters in Christ, but, no, I didn't trust them. Why was that?

The squeak of the door sounded, and I sucked in my breath. I wasn't ready. But that didn't matter because they were here.

"Gloria's sure growing fast!"

It was a shrill voice, and it sliced through my thoughts.

"Isn't she! I feel like I just switched out her clothes for larger sizes. But this morning the first shirt I pulled from the dresser wouldn't go over her head."

"Time to drag out the hand-me-downs."

I didn't care who it was. My head was now aching from crying. I couldn't come out yet.

The door squeaked as again it swung open. I knew a lineup for the stalls would soon form, and I needed to hurry, so I wiped my eyes with my sleeve. The tears left dark splotches on the light green fabric.

Just breathe. Stop crying. My next few gulps stopped the flow from my eyes but not my invisible wounds. *God, I need to get out of here. I need to grab James and go home. I just want to go home.*

"Mary, is this your bag all over the floor?" The voice was new and gentle knuckles tapped on my stall. "Are you okay?"

"Ya ... yes! I kicked it by accident. I'm fine." Could they hear the strain in my words? Did they know I was lying? "I was in a hurry."

I heard shoes shuffling around on the floor. *Deep breath. Smile.*

Removing myself from the stall was awkward. I barely fit.

"Oh, don't do that, Beth. It's my mess, I'll get it." The small elderly woman just smiled at me as she handed over a toy car, my pack of tissues, and a tube of lip aid.

As I stooped down to retrieve my bag from the floor, she smiled.

"It's not a problem, dear. We all have moments when 'we need to hurry.'" Her eyes twinkled as she laughed. "I have to 'hurry' a lot more these days. Thank God for my 'extra protection.'"

The laugh we both shared as she patted her hips and the "extra protection" she wore was good for my soul. My tears of humour hid the evidence of my tears of pain.

"Thank you, Beth."

Thank you, Lord, for unashamed grandmas.

Beth's hand on my arm grounded me. Her eyes were sincere and free of judgment.

"See you next week, Mary."

Did she know? Had she somehow sensed my lies? Did it matter if she had? The next moment I was out the door, my steps a bit more sure, my invisible wound starting to scab.

As I entered the nursery, James opened his arms and yelled, "Mommy!" His big brown eyes were a haven despite his smelling of cheerios and slightly wet diaper. I scooped him up and cradled him for a moment.

"He was so good today." Hillary, a nursery volunteer said while grinning at James like a proud grandma. I thanked her and, after determining James' diaper was just wet and not 'dirty,' carried him over to the changing table in the next room.

"Mommy, I hungry."

"I have a snack for you in the car, baby."

"Want to stay here."

Tired eyes and red cheeks told me he was past ready for a nap. He didn't protest as we exchanged his wet diaper for dry.

"What do you think Daddy is doing at home, James?"

"Want stay, Mama."

"We can't stay, James. It's time to go home. All done! Now, we need to get our boots on and our coats."

"No coat. Want to stay here."

With the blink of an eye, whining turned into war.

"Want to stay!" he screamed as I carried him from the nursery. Tears to match mine from moments ago slipped down the toddler cheeks, leaving red, splotchy streaks. The foyer was swamped with other mothers zipping up coats on their own small ones, grandmas chatting in corners, and friends calling goodbyes.

The battle of getting a winter coat on my toddler left me huffing. I grabbed his comfort blanket from the diaper bag.

"Look, James."

He grabbed for the bundle of blue and yellow fabric.

"Sucky?"

He was lying on the ground with his feet on my knees, ready for boots. Again, I rummaged inside the diaper bag.

"Mama! Sucky!"

My child's desperate, needy pleas grated on my nerves. I was doing the best I could, but for him, it wasn't good enough.

Tears rolled fresh wet tracks down my cheeks as I clutched the sought-after bit of blue plastic.

"Mama!"

Now he was desperately tired-angry, and his limbs flailed as I struggled to give him the comfort object.

"James, stop it!"

It was too late. My hand smarted from his assault, and the sucky flew. My belly shook again. But I held in the frustration and defeat I felt.

God, this is ridiculous.

As I prayed the words, I knew I was whining just like James. My head repeated lessons often repeated to me by my mother. *"There is never anything too small for God." "Cast your cares on Him, for He cares for you."* Her words were snippets of scripture planted deep into my psyche that sprouted and waved their reminder-filled blossoms under my nose when most needed. But their bouquet also nagged like thistles ringing the edges of a flower bed. Reminders I still had a lot of work to do in my mind and heart.

"Here, James!" a little girl named Gloria said as she shuffled close and popped his sucky back into his mouth. Again I was blessed by a child. Her baby chub may have only recently disappeared, but her mommy vibe was strong.

"Thank you, Gloria."

I ignored the fact she'd plucked his sucky right from the floor and placed it back into his wailing mouth without a cleaning. She patted his head and smiled a toothy grin at me.

"Welcome!"

Sliding James' feet into his snow boots became much easier with his friend peering down at him.

"Did you have fun in nursery today, Gloria?" I asked.

"Oh, yes! James, don't be sad."

He stared back at her, his tired eyes doing a dance that promised encroaching sleep.

"Come on, little man. Time to go." We waved at Gloria as I shuffled towards the door.

James was heavy, and I felt the strain as I balanced his diaper bag and my own belongings along both arms. A flurry of others whirled around me as I set down the bags and opened the car door, and I felt alone as I strapped James into his seat. Was I imagining the goodbyes flying over my head? Was I missing the ones meant for me? Or was my heart right, and there weren't any sent my way? I told myself it was alright and it didn't matter.

Your mood is a raw red. Don't look for connection when all you want is to get home. You won't find any because you don't really want to see it.

The truth hurt, but I was good at reminding myself even when its spines poked like cactus needles. I adjusted the car steering wheel and started the engine.

Seat belt!

I rolled my eyes at my distracted forgetfulness and pulled the strap across my body. It didn't reach the fastener.

She's right. You are even too fat to sit in a car.

I fed the belt back into the retractor then pulled it all the way out again, holding it tight so I didn't lose any length while fighting with the buckle and flesh at my hip. As I heard the connection click, the muscles in my chest and shoulders unkinked in a wave of relief, laced with humiliation. Time to ask Jeff to install that extension for me.

Two

"How are the roads?" Jeff asked as I cracked open the front door. The nature of a Canadian winter made this question a regular greeting, and the sound of his voice soothed my wounded heart.

"The highway's fine, but the intersections in town are nasty. They still haven't sanded them," I answered as I walked into the living room to lay my sleeping human bundle down on the couch and pull off his boots.

"How was the Bible study?"

"It was good," I muttered, half hoping he wouldn't push for more information. The clink of a spoon against the metal inside of a travel mug announced his presence in the living room entrance.

"What happened?"

"Nothing," I replied.

"Yeah, that's a lie, Mary. I can tell by your tone."

"It's nothing important."

I turned away and headed back outside. Was he watching me as I waddled down the path between the snowdrifts? The sun shone brightly, turning the snow into shades of blinding white and yellow.

I collected my bags but hesitated after hearing the satisfying *honk* from the car, telling me the doors had locked successfully. I could hear Jeff stirring his coffee again from the front door.

"What happened?" His tone was quiet, and I knew he wouldn't let this go.

I took a deep breath and glanced past him to the mess of bags and cast-off snow clothing strewn around the entrance.

"You have a fat wife, and she's been reminded again that it's her own fault but in the nicest way possible."

Jeff grimaced while sipping his coffee. We both knew he didn't have time to start an argument. His overnight bag was already packed and lying beside the entryway closet, ready for his next shift manning the freight trains that left from the local station.

"I have a wife that fits my arms just to my liking, thank you. Was it Tina?"

"Yes."

He sipped at his coffee again while his deep brown eyes looked out over the rim of his cup. "You need to talk to her. You come home from Wednesday morning Bible study upset about something she's said at least once a month." He stepped aside to let me back in the house.

"How about we just not go back?"

He looked at the ceiling and laughed, his eyes dancing when he pulled his gaze back down to me.

"I bet no one would even notice we aren't there," I added.

"That's another lie, and you know it. Beth would be over here knocking at our door in two weeks if we stopped going. I bet she would even bring cookies. Hum, cookies ..."

He sat down and, after taking one more sip of his coffee, peeled James out of his coat.

"Wake up, little buddy. Daddy has to leave soon."

He was right, someone would notice. Even so, the thought lingered at the back of my mind. Would they care? Then again, did I really want them to? My gut was still sore, and I rubbed at the invisible wound.

"Are you going to want more coffee?"

"Nope. This is my second cup."

I wandered into the kitchen. Jeff had left a mess of crumbs on the counter. But his lunch cooler was all ready to go along with his water jug. It would take only a minute to wipe away the remnants of his meal prep. He never expected me to make lunches for him, and when I did, he always left a fresh kiss on my cheek as a tip.

I shrugged at the crumbs and left them for later, choosing instead to pour the rest of the coffee into my favourite oversized mug. Its deep blue, smooth porcelain always felt good against my skin, the weight satisfying.

"What time are you leaving?" I called down the hall.

"In twenty minutes. You should eat lunch while I wake James up."

"I'm not hungry."

"Mary ..."

"No, really. I'm just not hungry. Beth brought cookies this morning."

"And you didn't bring me one?"

"Ha! No, I enjoyed two all by myself."

A smile spread across Jeff's face as I walked back into the living room.

"Maybe we should stop going to church, just for those two weeks, so I can get my own cookies from Beth."

Now it was my turn to look at the ceiling, faking exasperation while I laughed. "I love you."

"I love you too, and don't forget it."

It was a joy to watch my boys. James giggled as he bounced on his dad's knee, and then once fully awake, he dug through the toy box to show us all his treasures for the umpteenth time.

Too soon it was time for Jeff to leave, and James followed him as he picked up his cooler, water, and last, his overnight bag.

"This week it's supposed to be a short run, and I'll be home Friday or Saturday night, James. You take care of Mommy while I'm gone, okay?"

"Okay." James' voice warbled as goodbye tears slid down his round baby cheeks.

Jeff slid his free arm around me as I leaned in for a kiss.

"I miss you already," I whispered.

"I miss all of you."

He smelled like the coffee he'd been sipping as I curled my fingers into his shirt.

"You're beautiful," he added, lips pressing against my forehead.

"You are too."

We ignored James' squeals for attention as I sank into his kiss and absorbed his true scent, hidden under the coffee fumes.

"Stay safe."

Goodbye kisses never lasted long enough, and I blinked away tears after picking James up. We waved as the winter cold slipped into the house. But we both ignored it. James laid his head on my shoulder.

"Want Daddy."

"I know. But he has to go drive the big train today. Shall we make cookies for him before he comes home?"

"Yes! Cookies. Chocolate cookies. Now, Mommy?"

"How about we make them tomorrow? What should we make Harmony and Joshua for supper?"

James rattled through all the things he wanted to cook while I watched his father drive the car down the street. I couldn't help a last wave as he turned the corner and disappeared. The desperate longing to go with him squeezed my heart while I squeezed James. The life of a cargo train engineer's wife was often lonely. But I couldn't deny how blessed I really was.

I filled the next few hours with meal prep and toy tossing. I should have sat down and eaten lunch, but crumbs and vegetable bits sustained me as school sandwiches for tomorrow morning were made and wrapped. We chose chicken noodle soup for supper, and James stirred water in a plastic bowl while I chopped vegetables and added powdered stock to the pot on the stove.

I skirted the chair he was using as his kitchen, his need to be in the centre of the room greater than my need for direct access to the stove and pantry. After turning down the element to ensure a slow simmer, it was time to grab the other kids from the bus stop.

"I want Marvin!" James insisted as I wrapped his coat around him, sliding his arms into its sleeves and gently tilting his chin up so the zipper wouldn't nip his nose.

"You might lose him if you bring him outside, James."

"Please?"

"Alright, but keep him in your pocket while we walk, okay?"

As I wedged his hat onto his little head that didn't seem so little anymore, I made a note we needed a new one for him.

"Did you find him?" I asked as he searched the ground for his favourite toy truck.

"Yes!" He beamed up at me as I slid on my coat. This was always an awkward dance, as I had to lift the bulk of the fabric above my gut to get the bottom to zipper then pull it down like a shirt around my middle.

I checked the wall clock before squatting down to help James with his boots.

"We need to hurry, James. Five minutes before the bus comes. Did you put Marvin in your pocket?"

My heart skipped a beat as I heard a popping sound then felt a disconcerting freeness around my middle.

"Mama needs a new coat!" James laughed.

I held in words of pure self-disgust and frustration while pulling up the back of James' boots. I ignored the indignity of my broken coat until he was ready and then looked down at myself. The zipper had completely released. I examined it, blinking a tear of frustration away.

"Oh, well, James. Let's go."

"New coat, Mom!"

"Yes, I know, but we have no time right now."

I fiddled with the zipper fastener, but it was stuck at my throat and refused to be pulled down against the open teeth. Winter's winds were gentle today, blowing only enough to send a slight chill past the flapping edges of my coat and ting James' nose with red. His mitten-covered hand felt warm as I clasped it to cross the street.

Ice buildup in the gutters brightened our surroundings, the flashes of light distracting me from my dark mood. Crisp air always cleared my head and kept me in the moment. This time it opened my mind enough to enjoy the sight of the school bus as it turned down our street. We were just in time to meet it.

"Mom!" Joshua yelled as he jumped down from the last step and threw his backpack at me. Its weight hit me like a brick. "Oh, good catch, Mom. Can I have a snack?"

"We'll see what your lunch looks like first."

His rolling eyes and groan carried a healthy hint of humour as he raced past me and up the sidewalk towards the house.

"Are you okay, Harmony?" I asked as she trudged past, her exit from the bus eclipsed by her brother's gusto.

"Fine," was her reply.

"Oh, no. Are you cranky too?"

"Too?"

I scrunched up my nose and threw her a grumpy face. She struggled to hold back a grin at my comical expression. "Just tired, Mom."

"Harmony, I make you soup," James announced, his little mitt leaving my grasp and seeking his sister. The years between them melted as she let a smile break across her face.

Neither would ever know how much watching them blessed me as I clutching my broken coat, holding it closed.

"I don't like soup."

I rolled my eyes at Joshua as he slumped down in his chair, nine-year-old eyes half-glazed over with sleep as they scowled at me.

"Too bad. It's delicious," I said, spoon in hand, soft chunks of celery and carrot cooling as I gently blew on them. Supper was simple and wholesome, just what my body needed after depriving myself for most of the day. Beth's cookies could only take me so far.

"*But* I don't *like* soup." He emphasized his words by sliding farther down the seat.

"Whining won't change the fact that soup is what we have for supper."

Harmony and James had long since finished eating, and their empty bowls sat on either side of me.

"But I'm *hungry*."

"Then, please eat your soup."

"*Fine.*"

I held back laughter as Joshua sat up in disgust. His nose wrinkled as he sniffed his spoon, stuck his tongue out, and touched it to the broth. I watched the shiver of revulsion ripple through his shoulders and arms. He looked up at me.

"Be brave," I encouraged.

In that split second, I could tell he really hated me. The loneliness of being a part-time single parent bubbled up for a minute. His stare of revulsion was heavy on my shoulder. But then in an over-dramatic fashion, he ate the spoonful.

"Now, was that so bad?" I asked.

He shrugged and picked at a large chuck of carrot with the empty spoon.

"I still don't like it."

"And that's okay. But if you're hungry, it's what we have for dinner."

He ate a second bite, and though I could tell he wasn't enjoying it, the revulsion decreased and his eyes lost their hate.

"Thank you, Joshua."

I returned my attention to my bowl, taking a bite of the now lukewarm liquid.

"Mom! James pooped!"

My sigh was deep, the expelled air drawn right from my toes and hanging in the air in front of my face as I ignored Harmony's first cry.

"Mom!" she called again. "Oh, man, it stinks so bad."

I gave up on eating a warm meal and pushed away from the table.

"Try to finish that, please," I said to Joshua as I walked from the room.

"Do I have to eat the carrots?"

"How about you just do your best, okay?"

A wall of stink slapped my face as I entered the living room.

"Man, you weren't joking about that smell," I said.

Harmony was curled up on the couch with a blanket, a book held high before her face to catch the side lamp's light. She held her nose as she nodded at me and puffed her cheeks out.

"Can't. Breathe."

"Oh, come on. It's not *that* bad." I chuckled.

"Yes. It. Is."

I took James to the bathroom to change him. The shower rug shielded his back from the cold tile floor, but my knees knew no such protection. I felt the transition lines cutting into my knees.

"Remind me tomorrow to put my fuzzy pyjama pants on before we do this again, James. Okay?"

He giggled as I rubbed the indentation in my skin before letting him up.

Three

Bedtime was one of the best times for me. James was a great sleeper, and once he settled, he rarely woke up before his siblings had prepared for school the next morning; but the older two did a bob between bedroom and living room for an hour before settling in. Even Harmony with her quiet moods didn't like to be all alone.

"Mom, can I have a drink?"

"Yes. Just water!" I whisper-yelled when Joshua asked.

"Mom, do you know where my orange sweater is?" Harmony asked as she sifted through folded laundry in a basket at the base of the staircase, waiting to be carried up the steps and put away.

"What orange sweater?"

"The one with the little white flower on it. I want to wear it tomorrow."

"Check in the basement. I didn't get it pulled out of the dryer today. Oh, and remind me to do that in the morning! Oh, *oh*! Next time, don't wait so long to look for it."

They threw eye rolls at me right and left as the evening wore on. I'd forgotten about my cold soup and now contemplated whether I wanted to warm it up or grab something from the freezer to pop in the microwave.

That's not healthy

You need to stop buying those. They're too expensive.

It's just going to make you bigger.

It felt like being poked by a large stick as my brain refused to leave my wound from the morning alone. All the little things piled on top of each other, putting weight behind the stick. Fresh, hot tears spilled, and there I was, a mess, holding my cold bowl, trying not to let it spill over my hands until I finally reminded myself I could set it down.

"Mom? Are you okay?"

Harmony's voice was a whisper beside me.

"I will be, baby," I managed. "Just having a sad moment."

"I was sad today, too."

Her arms slid around me. They weren't long enough to close the circle, but she tried, and her closeness was like a bandage binding me up again. I kissed her frizzy hair, not quite messy enough to tell the story of sleep, but the stray wisps that tickled my nose whispered how they flirted with her pillow for a moment.

"Do you want to talk about it?" I asked.

"Tomorrow. Maybe. You?"

I shook my head.

"I'll be okay. You've already helped a lot. Did you find your sweater?"

She waved soft knit material at me and silently smiled as she made her way to bed.

I discarded my cold soup and chose my favourite all-in-one tray from the freezer, pouring a cup of coffee to sip while waiting for my late meal to warm in the microwave. The coffee was bitter from sitting in the pot all evening, but I didn't mind. After the microwave chimed, I made my way with my food and drink into the living room. A Bible lay on the far end table, and I placed my comforts down beside it, snuggling in under a lap blanket and doing a fair impression of an antisocial teenager. I opened the Bible and flipped past highlighted passages, unsure of what I was looking for.

> *"My beloved is mine, and I am his;*
> *he grazes among the lilies."*
> *- Song of Solomon 2:16 ESV -*

The verse gave me the mental image of Jeff sitting in a field eating lilies. I giggled at my imagination, knowing the verse meant something different, but still. Love was like that, beautiful and ridiculous at the same time.

> *"...bearing with one another and,*
> *if one has a complaint against another,*
> *forgiving each other; as the Lord has forgiven you,*
> *so you also must forgive."*
> *- Colossians 3:13 ESV -*

I closed the Bible, not wanting to read anymore, as Jeff's words repeated in my mind.

You need to talk to her.

I didn't want to think about Tina and her stylish outfits. Tina and her perfectly applied makeup. Tina and her slender frame. Deep in my heart, I knew her words hadn't been meant to hurt me. But, they had, deeply. Did it matter? Where did this disdain come from? Was I jealous?

My hand probed the rolls of my gut as I sat tucked under the lap blanket.

"God, I don't want to talk to her. I don't trust her."

Like a lightning bolt, I knew that was one of my biggest problems. I didn't trust. It wasn't just Tina that I didn't trust, it was all of them. Every person who stepped into that church building regularly, everyone I called "brother" and "sister." Even sweet Beth and little Gloria. Why didn't I trust them?

Because you don't trust Me, Mary.

And there it was: truth echoing through my head to resonate in my heart. I heard the wall clock ticking up above me, counting out the seconds as I refused to answer.

"I do."

No, you don't.

"But I want to. I want to trust You, God, and all of them, too."

I know.

I felt no condemnation of the emotions I experienced as a wave rippled through my mind and body. I struggled to trust my brothers and sisters in Christ, even the God I claimed to love, but could I learn to?

"I don't want to talk to her. Can't I just forgive and forget?"

Can you forgive and forget? What will you do if it happens again?

You come home upset about something she's said at least once a month. Again, my husband's words echoed through my mind. He was right. This wasn't the first time Tina had said something that pierced past my defences.

It's your own weakness that hurts you, not Tina's words.

She's right. Just get over it and move on.

You're too sensitive. That's not her fault.

The negative words crept in like a terrible headache. They wormed around and gnawed on my revelations of truth until it was hard to tell one from the other.

"Okay, so what if I talk to her, and then she hates me? We'll really never be able to go back to church."

You're going crazy talking to yourself like this.

That's right. She'll probably tell everyone, and then they'll all hate you.

It's not worth this drama!

In a way, the voices were right, but they pushed me closer to giving up that part of my life. Could that be good?

You know it's not a good thing. You know what you need to do.

The confusion, my hesitancy, the jumble of noise in my head. It hurt, and I felt my headache switch from a dull ache to a hard, unforgiving vice.

I wiped the moisture from my eyes and pulled the blanket up to my shoulders. My microwave tray was getting cold, but I didn't care. So was my coffee. I shouldn't have grabbed a caffeinated beverage so late in the evening, and as I reached for it, my hand bumped my Bible, knocking it to the floor.

Just leave it.

You know what you need to do.

I picked up the floppy book, and as I laid it on the couch beside me, my notebook slid out from between its pages.

"I don't want to talk to her."

But I didn't have to, not at first anyway. I turned away from the page filled with last Sunday's notes and uncapped the pen that had rested snugly in the spiral binding.

Dear Tina,

The pen wrote in thick, undeniable black.

Four

The letter in my coat pocket weighed on my mind like a lead brick. My hand wandered to it, feeling the sleek edges of the closed envelope.

"Are we there yet?" Joshua asked from directly behind Jeff.

"Really?" My husband replied from the driver's seat. "Do you see the church building?"

"No," Joshua whispered back as he crossed his arms over his chest, slipping his hands into his armpits.

James had drifted off to sleep in his car seat, and I hoped a few minutes' nap would do him some good. But Harmony worried me. I watched her blank expression in the rearview mirror as she sat quietly in the back seat. She hadn't come to me with her problem yet, and I'd put off asking her directly. I made a mental note to visit her in her room when we got home from church.

I reached over and slid a hand into Jeff's free one. He glanced at me with tired eyes as I curled my fingers around his and smiled while I mouthed, "I love you."

He'd arrived home this morning—two days late. It was lucky he'd made it home at all, and since he was determined to come to church with us instead of going to bed, I hadn't asked what had happened. His daily phone calls had been short and explanations lacking. But I didn't mind. He'd be home for four days now. We would have time to talk later. His hair was damp from his quick shower before leaving the house, and I hoped he didn't get chilled because of it.

"They might not allow us back in the church after this," I whispered.

"Don't be overdramatic. It'll be fine, Mary."

I was scared and making jokes to cover it up. But I wasn't fooling Jeff.

"People can't fix mistakes they aren't aware they're making," he reminded me.

"I could just throw the letter out the window."

"Could, but you won't." Half an eye roll was all he could manage while watching the road ahead of us.

"Joshua! Don't kick the back of the chair, please." Jeff's sudden and loud objection made me jump.

"Sorry," Joshua replied, and I watched him slump when I turned to give him a "Mom look." "Are we there yet?"

"Yes," I replied as we pulled into the church parking lot. "Thank goodness."

After the service, Jeff went to get James from the nursery, and I scanned the back of people's heads for a Tina-looking updo. The line out the sanctuary doors and into the fellowship hall was long. Everyone was chatting, children weaved in and out of the coffee line, but I didn't see her.

Alternating waves of relief and doubt rolled over me as my eyes darted here and there. She had to be here. She was always here. I nodded hello to Rose Grill, the pastor's wife, before walking into the foyer. The doors to the fellowship hall were wide, and the line started barely out of the sanctuary and ran right up to and past the kitchen.

There she was.

"Of course, kitchen duty," I muttered, checking my attitude as I stepped past a bulletin board. The disarray of flyers, notes, and pictures called to me. Be a Nursery Helper, Sign Here. Come Sing at the Hospital, Sign Here. So many needs glared at me from white sheets of paper. Tina was one of those people who had her name on every list. I was one of those people who barely made it in the door with my children in tow every week.

The letter in my pocket turned from a lead weight to a burning flame. I wished I could watch its edges crisp and flake away as ash.

You know, you could just grab some coffee and walk away. She doesn't have to know you even wrote it.

It would be so easy to follow the voice of my inner doubt. But I knew Jeff was right. If I let my pain build up, it would drive me away from this building, these people.

A bead of sweat trickled down my back as I stepped up to the kitchen window, and the delicious smells of fresh coffee and baked goods greeted me.

"Clean cup for coffee? Hot water for tea?" Tina asked from behind the counter.

I glanced at the open basket of tea bags and shook my head.

"A clean cup for coffee, please."

Now, Mary, it's time to give it to her.

But what will happen? I don't want to. I change my mind.

Mary, trust Me.

Tina smiled at me as I reached over the tea basket and cookie plates and handed her the letter with trembling fingers. I grabbed one of those cookies and popped it into my mouth as Tina took the envelope. My hands trembled as I clutched the cup and stepped down the line towards the oversized coffee pot.

I felt her questioning eyes follow me but didn't turn to watch her slip my offering into a pocket or tuck a stray hair behind an ear with an immaculately manicured finger.

Once in the car again, I blew my nose on a leftover napkin I'd found in my purse.

"You okay?" Jeff asked as he strapped James into his car seat.

"I will be."

"Mama, I *hungry.*"

With that, I set about digging through the diaper bag in search of James' cheerios.

"Trust, Mary," Jeff whispered to me as I passed him the plastic bowl.

All I could do was nod. God only knew the outcome, and He had called me to trust Him, even in this small thing.

The Letter

Tina

One

THE LOW RUMBLE OF the car engine covered my sniffling tears. Giving in to them was stupid, and I wished I didn't have to hear myself whimpering. I held the letter against the steering wheel, its torn envelope in my lap. I wanted to crush it then tear it to pieces. Emotional bubbles were popping in my gut, releasing bursts of anger, doubt, disgust, and regret. I couldn't sort them out. Not right now.

Dear Tina,

I could hear Mary's voice as I read her words.

I know you never meant to hurt me, but you did.

I threw the letter onto the passenger seat beside me and turned off the car engine.

My feet had never warmed after the switch from my high heels to my black fur boots. The heels had pinched my toes as I stood serving in the church kitchen. I had flats that would have been more comfortable, but my legs went on for miles in a pair of heels and a knee-length skirt. I liked that feeling too much to give them up during the winter months. My toes stung as I wiggled them before stepping from the car onto the snow-dusted pavement of my driveway.

I glanced back at the letter, its envelope now on the car floor, and decided I didn't care. Let it stay there. Who did she think she was? I didn't have time for this drama.

The car door slammed shut. As the sound echoed up the driveway and through the open garage, I heard my husband's voice in my head.

Do you know how much it'll cost to fix that door latch? Keep yourself under control, Tina.

Why did Herald's constant correction follow me everywhere? I could picture his tall shoulders stiffening under the tailored blazer he always wore, his eyes looking me up and down from beneath his impeccably groomed eyebrows. It was something I'd loved about him, once.

I stopped and filled my lungs with cold winter air, closing my eyes as I slowly released carbon dioxide back into the world. The residual tear tracks on my cheeks froze before I stepped into the empty garage. I parked in the driveway so he could pull his car into its shelter.

I don't have time to scrape ice every morning, Tina.

He was right. He filled his days with law books and court cases, early mornings and late nights. Still, it would have been nice to have a frost-free car on a Sunday morning. He'd stopped going to church with me some time ago.

I'm tired. I need to rest on weekend mornings. Don't worry, I'll go to the second service.

But he didn't even do that anymore.

My shuffled steps echoed around the empty parking space. Had he left the door unlocked for me? No, of course not. The knob resisted my twist, and I fumbled in my pocket for the key.

I almost fell backwards as the door opened unexpectedly, leaving my extended key poised in midair.

"Hey, Tina," Kevin, my adult stepson, greeted me as his sandy brown hair fell into his eyes. His height towered over me.

"Oh! Hello, Kevin. It's nice to see you."

"I got in late last night," he replied to the silent question my tone cast at him.

"It's good to have you home. Where did Herald go?"

"He didn't say."

"I see."

Kevin's strained smile ushered me in like an icy wind.

"I'll make us some lunch. Soup okay?" I asked.

"Thanks, but no. I was about to head out."

He saluted me with a raised coffee mug, then turned and walked down the hall.

"Your dad said nothing about what time he would be back?"

A "No" drifted back to me as he stepped into his bedroom and closed the door.

"God, is it too early for a drink?" I muttered to myself.

It was, and I knew it.

It didn't take long for my condensed soup to warm on the stove. I poured a portion into an oversized mug. It always made me feel cozy sipping a cup of soup like tea. I needed some comfort after Mary's letter, and just listening to the wind pick up outside the kitchen picture window chilled me. I sat at the table sipping my soup and reading a book when Kevin appeared.

"Any word from Dad?"

I looked up in surprise and picked up my cell from the tabletop to check.

"Not yet. Knowing him, he won't be home until dinner now."

I set my phone back down and took a sip of the savory warmth from my mug.

"There is still soup left on the stove."

"No, thanks," he replied as his empty coffee cup found a home in the sink. "Tina?"

"Yes?"

"It's been about ten years now since you married Dad, right?" His voice was hesitant, and the catch in it made me set my mug down. His back was turned to me as he reached into a cupboard and pulled out a box of crackers.

"Almost. It won't be ten years until July."

"I was fifteen when you got married." His voice trailed off, but then he turned and looked straight at me, the cracker box clutched tightly in his hand as if he needed it for comfort.

"Is something wrong, Kevin?"

"I just ... I just wanted you to know that you're a good stepmom."

I was shocked. His deep brown eyes held a sincerity I'd never seen there before. I dropped my book on the table.

"Thank you." I didn't know what else to say. Emotion crawled up my esophagus like a sore throat. "What's going on, Kevin?"

"Nothing. Just wanted you to know that's how I feel."

He turned to walk out of the room and didn't look back as he said, "I'm going out with the guys and won't be back for supper. Leaving again in the morning."

His back screamed tension at me as he made his escape. I got up to follow him to the door, but he looked back at me and said, "He doesn't deserve you."

His words glued my feet to the floor, and I let him slip into the shadowy hallway. The garage door opened and closed as I stood there at the table, my lunch forgotten.

It left me with a deep foreboding. Why wasn't Herald home yet? What was he doing all morning? What did Kevin know? The hours dragged on, and still, Herald didn't come home. My cell phone remained silent when I sent him a message asking what he wanted for supper. Disquiet bubbled over into anger as I chopped carrots and potatoes for roasting. The faint orange tinge of carrot juice left on my skin flashed to red, and I stabbed at a nearby onion as hot tears slipped down my face. What mistake had I made this time?

I knew Herald would come home with a list of grievances. Like the bathroom wasn't clean enough when he unexpectedly invited his coworker over last week. Or last month, when the washing machine broke down, and I hadn't noticed the water all over the utility room floor. Or maybe he would find something new and tell me I used too much lemon on tonight's chicken or maybe not enough.

"We could all improve ourselves if we tried harder, couldn't we?" Mary had said at Wednesday morning Bible study.

We had all been sitting together pleasantly chatting and drinking coffee when she'd said those words. She hadn't meant them against me, I was sure, but here they were, back in my brain, a slap in the face.

Dear Tina,

I know you never meant to hurt me, but you did. See, there are a lot of different factors why I'm, well, "fat." You don't deal with anything like this, so you wouldn't know. I've also never told you … So you didn't know to be sensitive. But it really hurt when you implied that I just wasn't trying hard enough.

I still didn't know how to take those words, but they echoed through my brain. I should have known to keep my big mouth shut. But she'd sat there, her huge self hardly fitting on the fellowship hall chair. Granted, they were kind of small.

Why did she have to hand me that letter *today*?

I'd been alone too long and didn't hear Herald's car pull into the garage or even the front door open and close. My swirling thoughts screamed in my ears.

"Are you making dinner?"

I jumped. His voice was irregularly husky, and I turned to see him standing with his hands folded across his chest.

I glanced at my watch to emphasize how close to dinnertime it was, and that he should know better than to be so late.

"Yes. It's lemon chicken and root vegetables. Did you get my texts?"

"Yes."

"Then why didn't you answer?"

"You can stop now." His eyes shifted from my shoulders to the floor as he ignored the question. "Cooking, that is. I have a visitor, and I want you to leave. I booked you a hotel room for the night. Here."

My jaw dropped as he produced a key card from his pocket.

"Go out. Get yourself some dinner."

"You did what?" I stammered.

"Her name is Lucy. My visitor." He stuffed his hands into his pockets and looked me square in the eyes. "Pick your mouth up off the floor, Tina. I want a divorce. The papers are already being drawn up. I booked the hotel for you for two weeks. After that, we'll talk."

My vision tunnelled as my hands shook. I noticed that he was wearing his silver suit, the one he usually wore to court. He never wore that on a weekend. His collar was also left unbuttoned, giving his appearance a risqué feel instead of the uptight lawyer he usually portrayed.

I felt an itch in the hand that held the kitchen knife and dropped it before I could give in to the urge to fling it across the room. In stunned silence I grabbed my phone from the table and then the key card from his hand, shivering at the feeling of warmth from his skin as our fingers touched.

Why aren't you screaming at him? You should be screaming and throwing things! But my breath seemed to have left my lungs.

"Goodbye, Herald."

My voice wobbled, but it didn't break despite being weak. I headed right for the garage door. My purse and church bag lay slouched against the wall under the coat rack. *Should I go back and pack something?* I asked myself as I slipped my coat on.

"No," I said aloud.

I passed his Lucy sitting in his luxury Mercedes, the engine still running and the exhaust fumes filling the cold garage with a pungent fog. She was flipping through her cell phone and didn't look up as I passed. I thanked God I'd only eaten soup earlier as my gut rolled, and I almost lost it all over the cement floor.

Just keep going, get in your car, and get to the hotel. Don't think until you're there.

After making it to my smaller Volvo, I threw my bags on the passenger seat and slammed the door again. The wind had blown straight into my open coat, and I shivered as I zipped it closed.

No, you don't. No crying. Not until you're in the hotel room. I rebuked the emotion closing down my windpipe.

"What hotel?" I clutched the key card. Best Western. I assumed it was the one just down from the church building and not the second choice closer to the airport. Should I go back in and ask him? I glanced up the driveway.

Herald stood just in the doorway, watching me. His "visitor" peered over his shoulder on tiptoes.

My God, how old is that girl?

Again, I almost lost my lunch but swallowed forcing bile past my sore throat. No, I wasn't going back. I did my best not to look again as I pulled out of the drive and started down the street.

Two

The metal door handle chilled my bare hands as I entered the hotel lobby. At first glance, the long room was all clean white tiles and precise modern lines. The receptionist was dressed in black and green, her hair pulled back in a professional bun. Not a single hair was out of place.

"Hello, my husband booked a hotel room for me but failed to mention which Best Western it was. Could you check for my name? It's Tina Hearth. He is Herald Hearth, the lawyer." The dull sound of a human finger plunking against a touch screen grated on my nerves as I knitted a strained smile across my face.

"Yes, ma'am ... It looks like you are in the right place. He booked you in and collected a key card already."

"I have the card but just realized he didn't give me the sleeve for it.. Could you tell me the room number?"

"He didn't tell you the room number? Could I see some ID please?"

I could tell the first question had just slipped out of the receptionist's mouth by mistake as I shrugged an affirmative to her and handed over my driver's license.

"Sorry, ma'am, room 205. Second floor. It looks like you will be staying with us for two weeks. We hope you enjoy your time here. The elevators are just straight down the hall and then to the left."

"Thank you."

Did she watch me walk away? Did she know the look of a woman who had just lost her entire world? She must have guessed something was going on. But what did it matter?

The room was chilly when I entered, so I pulled the thermostat cover open. "Eighteen degrees Celsius? Really?" I raised the programmed heat settings and shrugged off my coat. The digital numbers hit twenty-one degrees.

Sitting down at the small table by the window, I stared at the empty seat across from me. Kevin had been trying to tell me something was up. But he didn't know how to. I should've recognized it but had been too shocked by his unusual admiration. We'd never quite clicked, and I'd accepted that as the cost of marrying a man with an older son. His mother had left long before, and as far as I knew, neither he nor Herald had heard anything from her in years. It must have been difficult for him to say what he did this morning.

"He doesn't deserve you." The words rang like warning bells in my head, and then Mary's voice slid in behind Kevin's. *"We could all improve ourselves if we tried harder, couldn't we?"*

The war in my mind raged as I gave in to tears that started as a gasp and then poured hot and ugly down my flushed cheeks. Warm air blew from the wall heater behind me. It was one of those big clunky ones attached under the window. They always made it hard to sleep with their late-night transitions, but right now I was thankful for the heat.

What had I done wrong? I was a good wife. I took care of myself and dressed to impress. Herald had always made more than enough income, so I didn't have to work, but I wasn't idle. I volunteered whenever I could. I was always busy at church or in the community. People knew my name and knew whose wife I was. I made Herald look good. Why was it never enough? Where had I gone wrong?

I didn't have as many tears as I thought I should and was soon blowing my nose on thin hotel tissues and staring into space. There was no use whining or complaining. It was done, and I'd left without a fight. But what now? A deep cold settled over my anger and pain—an ice shield that chilled despite the blowing heat at my back.

"Go out, get yourself some dinner." As if I needed his permission to eat tonight. But was I hungry? I should be. I should eat ... But I didn't want to go out like this, not now. All I had with me was the church outfit I'd worn through the door, my purse, and my church bag. I got up and grabbed the bag off the bed.

Lying on the top was the letter from Mary.

Why didn't I remember putting it there? I laid it on the side table and dug deeper into the fabric bag's depths. There, I felt them: granola bars and breath mints. I pulled them out and looked around. The single-serve coffee machine called to me. I rarely drank caffeine this late in the evening, but what did it matter now? The rumble and bubble as it percolated was comforting.

I began to think ahead as the room finally began to warm around me, but a chill still filled my gut. Should I call someone? Did I want to? I should.

How could I tell someone my husband brought another woman home with him today? On Sunday. God's day.

"On a Sunday? Really Herald? You couldn't have kept her in a hotel instead of the woman you married?"

I knew I didn't want that either. But at least it wouldn't have shamed me as much as leaving my home. Why'd I leave so easily? I should have screamed at him. I should have made a scene and demanded my rights to our house. But here I was in a hotel room instead of the floozy peering over his shoulder. Maybe ... maybe a part of me had been expecting this, wanted this.

"Well, maybe she isn't a floozy ..." I told myself. Herald had a way of using his words to get what he wanted. If it worked on me, it would work on her, too. But again, who could I tell?

I went through a mental list.

My mother passed away when I was a teen.

My sister? We couldn't stand to look at each other. There was no way she would help.

Kevin? Well, he already knew something was up. But no ... That was not what a stepson was for.

Someone from church? It was right around the corner.

Should I call Pastor Arthur or Rose, his wife? My gut did another flip-flop at the thought.

Your husband did what?

How on earth could you let him do that to you?

How long has he been sleeping around?

Have you been doing your marital duty to him?

I stopped myself from putting my imagined words into their mouths and didn't let my mind weave another sentence. No.

Should I call Beth? She was a sweet woman and always walked around with a smile on her face. No. I imagined her patting my hand and handing me cookies and milk. That isn't what I wanted or needed.

I downed my coffee before it got cold and told myself I would have to just do this alone.

After reaching that revelation, my face felt cold, and I wiped away the tears, reaching for another tissue from the bedside table. Mary's letter and its contents slipped into my grief.

Dear Tina,

I glanced at the words exposed to the ceiling as I wiped my nose.

I know you never meant to hurt me, but you did. See, there are a lot of different factors why I am, well, "fat." You don't deal with anything like this, so you wouldn't know. I have also never told you … So you didn't know to be sensitive. But it really hurt when you implied that I just wasn't trying hard enough.

I'm trusting you to hear me and understand when I ask you to be more careful with the words you say to me. I know we are not close and don't really know each other like we should. But I still trust you as my sister in Christ. Thank you.

- Mary -

As I read her words again, they didn't seem as harsh as I'd taken them at first. *I'm trusting you.* No, they didn't seem harsh at all now. Had it all been me? I'd let my attitude get in the way. I picked up the letter and reread it.

I'm trusting you.

I tried to think back to the last Bible study. What had I said to her exactly? I couldn't remember and hadn't realized anything I'd said could have hurt someone. She was right, though. I didn't know what it was like to live in her body.

I looked down at myself and smoothed out my skirt. It draped my hips in pleats and the cut hugged my torso. I'd taken it to a seamstress to have it fitted. I looked good and knew it. As I aged, it wasn't easy keeping it all in line. I'd worked hard for this fit.

Mary? Well, she had kids. It wasn't just her more than generous girth that she'd let go, though. She often showed up to Bible study looking like she'd walked through a tornado: clothing that didn't fully button up or was missing said buttons, hair that looked like she'd woken up and just thrown it into a ponytail without a brush, unplucked hairs protruding from her chin. But, when I really thought about her, it was her soft voice I remembered most, even when that not-altogether kind sentence bubbled up in my mind.

"We could all improve ourselves if we tried harder, couldn't we?" It was in response to something I couldn't remember saying, but I remembered it, and it stung. It stung because it was true, and here I was in a hotel room, alone, because I wasn't good enough anymore. But I couldn't try harder when I didn't know what I was doing wrong. What had I done wrong?

I wouldn't get another chance with Herald. I didn't think I wanted one ... Was that even okay? Separation, divorce—these were shunned practices in my church and social circles. Sure, couples broke up all the time, but those who followed the moral high ground never quite looked at them the same way. Including myself ... Why did this break feel so final, so fast? Why didn't I want to fight for my marriage? It was evil to give up ... wasn't it?

I should have realized what was going on a long time ago, when there was time to fix it. But we'd already stepped off a cliff, and now I lay in pieces at the bottom.

"Enough, Tina!" I almost shouted it at myself. "Enough of this."

Maybe I should go out. I needed things. I didn't want food, but a woman needed more than one pair of underwear and socks. Right about now was the perfect time for some shopping therapy. Did this hotel room have a fridge? I'd forgotten to look. When I got up, I found one hidden in the cupboard.

Clever.

At least I could grab some essentials and not starve to death if I needed to hide from the world. I picked up my purse and slid my phone inside. Time to forget for a while. Maybe I would buy something a little nicer than plain cotton underwear ...

The fancy stores were closed after dinner on Sundays, but the Super Store was still open, so here I was. So much for classy underpants. But that was okay. In times like this, a woman needed something she could depend on. Granny panties would work just fine.

It was getting late, but I noticed a few shoppers with children in tow. Didn't they have school in the morning? Maybe I was just getting old, and that's why I thought it was late. Maybe that's why Herald had chosen a child over me.

"At least I don't need Depends yet," I giggled to myself while heading for the intimates section.

I found my size easily and stood there trying to pick between pastel colours or fun prints when I felt a tug at my sleeve.

"Hello, Coffee Lady."

I looked down in surprise at the sweet little cheeks turned my way, their dimples exposed as she smiled up at me with a full grin and squinting eyes.

"Hello, Gloria. Where's your mommy?"

"Over there." She pointed down the aisle as a cart rounded the bend.

"Gloria, there you are. Don't run away like that, please. Oh, Tina!" Her mother's eyes lit up as she saw whose sleeve her daughter was affectionately holding. "Funny seeing you here! How are you? I'm so looking forward to this week's study, are you? This last week was wonderful."

Debora was a chatterbox, and I politely nodded and slipped in my yeses and noes as fast as I could so as not to interrupt her waterfall of words.

"Thank you so much for helping in the kitchen at church today," she continued. "The coffee is always extra strong when you're on kitchen duty. A mother like me needs a good strong cup after sitting in services all morning. How is Herald? Do you think he'll come to church next weekend? It's been such a long time since we've seen him. I do hope he's doing alright."

"Oh, he's fine."

"Good! Now, have you signed up to sing at the hospital next month? Of course you have. You always go. You have such a lovely voice. Come, Gloria, let go of Tina's sleeve."

Gloria was still holding on to me and gently tugging to get my attention.

"Yes, Gloria?" I squatted down to look her in the eyes, doing my best to not bubble over with tears at the mention of Herald.

"I made cookies today, Coffee Lady. Mama helped me. Would you like some?"

"Cookies?" I asked.

"Uh-huh," she replied.

"Oh, that's right, we made a huge double batch today. But, baby, we didn't bring any with us. It's hard to share when they're still at home."

Gloria looked back at her mama. "Bring them to her tomorrow?" Her improper grammar was adorable and melted my heart, but my tears became real when I realized I was going to have to tell her no.

"You're so sweet, Gloria. I would love to try your cookies, but I'm sorry. I won't be home tomorrow."

"Now, isn't that sweet of you, Gloria?" Debora interrupted. "Don't worry, we can bring them over any day this week. What days are you home, Tina?"

"Um ... Well ..."

Gloria had noticed my tears and reached out her chubby, still half-baby fingers towards my face.

"Don't be sad, Coffee Lady."

Her sweetness was both healing and destructive as her touch peeled away my emotional guards.

"Oh, Gloria." My tears were now enormous drops that wet her hands. "I'll have to come to your house to get the cookies. I won't be at home for a long time."

I peeled the little girl off my neck as she had wrapped me in a hug when my composure slipped. Her mother stood there gaping at my outburst, and I physically lifted her child into her arms.

"Thank you, Gloria. I'll call your Mom."

Then I ran, my purse bouncing on my hip, my shopping therapy forgotten.

My shoulders shook as I slammed my car door closed.

"Damn." I had no other words to describe my frustration and pain. The curse rolled off my tongue in repetition. "Once Debora knows something's up, everyone will know."

She wasn't an unkind woman, but her constant chatter was her biggest weakness, and everyone knew it. Thank God I hadn't blurted it all out at her feet.

"I'm sorry, Gloria," I whispered, though the child would never hear me.

I drove back to the hotel and buried myself under the heavy blankets of the bed, listening to the window heater click on and off all night long.

49

Three

"Good morning, ma'am." The voice on the other end of the phone line was chipper despite the early hour. "Sorry to wake you, but there's a gentleman here at the lobby desk asking for you. Would you like me to tell him to wait, or should I send him away?"

"Did he give you his name?"

"Of course, ma'am. I'm sorry. He says it's Kevin. He says he's your stepson?"

"I will be right there."

What on earth was Kevin doing here?

I glanced at the bedside table clock as it shone a mocking 7:30 a.m. He'd said the day before he would leave early. Why'd he come here?

I dragged myself from the bed and redressed into my crumpled clothing. I'd no brush to straighten my hair, so I used my fingers as best I could while checking in the bathroom mirror. The bags under my eyes were bad. I grabbed my purse and the small cosmetics bag I kept in it. Cleanser, concealer, a bit of colour for my cheeks? No, no time. Just a touch of concealer. It covered the worst of the dark lines.

"I might as well have gone out drinking or something," I mused to myself as my head throbbed.

I'd never experienced the flood of emotions that had washed over me again and again as I huddled under the covers through the night. Had I slept? I must have, but I didn't feel rested.

"Buck up, Tina." I slapped my cheeks with hands freshly washed in cold water. "Get down there and see what he wants. Then you can take the time to sort yourself out. You still need that underwear."

Across from the lobby desk was a cozy living room set up, complete with an electric fireplace. I found Kevin perched on a couch, staring into the flames, an overstuffed reusable grocery bag between his knees.

"Good morning, Kevin," I said as I sat down across from him.

"Morning." The bags under his eyes looked even more pronounced than the ones I'd just covered. "Here. Dad said you didn't take anything with you last night. I'm sorry if I forgot something."

He handed me the bag, my favourite blue sweater spilling down the side. I also glimpsed my hair brush jammed up against the inside of the fabric.

"I, ah ... just grabbed a bit from each drawer. I didn't know what toothbrush was yours, so I grabbed a new one from the closet."

"Thank you." The woven material was coarse, but I hugged the bag to my chest, unable to look him in the eyes. "You didn't have to."

"It's not your fault, Tina. My dad's an ass. He always has been. I never understood why you married him."

"Kevin!"

"He did the same thing to my mom, you know ... Showed up on the doorstep with another woman. I would have gone with her if I could have."

I stayed silent and watched his face contort as he relived painful memories.

"He didn't deserve her or the woman he shamed her with either. I knew he was going out with someone when he got all dressed up on a Sunday morning while you were already out at church, but didn't know he was bringing her home … I wouldn't have gone out if I did. I'm sorry."

The tears rolled down my face unheeded. Why had it taken something like this to crack Kevin's shell?

"I should have been there … I should have told him off."

"Kevin Hearth, it is *not* your job to stop this or fix it."

"What are you going to do now?" he asked, reaching for the tissue box conveniently set out on a side table. "Here," he said as he handed me one.

"I should have known what was going on. I haven't been enough for him for a while." Verbalizing the reality of it all to another person stung terribly, but it was now my life, and one thing I knew was I couldn't run from it for long.

"Here." This time it was a paper he handed me.

I opened it and found two telephone numbers and an address.

"I'm not coming back," he said, looking at his hands and flexing his fingers. "Dad doesn't know it, but Mom lives out in Alberta."

I rarely thought of the fact that Kevin travelled across the country on a weekly basis. It was an embarrassment to his father that he'd chosen a trade—and truck driving at that—over a university degree.

"I didn't know if you had my number ... so just to be sure, that's the top one. Mom's at the bottom. I'll stay with her until I get my own place. We already started looking last time I stopped out her way."

"Thank you." I sounded like a broken record, but I had no other words.

His eyes had softened when he mentioned his mom. But right now wasn't the time to pry into that story.

"Well. I need to go." He stood and dusted his hands off as if ridding himself of the situation. "If you need me ... You're right, I can't fix things. But don't let him leave you high and dry. If you need me in your corner, call."

I was stunned. The unexpected kindness pinched as well as comforted.

"Thank you for caring, Kevin."

"You have people, right? I mean ... People you can trust? Like from that church you go to?"

"I think so."

He nodded and then walked away, his work boots thumping on the smooth tiles of the entryway. His back was straight, his shoulders broad. He'd grown into a good man. I should have made more of an effort to connect with him. I didn't deserve this support.

At the large glass doors, he turned and waved before disappearing into the early morning chill, leaving me alone with the question: *now what?*

My hairbrush, my toothbrush, my favourite blue sweater, and a hoodie I always wore lay on the top of the bag Kevin had brought me. A wad of mismatched undergarments and several rolled-up pairs of socks hid underneath my housecoat. It must have been the first thing he grabbed from the hook on the bedroom door because it was jammed into the bottom of the bag. My linen blouse would need to be rewashed and ironed as it was now deeply wrinkled, but it was one of my best shirts, and I was grateful to have it. Two pairs of my good jeans and miscellaneous t-shirts from my casual drawer completed the package.

As I retrieved each item from the grocery bag, I refolded it and laid it out on the TV stand. They were each a blessing, a thought from Kevin, who didn't owe me anything, as he'd asked himself what I would need. They were not what I would have packed for myself, but they were enough.

I still needed things, like a proper bag to carry my new life. This resignation was scaring me. But it settled in my bones like an inevitability I couldn't fight. So why try? I made a list of daily items and food I should buy. The little fridge was big enough to store a decent amount of fresh vegetables and fruits. It almost felt fun planning my own little world.

"Now for the big things ... I only have this room for thirteen more days. Where do I go from here?"

The mental image of Herald's face, as he watched me pull away from the house, flashed through my mind. I knew that look. It meant I was now considered a liability, and support wouldn't be offered to a liability. I had very little that was only mine. No matter how much it hurt, if I didn't take stock now, Herald would leave me with nothing.

I needed a lawyer. My gut bubbled, emotions popping on the surface, turning sour. I didn't know any local lawyers who weren't Herald's close acquaintances. I needed someone from out of town. But as a housewife, I didn't know anyone who didn't know Herald. How could I find someone I could trust?

You're not smart enough to handle all of this yourself.

There is no way you'll beat him in court.

You're going to lose everything.

The solitude of my hotel room was getting to me. But some of those bubbles popping inside me were fear—a real fear I had never felt before.

"You need to eat," I said aloud. It was still early morning, and I had no food to make breakfast. I also didn't want to go downstairs and face people in the hotel breakfast room. A drive-through was my answer. Monday morning was also perfect for grocery shopping if you wanted to avoid familiar faces.

The grocery bag Kevin had used was a sorry, limp sight, but it was just what I needed for shopping.

You need to tell someone.

The nagging need weighed me down as I walked through the quiet hotel halls and out to the parking lot to find my car.

You can't do this alone.

"Shut up. I have no choice." It felt crazy answering myself, but maybe I was going crazy. I didn't dislike the sound of that. If it got worse, I could check myself into a hospital and be taken care of.

You're not crazy. You're in pain. You need your friends.

"I don't *need* anyone. I don't trust them."

I was getting angry with myself now. Why couldn't I keep my emotions in check?

The drive to the local fast food/coffee shop was uneventful. I used the drive-through and then sat for a few minutes in a far corner of the lot.

I stared at my credit card still in my lap, and I wondered how long I would be allowed to use it. Maybe I should just fill up the gas tank and start driving. See how far I could get before Herald cancelled the card.

Running away won't help you.

True, but I at least needed to move my things from the house, and I couldn't do that until I had a semi-permanent place to live. I was looking up apartments for rent on my phone when the low gas light came on.

"Nice going, Tina." I'd idled to an almost empty tank. If Herald had been beside me, he would have given me a lecture about greenhouse gasses and how money doesn't grow on trees. I would have shot back that printed bills were paper, so, yes, technically, money grew on trees. Then I imagined him enlightening me about the plastic content in Canadian bills and grinding my silly argument to mulch.

I turned off the car engine, but it wasn't long before the winter cold started creeping its way through every crevice of my car. My toes felt it first then my fingers as my coffee chilled.

I'd never had to pay rent, but even in my privilege, the conversations about rising housing costs hadn't escaped me. What kind of work could I get that would pay enough? Should I be looking at going to school?

"Don't be ridiculous, Tina. You're too old to go back to school."

The one year of general college I'd taken after high school wouldn't get me far now. Herald had swooped in soon after, and I thought I'd be set for life. A handsome lawyer was every girl's dream, right?

My toes had gone numb from the cold, and no matter how much I wiggled them inside my boots, they refused to warm. There was nothing for it. I restarted the car engine and made my way to the nearest gas station.

My insides felt like an ocean of thoughts, all swirling together, emotion becoming sea foam across its surface, bumping up against rocks and the beach to burst and pop. I'd less and less control over it. I hated that.

I wrinkled my nose at the fumes as I opened my car door. Had I pulled up to the pump correctly? I huddled up close to the gasoline dispenser, arms folded across my chest to trap in heat, when I saw Mary out of the corner of my eye. The sidewalk was a sheet of packed snow dusted with sand for traction, and she was pulling her little boy in a sled behind her while a grocery bag almost as big as him sat in between his legs.

I flipped up the collar on my coat to shield my face from view.

What a childish thing to do. Heat flushed my cheeks.

I know you never meant to hurt me, but you did, her letter had read.

Amid the turmoil of my pain, I felt shame when I looked at her. Her heavy boots left deep imprints in the snow, even though it was well-packed. Her coat flapped about her. Why didn't she zip it up? Didn't it fit? I rolled my eyes and then immediately hated myself for it. Who was I to judge? She had a family, she had a husband who visibly loved her despite all her shortcomings. Here I was hiding from her—Tina, the lawyer's wife, with tailored clothing. Mary turned a corner, and I lost sight of her.

You need someone. Go after her.

"What, are you nuts?" I said to myself. "I'm the last person she would want to see or help."

You need someone, and she trusts you. She said so.

"I'm the last person she should be trusting."

I hardly knew her outside of Bible study and the occasional wave and nod after church services. Where was this urge to go to her coming from? I really was going crazy.

What do you have to lose?

I peeked into the living room as we walked down the hall, and after seeing the pile of toys in a corner and blocks all over the floor framed by blankets and unfolded laundry dumped across the couch, I was glad Mary had chosen the kitchen until she ushered me in.

The sink was piled high with dirty dishes, and the floor gripped my stockinged feet in an unsettling way. Mary pulled out a chair from the table and brushed crumbs from their morning meal into a palm.

"I'm sorry, Tina. I wasn't expecting a visitor this morning."

"Oh, don't worry about it, Mary. It doesn't bother me a bit," I lied. "How are Jeff and the kids doing?"

"Good, good." Mary made herself busy clearing space on the counter in front of a stained coffee pot. "Harmony and Joshua are both at school, of course. Jeff started his work week early." Mary sighed, and I watched her shoulders slump towards the table. "He was supposed to be home for four days ... You know he rides the rails all week, right? We already miss him. But some weeks are just like that. He assured me they are giving him extra time off when he gets home on Thursday or Friday. But, they said that last week too."

"It must be hard to have him gone so much." There was strain in Mary's face, and a flash of jealousy washed through me. Had I ever missed Herald that much? It had been a long time, if ever, since I felt that pull within my heart. Did Mary know just how much she had?

"Yes. But it makes his time at home extra special."

She sat down across the table from me, and silence spread thick, broken only by the running of the coffeemaker and the hum of the refrigerator that stood across the room from us.

"I'm assuming you read the letter I gave you, and that's why you're here." Mary stared at her hands in her lap, her shoulders slouched, her double chin poking out as she looked down.

I cleared my throat before blurting out, "I'm sorry, but sometimes your words hurt me, too." I winced at myself. "I shouldn't have followed that with a 'but'."

Now I was the one staring at my chipping fingernail polish. I didn't look up as the coffeemaker beeped, and Mary went to pour a cup for each of us. The mug she set down in front of me had the words "World's Best Mom" printed across the side. I took a sip before reaching for the sugar and milk she'd just placed on the table between us. The virgin black liquid was bitter and strong, just what I needed to shock my system back from the edge as my lip trembled. I started again.

"I'm sorry, Mary. I'll try to be more careful with what I say from now on. Thank you for the letter and for saying you trust me."

"You're welcome." Her words were only a whisper.

I could tell she was crying but didn't trust myself to look up at her.

"It was brave to come to my house so soon," she continued. "Especially since you've never been here before."

I nodded.

"I am sorry if I hurt you as well," she whispered, dabbing her eyes with the corner of a sleeve. "Just a minute. I left the tissues in the living room."

My anxious heart was settling, and a wave of exhaustion hit me. I dabbed at my own eyes with a tissue when she returned with them.

"I don't really know what else to say, Mary. Maybe I should just go ..."

"No, stay and finish your coffee. You're welcome in my home, Tina."

I finally looked up, and our eyes met. Hers were a soft brown, gentle, like her voice. Even when rimmed with red from crying, they were beautiful. I knew mine were light blue and sometimes appeared cold. I wondered what she was thinking as she looked into them.

Tell her.

The silence dragged out again. *My husband kicked me out of the house yesterday* wasn't something you just blurted out. But the words ached at the back of my throat.

"Do you have a busy week planned?" Mary asked over the rim of her mug.

She trusts you. Now, trust her.

But could I trust her? Did I want to? I realized I had to start somewhere and would be no worse off if Mary decided I wasn't worth the trouble. I felt a flicker of friendship starting, a light I wanted to feed, but was afraid I would squash with the weight of my situation.

"Honestly, I don't know what my week will be like. I had some unexpected family trouble pop up yesterday."

While I watched Mary set her mug down and look up at me with concern instead of the curiosity —or annoyance—I expected, I decided.

"Truth is, I spent the night in a hotel and won't be going back home."

Abigail's Prayers: Two

Dear Heavenly Father,

Today I saw brokenness, right in front of me.

I was too afraid to say something, or do something.

She cried as she told us what had happened.

I've never seen her cry before.

I had no words to give her.

I wanted to reach out and touch her hand, but I didn't.

I felt too far away.

I've failed …

Please, help me to be brave next time I see her.

Help me to be brave next time I see brokenness in someone else.

When I am broken, help me remember how brave she was.

Amen

Power Off

Harmony

One

MOM STOOD AT THE bus stop, wrapped in her winter coat with a broken zipper, James clutching her gloved hand in his bare one. He was chewing on the stray mitten, wetness spreading down from the thumb as a dark stain.

"What are you doing, silly boy?" I asked him.

"Waiting for you, Harmy!" He grinned up at me, proud of his attempt to pronounce my name.

"Mom, you okay?"

"Oh, yes!"

It was like my question woke her from sleep. Her eyes slowly focused on me, and she laughed at Joshua, who was already halfway back to the house.

66

"How on earth did he get up there so fast?"

It wasn't a question to me but to the wind, and I let it slide past as she turned and gently pulled James along the snow-packed sidewalk.

It worried me a bit. Usually, she would throw me a joke or enfold me in a hug. But then, I had something on my mind as well, a weight I was hiding in my blue jeans pocket, and I was glad she didn't grab me and pull me close enough to feel it. I couldn't wait to get home and see if I could get it to work.

My backpack dragged on my shoulders as I followed my family. I'd squashed my snow pants into a tight roll to fit them inside with my books and lunch bag, and it had puffed out my backpack to a roundness that pushed against my back. Maybe I should ask Mom for a bigger bag? How long had I had this one for? A few years at least. Maybe I should ask ...

"Come on, Harmony!" Joshua called from the house steps. He was doing his usual "I beat you home dance." It made him look like a baboon, and I giggled at the sight. We'd piled the snow high on either side of the steps when we helped Dad shovel the walk. Gravel flecks now dusted over the packed snow, Mom's way of preventing any ice that formed in the walk from causing a bad fall. I ignored Joshua "The Baboon King" as I finally got to the steps and pushed past.

"Mom?"

"Yes, babe?"

"My snow pants don't fit very well in my backpack. Could we look for a bigger one this week?" I asked as she stripped James out of his snow clothes.

"Why haven't you been wearing them home like you used to?"

"None of the other older kids do. It takes too long to put them on before the school bell rings."

"Oh," was her only reply.

"Harmony just wants to be like *Amy* and her friends. They're always talking about their new jeans or something *stupid* like that while we wait for the bus. They think they're *so* cool." Joshua placed his hands on his still snowsuit-covered waist and thrust his hips back and forth in mockery of a strut.

"They don't think they're cool, Joshua, they *are* cool," I scolded him.

"Okay, you two, enough. I'll ask Dad when he gets home on Thursday, Harmony. Until then, just wear your snow pants home, please."

"Fine," I grumbled under my breath while taking said pants out of my school pack and hanging them up in the closet. They'd been damp when I rolled them, and now my backpack held a musty odor. I left the bag's zipper open, hoping it would dry things out.

"MOM? CAN I HAVE A SNACK?" Joshua's voice boomed down the hall from the kitchen. He was *so* annoying sometimes.

"Did you eat your lunch?" she shouted back.

I threw my lunch box on the kitchen counter before making my way upstairs and away from the worst of the noise. I'd left half my mandarin orange uneaten, but Mom wouldn't make a fuss as long as some were gone. My gut gurgled, but I ignored it. Hunger meant nothing when the weight in my pocket kept poking me, a reminder that it was there, waiting.

The haven of my bedroom smelled like me. It might have been strange, but I found it a comfort to walk into. The boys had the larger room next door. I kicked my pyjamas out of my way as I flopped down on the bed then glanced behind me. Yes, I *had* closed the door. One could never be too careful with brothers who liked to barge in whenever they pleased. At least the squeaky hinges would alert me if they sneaked a peek at what I was doing. I could usually hear them walking up the stairs as well. The muffled noise of Joshua banging around in the kitchen assured me that for the moment, I was safe.

It felt good to pull my secret out of my pocket. I hadn't had time on the bus to get a good look at it as I'd searched for a hiding place. The screen was dark, but the pink of the safety case was bright and fun. Amy had given it to me. *Given.* I hadn't believed it when she told me she had an old phone I could have if I wanted it. But here I was, holding electronic *gold* in my hands, and it was mine.

I pressed the power button on the side, and the screen blinked to life. The background was a digital picture of pink bubbles and purple shadows. I had a hard time imagining Amy liking that kind of background, but she'd said it was an older phone. It wasn't as large as the new models she and the older girls flashed around the bus every morning. But it worked, and it was *mine.*

"Do you even know *how* to use a smartphone?" one of the older girls had asked when Amy had handed it to me.

"Of course, everyone does," I'd answered.

That hadn't been completely true as I'd never owned one before. Mom didn't even have her own cell, and Dad took his with him to work while we used the landline. Mom had a laptop computer she kept on the top bookshelf in the living room and only took it down when she had to pay bills or something like that. Often the dust collected on the cover was thick enough to make pictures in. She would never have said yes to getting me a phone, so I hadn't even dreamed of asking. My family was "tech resistant," and it was one of the most embarrassing things about them *ever.*

I held a button on the side of the phone down just like I'd seen Amy do. The phone's clock was off by an hour. I needed to figure out how to change that. My heart fluttered as I thumbed all the icons present on the home screen. I found a chat app, the camera, a social media app, and some games. An error blinked on the screen when I tapped one.

No DATA or Wi-Fi detected. Please reconnect.

I sighed. I'd forgotten about *that* part of owning and using a phone. Maybe accepting it from Amy hadn't been a good idea.

"You *do* know you're one of the only kids without one, right?" Amy had said one day last week. "Why is that? Don't your parents want you to contact them? Don't they *trust* you? Dad got me one so I can text whenever I want. He's like that, he cares. You know you could get *kidnapped* and never have a way to let your parents know you're in trouble? What's with your family?"

Amy was one of those people who liked to hear herself talk. Her words had resounded in my brain like the ringing of a gong, and it had hurt. I knew the reason Mom would give me: it cost too much. She would also say I wasn't old enough. They were dangerous if not used properly, and I didn't *need* one because I never went anywhere without her or another adult. Right there was the big difference. I was only twelve. Amy was fifteen. I guessed her parents trusted her.

Well, I needed access to the internet if I wanted to use this phone properly. I would have to figure out a way to get Mom's Wi-Fi password.

"Mom, why don't you have a cell phone?" I asked as I helped her pair socks after dinner that evening.

Joshua was still in the kitchen picking at his food like usual. Why did he never eat? He was so weird.

"Mom?" I waited for her to look at me. "*Why* don't you have your own cell phone?"

"I don't need one, Harmony. We do just fine without."

She sat on the couch while we both picked socks out of an overflowing laundry basket sitting between us. I had my legs crossed over each other as I sat on the floor, the circle my legs made slowly filling with rolled sock pairs.

"But all the other moms I know have one, and most of the kids my age too. Even younger ..."

"Well, maybe they need them. Remember, baby, that most other moms have jobs, and their kids have to go to daycare, or a sitter, or even might be at home alone if they're your age. Maybe they walk home from school all alone. Our family is always together, so we don't need one."

"But don't you ever wish you had one anyway? You're an adult. You could just get one if you wanted."

"Sometimes ..." Her answer drifted off as she laid two matching socks across a knee before rolling them together and folding an end over so they formed a neat little package.

I was holding one of James' socks, a green one with red spots. It looked like a Christmas cast-off, but it was one of his warm ones, perfect for the kind of weather we were having. I let my hand wander through the basket, not really looking at what I touched, just feeling for the same knit as I focused on Mom and tried to think up a way to get the password for the Wi-Fi.

"How come you never use the internet?" I asked.

Mom looked at me. Her eyes were deep brown and seemed all-seeing.

"Why these questions, Harmony?"

"I'm just wondering. All the other kids have phones and tablets and stream shows on their TV. We don't have any of those things ... We're weird."

"If you get Harmony a phone, I want an Xbox," Joshua stated as he slunk into the room and looked straight at me while sticking out his tongue.

"Joshua, don't be rude to your sister. And, *no*, just no," Mom groaned.

"Dad won't let you play those 'shoot them up games,' Josh. It's the only reason he wants one, Mom."

We all jumped at the sound of a crash from the corner of the room, followed by James' insistent giggles as he walked through the mess of blocks he'd just made.

"If I had a cell phone, I could talk to Dad." I said this under my breath, but I knew she heard me. She didn't look at me as she watched James from over my shoulder, but I watched her deflate and sink further back into the couch cushions. I didn't enjoy doing it, but making her and Dad feel guilty about him being gone all the time might work.

Now. I needed that password.

Two

I wondered what all the other girls were saying to each other over the messenger app as I sat on the couch and pretended to read my book now that the socks were all folded. Mom walked through the house, picking up James' toys, and Joshua clomped around upstairs, supposedly putting on his pyjamas. The blanket I'd thrown over my lap was warm, and the fleece backing tickled my toes.

I was procrastinating. I knew Mom would stick her head into the room and give me the "look" soon: the look that asked why I wasn't getting ready for bed without her having to ask. But it was Monday, and I knew every Monday, Mom got the laptop down from the top of the shelf and paid bills. I had no plan to get the internet password other than to wait for an opportunity. What would the girls say tomorrow if I hadn't figured it out? What would Amy say if I had to tell them I couldn't use her gift? I didn't want to even *go* there.

I was listening closely to the sounds of the surrounding house and the people inside. Joshua started to quiet down. Mom's footsteps patted around the kitchen, and the creaking of cabinet doors told me she was putting dishes away. I heard the furnace blowing through the vents, the air smelling of warm dust and us. The picture window was gathering frost around its edges. It looked like silver gilding from far away and lace from close up.

I listened to Mom's footsteps as she shuffled up the hall, then joined me in the living room, following her from corner of my eye, pretending to be reading my book and unaware of the time. She walked up to the bookshelf and pulled the laptop down, blowing a cloud of dust from its surface as she moved to the armchair.

"Yes, I see you, Harmony." She looked at me over the top of the open computer. "Finish up."

"I will, but it's just the exciting part."

"*Five* minutes," she warned. But the smile on her face told me she wasn't upset.

I scanned the page of words in front of me but couldn't concentrate. A grunt from Mom told me she was on her feet again, but I refused to look up. Then the sound of shuffling books got my attention, and more dust got blown into the air.

"Remind me I need to dust these shelves tomorrow."

"Huh?" I said, pretending to not have heard.

"I said please remind me to dust tomorrow when you get home from school, just in case I forget." She waved a little red book my way as she walked back to the chair.

"Okay. What's that?"

"This? My memory insurance for when this thing refuses to work." She laughed with me while tapping a finger against her temple, then flipped through the red book's pages. She found what she wanted and then typed something. Could that little book be what I needed?

I yawned and stretched then flipped back the lap blanket. I could feel a draft creeping in from the old picture window and rubbed my toes with a hand before stepping down onto the cold linoleum. Mom had told me once that they'd covered the hardwood flooring under it because kids meant constant moping.

The sound of my bare feet on plastic made her look up, and I stretched my arms out, asking for a hug. "Aw! Good night, Harmony." Her eyes twinkled with delight.

The little red book was between us, and as I pulled away, I glanced at its open page. *Important Passwords* was written across its top.

I smiled and waved good night as I walked to the hall, wondering if she knew I was snooping. If she did, would she guess what I wanted with those passwords? I didn't think so, and now I knew right where they were.

I was listening to the sounds of the house again. My eyes closed, but my bedroom door stood wide open, just in case Mom came upstairs. This way, she'd think I'd forgotten to close it.

I heard Mom dragging something then the creak of steps as she travelled to the basement then up again. She must have been carrying a heavy laundry basket one way, but I couldn't hear if she'd put a wash on or was just getting ready for tomorrow's chores. I heard the fridge door open and close, the kitchen tap run, then chair legs scrape the floor.

When would she go to bed? I stole a peek over at my bedside clock. It read 11:02. If Mom knew I was still awake, she would be *mad*, and I was getting tired. Keeping my eyes closed was working against me. Maybe I should sit up?

Then I heard the chair squeak against the kitchen floor again and squeezed my eyes closed. I pinched myself—not hard, just enough to make myself squirm under the pressure. My parents' bedroom was at the foot of the steps, still on the main floor. I needed her to be really *asleep*.

Come on, Mom, go to bed.

I never realized before how long it took Mom to clean up after us. I really hoped I didn't have to wait much longer.

I slid my fingers up under my pillow and searched for the edge of my phone. I'd tucked it in between my mattress and the bed box. Joshua might go through my drawers if he was really looking for something or mad at me, but he would *never* look in my bed.

Muffled footsteps from the base of the staircase paused then stopped altogether as Mom entered her bedroom. *Finally*. The blowing of the furnace was amplified by the quiet, but I didn't move until my clock flickered to 12:05. I was so tired, but my shoulders had tensed as I waited, and now I had a headache.

Perfect. If I wake Mom up by accident, I can tell her I need to take some pain medication, or I won't be able to get up for school.

When did I become so devious? I'd never snuck around the house at night before. I'd also never kept secrets from my mom, not real ones, not about things I *knew* she wouldn't approve of. Was a cell phone really worth all of this?

If you want to fit in, you need that phone working.

I knew I could never use it to actually *call* people. So the internet password was important. I was tired of feeling different and not knowing what was going on when the older girls would talk on the school bus or at church. They looked down their noses at little Harmony Cooper. We were all learning how to use email and upload our homework to the network classroom. But I didn't have a computer I used at home, and I'd never been allowed to use my Dad's cell except that once when he'd asked me to answer it while out in the garage fixing the car, his hands covered in oil.

My family was an embarrassment, and I was tired of it. I *needed* this cell phone, and I *needed* that password.

I tiptoed across my bedroom floor, using my discarded clothes as stepping stones. When I got to the stairs, I looked back at my dirty laundry. No, it couldn't help me with this part. I braced one hand on the banister and one on the side rail along the wall while holding my breath then placed as little weight as I could on the first step.

It was silent. I let out my breath slowly and gulped down more air. It felt like a tight bubble in my throat. I forced it down to my lungs with a half swallow and tried the next step. Again, I managed it in silence. Maybe I could actually do this without waking Mom up. I moved faster, keeping to the sides of the steps as I descended. The wood was strongest there and tended to groan less. I could hardly believe it when my feet touched the cold linoleum of the hallway.

Yes!

I wanted to shout but swallowed another gulp of air instead. Mom had turned down the furnace, and the main floor was uncomfortably cold. The hairs on my legs stood on end as my skin tightened with goosebumps. I needed to hurry, or I'd wake Mom up just by hearing my teeth chattering. I tiptoed down the hall in the darkness, knowing the way by heart. Mom always picked up James' toys before bed. My only obstacle would be the living room furniture.

I was *so* close to my goal, standing in the living room doorway. I closed my eyes and visualised the furniture scattered through the room. The couch was to my left, Mom's armchair to my right. The TV was on the wall closest to me and to my right, the bookshelf stood almost directly in front of me.

I stepped ahead, holding a hand straight out in front of me, and didn't stop until my fingers touched books.

"Now, how do I get up there?" I whispered, turning my face upwards towards the laptop and the little red book.

What shelf had it been on? It was smaller than the rest of the books, so I should be able to find it by feel, but then what? I would need a light to read it, and then once I found the password, I might need to write it down. I couldn't take the whole book ...

I stretched my arms up and felt the book spines just above my head. My fingers barely touched the tops of some as I measured their height against each other. *There.* The book I touched was short and slender. The cover was smooth but the spine well creased. I grabbed it and pulled it down to my chest.

I stuck a foot out, looking for the side of the couch, and knocked my toes against the side table. The sound of its legs scraping against the floor was painfully loud in the quiet. I froze and listened. The thumbing in my chest sounded like thunder in my ears. Had Mom heard me?

My concentration was met with only the sound of the furnace and the eerie ticking of the kitchen clock down the hall.

Thank GOD.

I was getting really tired, but now that I knew where the side table was, it was easy to feel for the light switch. I closed my eyes as the bright beams stabbed at me, then opened them a slit and waiting a few seconds before looking at the book I held. Yes, I'd guessed right. The red cover might as well have been gold, and I quickly flipped through its pages.

THERE! Mom had marked it with the built-in ribbon.

I stopped short of a giggle of glee when I saw just how long the line of letters and symbols was. There was *no* way I was going to be able to memorise that. I needed to write it down. "Well, that's overkill, isn't it, Dad?" When did my parents learn to be so careful? Did I dare walk back to the kitchen in search of a pen?

I tiptoed across the living room and checked Mom's side table. Nope. But then I had a thought. What if? I slid a hand down between the chair arm and the seat cushion.

Eww!

I cringed as I touched old cheerios and … Was that a half-eaten pretzel? Definitely not what I was looking for. I tried the other side and barely held down another bubble of glee when I touched a smooth plastic tube. Could it be? It was!

I retrieved the pen and checked to see if the ink was still running by making a small scribble next to a larger one on the side of a page. Mom had done the same thing, and she would never notice the new mark.

The ink flowed after a few dry scratches, and I quickly copied the password onto the palm of my hand.

I took the pen with me as I placed the little book back into its empty slot on the bookshelf. Then I switched off the light and stood in the darkness, hands clutched around the smooth plastic, wishing it was a flashlight. I counted to ten and waited for my eyes to adjust.

The walk back up the hall was slow. My feet were going numb from the cold, and I regularly stopped to wiggle my toes. I wanted to dash up the stairs and jump into bed, but I could never do that quietly. So the *slow* acrobatic dance of light footsteps and balancing my weight on the banister and handrail began. It was *much* harder to pull myself up the steps than it had been coming down. My arms ached by the time I reached the top.

My open bedroom door welcomed me, and I left it wide open, too afraid any squeak would wake up the rest of the house. I settled in to the bed, but instead of wrapping myself up in the blankets and drifting off to sleep like I knew I needed to, I dug for the phone and thumbed it on. Now, where had the internet settings been?

I tapped on different apps until I found the one that asked for a Wi-Fi connection. Would this work? I pressed the access option and really did giggle as the images and text on the screen shifted and I was taken to internet options. There were several names that popped up, and I chose the one called "Coopers." Using the light from the phone screen, I copied the numbers and symbols from my palm when the pop-up asked for a password.

Connected

Relief was followed by a wave of fear as the phone I held BINGED. I dropped it on the bed and muffled the mechanical outburst with my pillow.

STOP! STOP! OH, PLEASE STOP!

I heard James cry, and my heart skipped a beat. Then my world shifted into slow motion as Mom's door opened and her quick footsteps patted up the stairs. I fumbled to grab the phone from under my pillow and squeeze the power button.

Off

The screen went black, and I shoved the phone back down in between my mattress and the bed box as Mom's head appeared above the last staircase step.

Three

"I can't believe you stole your parents' password."

"I didn't think someone so ignorant could figure out how to use my old messenger app."

"The other girls will NEVER be okay with you chatting in our group."

"Don't wear that stupid sweater to school tomorrow. You know, the one with the dumb flower on it. It makes you look like a kindergartener."

"Don't wear that purple top, either. It shows your boobs too much. It makes you look just as big as your MOM."

"I never would have given the phone to you if I knew you were going to SIN with it."

"You're so bad, Harmony."

The messages had come all night after I told the girls on the school bus I'd gotten it to work, and Amy had helped me set up my own accounts for the messenger app. They buzzed like angry bees in my brain.

I could feel the weight of the cell phone whether it was in my pocket or school bag. Even when it was in my room and I was downstairs with my family, I could feel it pressing down on the boards of my bed and the floor. Sometimes I looked up, afraid it would break through the ceiling and crush me. Sometimes, I wished it would.

"Tina is coming over for dinner tonight, kids," Mom said as soon as we all walked into the house a week later.

"Tina? You mean that lady from church you gave the letter to?" Joshua asked.

He was looking at her, his head cocked to the side, his eyebrow raised.

"Yes, that lady."

"I thought you didn't like her. I thought she was *mean*." He left his coat on the ground as he hurried to the kitchen for his after-school snack.

"DON'T forget to hang your coat!" Mom sighed as she followed him. "Let me check your lunch first, young man."

Her raised voice carried back to me with a snap, and I picked up my brother's coat, shaking half melted snow from its shoulders. It dusted the entryway mat and melted to water drops as I quietly watched. It made me smile to see them melt even though it probably meant wet socks were in my immediate future.

I hung Joshua's coat up beside mine in the closet and pushed all our boots to the side. If Tina was coming, she wouldn't want to walk over them.

It was strange that she was coming over, but I knew Mom had chatted with her earlier in the week. Were they friends now? She'd made Mom cry more than once. I'd seen the tears and heard her tell Dad about Tina's unkind words. I guess adults picked on each other too.

The cell phone was in my back pocket, burning like a hot coal while it weighed me down. I'd worn a belt today, afraid that the weight would cause a wardrobe accident. I knew it really wasn't that heavy, but still.

"Mom, do we have orange juice?" I called down the hall.

"No, Joshua just drank it. Sorry, babe. Do you want me to make you some grape?"

I nodded a yes as I entered the kitchen and laid my lunch kit on the counter.

The sound of the freezer blowing seemed louder than usual when Mom opened it to grab some frozen concentrate.

"Where's James?" she asked.

"Living room," I replied.

I sat down at the kitchen table to wait for the juice, thankful she hadn't asked me to make it myself. The phone was in my back pocket, digging into my leg. I needed to ditch it in my room.

"I'm *so* hungry," Joshua trumpeted while standing at the counter, spreading peanut butter onto some bread.

Mom rolled her eyes at him. The frozen juice slush now rested in a pitcher she took to the sink and began filling with water.

"Joshua, grab me a spoon from the drawer in front of you, please," Mom asked.

"Why is Tina coming over?" Joshua asked back.

Mom paused before answering. She squinted at the pitcher of juice as she stirred the frozen block resting at its bottom.

"She needs a friend right now. So we're going to be her friends."

"Even though she made you cry?" I asked.

She turned to look at me, her thoughts swirling behind her eyes.

"Yes. Some people don't realize when they're being mean. Sometimes we don't realise we're being mean. Most of the time when people say and do mean things, it's because they're hurting inside, and they need a friend. Tina needs a friend."

"Oh."

"Are you okay, Harmony?" Mom asked as she looked directly at me.

Did she know I was hiding something? "Just tired, Mom."

She handed me a cup of juice. "You've been tired the whole week. Aren't you sleeping?"

I shrugged, not wanting to answer the question and hating the feeling of her worried eyes moving over me.

"No reading late tonight, okay? Early to bed."

"I don't have to go to bed early too, do I?" Joshua asked between bites of bread.

"Nope, but only because you're going to be sweeping the basement for me after supper."

"WHAT? No!" he protested.

I giggled at the faces he made in between his last few bites of sandwich. Sweeping the basement really wasn't that bad of a job, and he knew it. But being Joshua, he had to amp up the theatrics, just in case Mom got sick of it and told him to "never mind."

"Well, what are you going to make *Harmony* do?"

"She's going to help me set the table then clear it after dinner."

I knew not to fight the inevitable but needed a rest. "I am going to go lay down for a few minutes first, Mom. Is that okay?"

She nodded as I got up and dropped my empty cup into the sink. "I'll have Joshua call you when I need you."

I groaned as I walked up the stairs, knowing full well Joshua's call wouldn't be verbal but more of a jump on or shake awake. Suddenly, a buzzing sensation shook my back pocket. I jumped, skipping a step and almost face planting into the staircase.

"Ouch!"

"Harmony, are you okay?"

"Yes, Mom!"

"What was that?" Joshua asked.

He stood right behind me on the staircase, arms crossed.

"*Nothing.*"

I skipped up the last few steps and closed my door behind me, crawled into bed and dug the phone out of my pocket. "That was close."

I was going to have to be way more careful. But, man, it was a good thing I was keeping the phone on vibrate only for notifications.

I rolled into the blanket and pulled it over my head. My quilt was overstuffed, a cloud of warmth, a cocoon of safety, a guard for secrets. But I left a hole above my head to let fresh air in as I thumbed the phone on. I was greeted by pink and purple bubbles.

"I need to change that background," I reminded myself. "It's just horrible."

I sighed again as I pulled down the notifications tab to see what had scared me so badly.

They were talking again.

"I know you're hiding something," Joshua whispered.

He'd snuck into my room and was poking my ribs through my quilt.

"What are you doing under there?" he added.

"Nothing, go away."

"I will not. It's time to get up and help Mom."

"Already?" I moaned.

"Yep, come on. What do you have under there with you?"

"NOTHING!" I threw back the covers and stuck my tongue out at him. I could feel the static from the blanket holding my hair up on end.

Joshua let out a snorting laugh.

"You look hideous!" he yelled as he ran out of the room.

Before I could take a deep breath and straighten my crumpled clothing, he stuck his head back through the doorway.

"Why are you crying? I wasn't that mean, was I?"

"No, and I'm not crying," I lied.

I wiped the last of my tears away as he disappeared down the stairs. It felt like the messages the girls had sent had burned my eyes. I squeezed them shut and held my breath for a second against the pain. Then I let it out to suck in clean air. If I didn't get over this, someone would find out, and *Tina* was coming soon. She might even be downstairs already.

It was a good thing I'd put the phone away, leaving the messages unanswered. Reading them had hurt enough. I pulled the blankets up over my pillow, a halfhearted effort at making the bed, then made my way downstairs.

The kitchen was abuzz as Mom put the finishing touches to her soup. A large bowl of chopped salad was ready as well.

"Can you grab a basket for the breadsticks, Harmony? They are just about to come out of the oven. There are a few at the bottom of the pantry, I think."

I stuck my head into the corner pantry and dug through the collection of plastic containers.

"How big?" I asked.

"Um ..." She paused, her fingers poised over the bubbling pot, just about to sprinkle in some salt. "Medium-sized."

I looked at the mess in front of me and the three old wicker-style baskets at the very back of the pantry.

"I think we need new baskets, Mom."

They were all stacked together when I pulled them out, but the side of the largest was crumbling, and the small one was filled with dust. I didn't want to think about what the other particles were.

"Oh? Let me look."

I lifted them above my head to show her the mess.

"Ewww ... Yeah. Never mind. Grab the big silver bowl then, babe. You can put *those* in the garbage."

I wiped out the big silver bowl and lined it with some paper towels before setting the table. The doorbell rang, and I heard James yelling at Joshua, "Hurry! Open!" Then Tina walked into the kitchen, her blue cashmere sweater and stylishly faded jeans sticking out like a neon sign that blinked "HIGH CLASS" amid our mess.

"I brought cookies," she said, lifting the plastic package above James' head as he tried to grab them from her.

"Cookies, Mama!" he squealed.

"*After* supper, James," Mom replied, a smile on her lips. "Welcome, Tina. How are you?"

"Doing, Mary, I'm doing."

The meal was a mix of silly and awkward moments like Joshua's exclamations of "I *hate* soup" and "I thought you didn't like my Mom?"

Followed by Tina's heartfelt, "I don't. I *love* your mom."

"Not as much as my dad loves her." Joshua sank down in his chair.

"You're right. Definitely not as much as your dad."

I'd *never* seen Mom blush so much. It was the strangest thing to see the awkward conversation and unsure glances between two adults slowly shifting to acceptance and companionship. Mom and Tina had never been enemies, but they were so different. How could a friendship like this ever work?

Some of the unkind things Amy and her friends had said were still floating in my brain, embers that burned as they bounced up against the edges of my skull.

"Why is your Mom such a mess? You're going to be just like her, you know."

"Take a shower before you come to school tomorrow. You smell funny. I want to know if it's your soap or just YOU."

I sniffed to hold back tears.

"Two breadsticks left. Joshua and Harmony. Who wants to finish them?" Tina asked.

"OH, ME!" Joshua said while grabbing one.

I poked at the salad on the plate.

"No, thank you."

"Harmony, are you okay?" Mom asked.

"I'm fine."

"She's lying," Joshua said. "She was crying in her room when I told her to come downstairs."

I could've cursed the existence of little brothers as concern drifted across Mom's face.

"Be QUIET Joshua! I said I was FINE." I pushed away from the table and ran for the stairs. How could he, right in front of a guest?

"Should I leave, Mary?" Tina asked, and I felt my heart constrict.

"No, not yet, Tina. Could you take James into the living room? I think right now is a perfect time for cookies."

The sounds of their voices faded under the pounding of my feet on the wooden steps, and I slammed my bedroom door for emphasis, knowing they'd all wince as they stared after me. First, I crawled into bed and then covered my head with the blankets. A tightness formed in my chest, squeezing out the air. I took in small gasps, but it felt like I was slowly suffocating. My blanket cocoon soon became oppressive, and I threw it aside.

Footsteps at the bottom of the stairs sent me into a panic. I did *not* want to talk. I did *not* want to see *anyone*. I knew it was Mom as soon as the steady squeak reached me. Joshua would have run, and James would have crawled, slapping his hands on the steps. I jumped off the bed and grabbed my door handle, bracing my feet against the floor and pulling back with my whole weight. No one was going to come into my room. Not even *her*.

I felt it when she tested the door handle. The silver knob tried to turn, but I squeezed it as hard as I could, praying she wouldn't fight me.

Instead, she stopped and knocked gently on the wood. "Harmony, can I come in?"

"NO!" My answer came out as more of a growl than a word, my throat threatening to close up with emotion. "Go away."

"I'm sorry your brother embarrassed you. But ... Is there something you need to tell me?"

My fingers had blanched as I clenched the door handle. "No."

"You know I love you, right?" Was that a hand brushing against the wood of the door? Would she try to push her way in, after all?

I tried to hold the door even harder. My fingers greased with sweat, forcing me to shift my grip.

"Please, just go away, Mom!"

I wasn't ready for this. There was nothing I wanted to tell her. My mind's eye could see the cell phone tucked away against my mattress, a lead brick that threatened to collapse the house like an earthquake, if I wasn't careful.

"Okay. I'll finish my visit with Tina and then get James to bed. We will talk later, Harmony."

I knew Mom's voice and the shifts in her tone told me she would not let this go. I had to make a plan.

Four

I didn't let the doorknob go until I heard Mom step off the steps and into the hall downstairs. My fingers throbbed with my heartbeats as I released it, flexing them as I wiped my face to dry my tears. I would need to change my shirt. I pulled it off and blew my nose on the hem before throwing it in the dirty laundry hamper. What next? pyjamas. I immediately looked for my favourite pair by digging through my dresser drawer to find them, neatly folded and ready for me.

The soft blue material felt like a hug as I slipped it over my head. After shimmying out of my jeans and throwing them towards the dirty clothes hamper, I again cocooned myself in blankets, leaving a hole just big enough to breathe.

The blanket muffled the sounds in the house. How long did I have before Mom came back? I pulled the cell phone from its hiding place and thumbed it on. The brightly coloured background of pink and purple bubbles greeted me, as well as a full notification bar. I swiped to the side, sending the previews cascading into nothingness.

You shouldn't have taken the phone from Amy.

You can't tell your Mom.

You're going to be in so much trouble.

The voices in my head started bouncing around again.

You stole *the password.*

You *kept secrets.*

You deserve the things Amy and the others say about you.

It's all *true.*

Was it? I knew not all of it was, but it was becoming harder and harder as the days passed to sort it all out. The words were tying themselves around my heart.

"I should just throw this thing away and forget about it."

But I knew Amy would never let me forget about it. She would want to know where the phone was. Could I just give it back to her? Maybe ... But if I did, she wouldn't let me forget what I'd done. It wouldn't stop the unkind words. What should I do? I could never sit at the back of the bus quietly listening to the older girls again. I wasn't invisible anymore. Amy's gift had been more than an invitation to join them. I now realized it marked me as her target.

You should have known.

But I wanted to be like the others so much, I'd ignored the truth.

"You really are stupid, Harmony," I whispered.

I wondered what Mom and Tina were doing downstairs. I still couldn't believe someone like *Tina* wanted to be friends with *my* mom. How could Mom accept that after the mean things she'd said to her? Should I just forgive and forget like she had? If I did, was there hope that someday Amy would accept me as "one of the girls?" Did I still want that?

The longer I held the cell phone in my hand, the heavier it got. Or was it my heart? Either way, it was weighing me down. I wished it would drop me through the floor and hide me under the basement's foundations. It felt like such an end would be easier than talking to Mom or facing another morning on the school bus.

If only we had two cars, then I could ask Mom to drive us to school instead. But no. Just like cell phones, my parents only had one, and Dad took it with him every week.

We walked everywhere when he was gone. Even when the temperatures dipped below -20 degrees Celsius.

"You can always put an extra layer on," was what Mom said when we complained about getting groceries together on cold evenings.

I sighed. My room was dark. I hadn't turned on the lights, and the winter sun had set hours ago. Was that the front door closing? Did it mean Tina was gone?

The sounds of the boys running around soon drifted up through the floor. Mom sure was having a time with them ...

Joshua's voice stabbed its way through my quiet as he walked up the steps. "It's not fair I had to do *Harmony's* job. She was supposed to clear the table."

"She'll sweep the basement for you tomorrow since it's too late now."

"FINE." A door slammed, and I heard James knocking around the boys' bedroom as Mom dressed him for bed. Then the notes of a lullaby drifted under my door.

I closed my eyes, wishing I could go back in time and be the toddler getting ready for bed, not worrying about having to give Mom an explanation for anything. When I opened them again, not wanting to fall asleep, the shadows around my wall posters caught my eye.

It was just light enough to see the edges had started to curl up. I knew the words on the one right across from my bed by heart.

Trust in the Lord with all your heart,
and do not lean on your own understanding.
In all your ways acknowledge Him,
and He will make straight your paths.
Be not wise in your own eyes;
fear the Lord, and turn away from evil.
It will be healing to your flesh
and refreshment to your bones.
- Proverbs 3:5-8 ESV -

It was one Mom had given to me, one of her ways of teaching me without "teaching" me. Trust ... Trust in God, trust my Mom, trust myself. It was hard.

I didn't feel I was very good at trusting God. I honestly didn't think of Him very much. He was just there. I clutched the cell phone as I thought about Him, shame burning in my heart and fingertips.

"Harmony, are you still awake?" Mom's gentle voice drifted under the door.

"Yes," I croaked, my throat dry and sore from tears.

Instead of coming inside, I heard her tiptoeing down the steps. Had she not heard me? Was I going to get out of talking to her? Maybe she was too tired to deal with a troubled daughter …

But no, I heard her climbing back up, and soon my bedroom door creaked as she opened it. I hid the cell phone deep in the folds of my blanket.

"Here, baby." She handed me a warm mug, the scent of lemon and honey rising with the steam.

"Thanks." I sipped it and winced. The lemon was stronger than I liked.

"James helped make it before bed … Sorry," Mom said as she sat down beside me. The mattress compressed under her and pulled me closer until our legs touched.

I wiggled around so as not to be pulled onto her lap, and we both giggled at the ridiculousness of it.

"At least we both still fit in your room, right?" she joked.

"Oh, Mom." I rolled my eyes at her.

"What?"

When I looked at her, her eyes twinkled. It didn't look like she minded her body being awkward. Not right now, anyway.

"Now, what's going on with you, my girl? Don't say it's *nothing* because I know that's not true. It's been over a week that you've been moping around. I should have asked you last week what was up. I'm sorry I didn't."

At first I said nothing. I just looked around at the shadows while sipping my lemon and honey water. Mom let the silence drag out, but I could feel her watching me, waiting.

"Do you like yourself, Mom?" I finally asked.

"Sometimes, but not all the time. I'm not perfect, am I?"

I shook my head no.

"Do you like yourself, Harmony?"

I shrugged. "Not really. The girls at school think I'm weird."

I heard the frown in her voice when she asked, "Oh? Why do you think that?"

"Because I'm so different. They have cell phones and skinny jeans. They go places ... Their parents have cars and ..." I shrugged again.

"You know those are just *things*, not *you*. Are you sure they don't like you? Avery does, doesn't she, and Karmen?"

"Yes, but those are the little girls. Not the *older* ones. Not the cool ones ..."

"They are the same age as you, aren't they? Twelve isn't little, Harmony." I heard the growing concern in her voice. "And who do you mean by the *older* girls?"

"Amy and her friends. I like them ..." My voice caught as I asked myself if that were still true.

"Amy, Pastor Grill's daughter?"

I nodded yes.

"She is a lot older than you, isn't she?"

"She's fifteen ... But she's the pastor's daughter, and everyone likes her! She is so cool. She knows a lot, too."

"What do you mean?"

"About adult stuff. She knows a lot, and she is really pretty. Even the boys like her."

"And you like her too?"

"Yes! Or, mostly."

"Mostly?"

I bit my lip.

"Why is your Mom such a mess? You're going to be JUST like her, you know." I rolled the words from one of her messages over in my mind.

"Sometimes she doesn't say nice things," I told Mom. "Sometimes she makes fun of people. All the girls do it. They do it to each other. They don't mind. It's just jokes."

"But do you mind?"

I shrugged again. Hot tears dripped down my cheeks.

"What things do they say to you, Harmony?"

I swallowed and looked into my mug. It was almost empty, and I silently wished for more.

"Harmony?"

The concern in her voice pulled it into deep tones. I could tell that she wasn't trying to rushing me, but I didn't know how to say what her eyes were asking me. I didn't want her to know.

Tell her.

NO!

Show her.

Don't be crazy. She'll take the phone away.

You need to tell her.

She will NEVER let you have another phone EVER.

They are bullies, and it's not okay.

They will never let you be their friend if you tell her.

You don't really want that anymore ... Do you?

I felt Mom's arms wrap around me as my tears spilled faster. The cell phone felt like a brick against my leg. I hated it. I loved my mom, but I knew she was going to be furious if I told her my secret. My heart raced as my thoughts battled.

After what seemed like an eternity, I felt too tired to fight myself or Mom any longer. I fished the cell phone out of the blankets and handed it to her, refusing to look at her face. When she took it from me, I pulled the blanket over my head. If she could forgive Tina, maybe she could forgive me too.

Apology

Amy

One

My vision was red. I saw the hue everywhere I looked, and even the shadows in the corners of my room had turned dark like blood.

"That little BRAT!"

I didn't care who heard me yelling through the door. Let them all know I was livid and to stay away. None of them cared what we did in our own house as long as no one else knew.

Say the right things.

Look the right way.

But when you're home, you can play as you may.

The rhyme swam behind my eyes, making me giggle in disgust. I'd come up with it myself one day when Mom told me she didn't care how I behaved once we were home. "But for the LOVE OF

GOD, you will act properly at church!" I wrinkled my nose at the memory.

She'd confronted me as I walked in the door from school today.

"I got a phone call from Mary Cooper." For a moment, the steel in her eyes had locked me in place. "She told me all about how you gave Harmony a cell phone without permission, encouraged her to use it without permission, and then bullied her for a week. I won't even go into the horrible things you've been saying about Mary herself, but I know about them. She sent me the copies of your messages. What were you thinking?" The last bit she'd almost whispered, her eyes burning with anger.

"What?" I replied. "I simply gave the girl a gift. It's not my fault she didn't tell her mom about it. I didn't *make* her use it. Besides, she practically begged me for it."

That wasn't exactly true. Harmony had never asked me for a phone. But the kid's puppy-dog eyes had been following me around the bus and school for months, and being generous made me look good. She wanted to be part of the "in" crowd. I simply gave her a way to do it.

"I thought we were supposed to be generous with people 'less fortunate' than us. I *thought* I was being kind." With that, I'd walked away from her while her eyes burned holes into my back, but the spiteful prayer on my lips was interrupted as she called down the hall.

"Your cell phone, Amy, now. You lose that privilege until I've had a discussion with your father." She meant it as a threat, but I knew it was a joke. Dad wouldn't do anything.

I'd fished my new cell phone out of a pocket and tossed it to her, watching her fumble to catch it before it could hit the hard floor tiles. I'd laughed then and again now at the thought. Dad wasn't the only one who was a joke.

But now sitting alone in my room, my hands ached for that phone. What would the girls be talking about without me? Or saying about me while I wasn't there to police them? How high was the notification number going to reach while I waited for Mom to do her parental duty and "talk to Dad?" How long would I be waiting?

I grabbed a book from my bedside table and chucked it at the wall.

"Just wait until tomorrow on the bus, Harmony. Just you wait."

I glared at the dent now showing in the drywall. Dad would be mad about that. We didn't own this house, the church did. "Perks of being in ministry," he always said.

Ministry: another joke. Always busy, but doing what? Sitting and listening to people moan and groan about how horrible their life is? Watching old people die? Writing sermons and reciting them on Sunday mornings while half the congregation sleeps? Arguing with a group of old people at council meetings? What a drag.

My fingers itched like crazy to hold my cell phone, but I knew there was no use in asking for it back. Dad wouldn't be home until six. They would talk after dinner, and I was sure Dad himself would return it before bed. I just had to be patient.

I switched from sitting on the bed to sitting at my computer desk. The monitor was dusty, and I brushed my shirt sleeve across the screen then used the hem to clean around the edges. I wondered if I could remember the passwords to my socials and access them through the browser instead of my cell. It was worth a try, right?

I pulled my books from my backpack as the computer booted up. It seemed slow to me. I should ask Dad when I could get a new one.

The *click* of my mouse satisfied the itch in my fingers. It wasn't the same as holding the whole internet in my hands like I did with my cell phone, but it still felt good. I clicked around and opened the browser, bringing up my favourite social site.

"Now ... What was it again?"

I tapped my fingers against my lips and looked at the ceiling. As I blinked, the red retreated to the edges of my vision, and true colours returned.

"Ah! Maybe this."

My typing was rhythmic. I tried one phrase and then another, but the "incorrect" symbol flashed at me. The red crept back.

"Shit! What is it?" I would've gotten a scolding from my parents for my language choice, but this was my room, and I would say whatever I wanted.

"Shit!" This time I yelled it as the "incorrect" symbol refused to disappear.

I gave up and trudged over to my bed, falling face first into the purple folds of my duvet cover.

I made Mom call me twice for supper before dragging my feet the whole way to the dining room. The chair legs screeched as I dragged it out and sat down. Mom glared at me. I rolled my eyes.

"What's wrong?" Dad asked.

"We'll talk about it after dinner."

"Where's Ashley?" I asked as Mom picked up the bowl of salad and handed it to Dad.

"At a friend's house. She asked to leave when you started screaming in your bedroom."

My older sister was as quiet as a church mouse, the perfect pastor's kid, and two years older than me.

"Oh, I didn't know she had any friends to go visit."

"AMY!"

"What? It's true."

Dad handed me the salad, a bland look on his face.

"No, it's not, Amy," he said. "She might not have a crowd that follows her everywhere like you. But she has friends."

I rolled my eyes again as I filled my plate with spinach and iceberg lettuce.

"What's this?" I held up a curly, leafy bit.

"Kale," Mom answered

She didn't look at me for the rest of dinner, politely passing the potatoes and baked chicken breast to Dad when I asked for it. Then she went in search of the ketchup when I wondered aloud why it wasn't on the table, placing the bottle beside my arm as she passed me to sit back down. I called her lack of attention "the cold shoulder punishment." As a child, I hated it. But my fifteen years had taught me she wasn't able to keep it up for long. Soon her fiery eyes and whispered threats would blaze at me again. I told myself to enjoy this break.

She chitchatted with Dad about his day, how his sermon was coming along, and what the weekend would look like. I drowned out their conversation by humming to myself. The noise my fork made against the dinner plate, cutting white potato flesh and stirring around my salad, was fascinating. Or at least, I thought so until Dad asked me to stop.

I obeyed for a while, but it was all so boring that I just couldn't resist starting again a few minutes later. My knife sent out a terrible screech as it slowly scraped the porcelain.

"Amy, if you won't eat, go to your room." I'd known she wouldn't be able to ignore me for the whole dinner.

A smirk crawled across my lips. "What? I *am* eating. I'm not doing anything but cutting my food."

"Amy, go."

I looked at my dad with hurt eyes. But I listened, making sure the chair scraped the floor as I pushed it backward.

"I don't know what to do with her anymore, Arthur. I feel so lost."

I heard frustrated tears in my mother's voice as I walked away, but I didn't care. My fingers were itching again. I rubbed them against my jeans.

Without my cell phone, I had nothing to do but stare at my homework now scattered across my desk. I didn't have much of it, and didn't feel like doing it, so I didn't. The numbers and equations swam on the page in front of me. I didn't think I could focus even if I wanted to.

Sitting on my bed, my pillows pulled around me like a cocoon, I waited, knowing I should have actually eaten my dinner when the red vision returned with the rumbling of my stomach.

I heard Ashley come home at seven-thirty p.m. Her call for Mom echoed in the tiled entryway and down the hall to my room. Then someone started rummaging in the hall closet, and that was *strange*. So I got up and opened the bedroom door.

"What're you doing?" I asked the back of my sister's head.

"Packing," she replied as she pulled down a small duffel bag from the top shelf.

She was tall and slender like me, but her hair was a dull straight brown, not blonde and curly like mine.

"Packing for what? It's a school night."

"Ask Mom," was all she said as she entered her own room and closed the door.

I shrugged, not really caring what she did with herself but jealous she was getting out of the house.

Where was Dad, and why was it taking them so long to have a chat and bring back my phone? Then I saw him down the hall, walking from the living room to the kitchen. He ran his hands through his hair and turned his back to me. Was he upset?

I stepped back into my room and closed the door. Better to wait this one out.

It was eighty-thirty, and I'd already changed into my pyjamas when I heard the soft tapping at my door.

Good Lord, it's about time.

"Amy? Can I come in?" my dad called.

I didn't wait for him to open the door but stepped across the room and found him standing next to my mom. My heart skipped a beat. This was not what I was expecting. Why were they both here?

"Sure," I said in reply and let the door swing wide.

The look I gave my mom was nasty.

I don't want you here. GO AWAY! the red inside me screamed at her.

My dad grabbed the computer chair and sat down.

"Come here for a minute, Amy. We need to talk." His finger pointed to the bed, and I obeyed, my heart doing flip-flops.

"Can I have my phone back now?" I asked.

Mom remained in the doorway, her arms crossed, her face tired. Dad and I both looked over at her as he paused before answering.

"No."

"WHAT? Why not?" I yelled at him before turning my red vision onto my mother again. "This isn't fair!"

"Amy, stop it!" Dad yelled back.

I would have bolted from my bed, but Dad manoeuvred the computer chair to block my route to the door, placing himself in between me and Mom.

"Your mother and I are very concerned about your attitude the last few months. I thought giving you space to go through these teen years would help you learn to regulate yourself, but it's clearly not working."

He took a deep breath. Was that fear in his eyes?

Dark red tendrils reached out from the glands at the edges of my vision to wave horrible fingers in front of me, half obscuring Dad's face.

"So, there are two things you will have to do before you're allowed to have it back."

I sucked in air. "So I will get it back?"

"Maybe," Mom said from behind Dad. She'd stepped forward and placed a hand on his shoulder.

"You will apologize to Harmony Cooper, in person, and in front of the girls at school."

I gaped at him.

"Second. Your mother will contact the school tomorrow and set up meetings with the on-staff counsellor. You will go to as many meetings as the counsellor thinks you need."

My vision changed from red to black. I couldn't see either of them. I could barely hear them with my heart pounding in my ears.

"I will not." My whisper mimicked Mom's from this afternoon in the hallway: quiet and pointed.

"Then you will not be getting your phone back." It was Mom's voice. I could tell she was pinning me with her gaze even if I couldn't clear my head to see it.

I could still do better.

"I hate you," I breathed.

She gasped, followed by a swallow as my words pierced her heart.

Next I screamed at them both.

Two

I couldn't remember standing up from the bed. But here I was, on my feet, toes curled into the carpet, fists clenched as if I were ready for a fight.

I blinked and looked around me. Where had they gone? I hadn't realized they'd left the room. What was it Dad had said before I stopped hearing him?

"You have the rest of this week to apologize to Harmony. If you choose not to, I'll cancel your phone plan."

"That little brat!" I screamed at the surrounding void. I swam in more shades of red than I could count. My breath came fast. I couldn't believe it. What had happened to my pushover dad, usually too busy to do anything but throw me a few dollars when I asked for it? What had happened to Mom? She was usually too worried, thinking about what others would think of us. A counsellor? Are you kidding? What would her friends think when they found out her daughter, the pastor's daughter, was going to therapy?

She thinks she can keep this embarrassment a secret.

Confidentiality. They think it will protect them.

They think you're going crazy.

Maybe you are going crazy.

What will YOUR friends think?

I heard laughing behind me and jumped, spinning as I did.

See, next thing will be the psych ward.

My heart skipped a beat, fear arresting its racing with a frozen draft from the window. I shivered. When did I open the window? It was just a crack. The chill ripped through the red haze to let me see.

I walked over and pushed it closed, waiting for the satisfying click of the latch as I locked it.

The red drained from my vision as my heart slowed. I was so tired, and my arms felt like logs as I crawled under the welcoming hug of my duvet. I pulled it up over my head before letting go of a wave of emotion with another scream and water that stung my eyes. My throat was sore. It was like the red haze was trying to claw its way back into my body.

YOU'RE *the one who's the joke.*

They hate you.

You make their life difficult.

You're an inconvenience, a stain on their perfection.

Ashley knew what was coming and ran away from it today.

You disgust them all.

I couldn't tell if the horrible whispers came from my head or were floating around me like a pack of ghosts on an invisible prowl.

I coughed. The air under the blanket was too warm; I needed a drink.

As soon as you walk out that door, SHE *will be there.*

Better to stay here in the dark where you belong.

How late was it? I poked my head out from under the blanket to check my bedside clock. 9:48 already? Where had I gone for the last hour? The red was gone, my tears running clear and fast, my nose dripping with regret.

Regret?

Yes, I could recognize my regret. I'd said and done horrible things. Was I sorry for them? I wasn't sure, but I definitely regretted it. I hated being called out.

I swallowed again. An itch added to the soreness. I had no choice. I would have to risk bumping into Mom again.

The door squeaked on its hinges. The hall was dark but for a soft light flowing down the hall from the kitchen, leaving corners and the end of the hall by the bathroom in shadows. Now, did I risk the kitchen or hope a cup sat on the counter in the bathroom?

Yeah, bathroom it was.

I tiptoed down the cold hall. My bare feet were silent against the chilled tiles. That chill travelled up my heels and ankles. I hated it.

"Why don't we have a rug laid down in this hallway?" I muttered.

The bathroom was lit by a nightlight plugged in beside the washstand. I sighed from relief when I saw the plastic cup sitting beside the tap. I picked it up and eyed its edges. It looked clean ... How many people had already used it to rinse toothpaste-filled mouths, though? The light in the hallway flickered. I poked my head out the bathroom door and watched shadows dancing around the kitchen entryway.

That made my decision. Mom or Dad or *both* were still prowling around.

"Get it over with, Amy. You have school in the morning," I muttered.

I gave the cup a good rinse before filling it and gulping down the cold liquid. I then filled it again to bring back to my room, just in case.

The dance of shadows from the kitchen had stopped, and I was just about to turn to my bedroom when I heard a strange sound, like muttering and sniffling. I stopped, one foot suspended over my carpet, one still planted on the cold tiles.

Get your butt back into bed, Amy. You don't need to go investigate.

But I did, I really did. The curiosity gnawed at my gut. I *needed* to know what was going on. So cup in hand, I crept up the hall.

As I peered into the kitchen, I saw Mom seated at the table in the centre of the room, her face in her hands. She was the one making strange noises, shoulders shaking in between hiccups and sniffles.

I stared, not used to seeing such emotion seeping from my mother. Then I caught some words she was whispering to the ether.

"... not good enough ... failing ... Oh, God! Help."

I felt fresh red creeping up my face. She was praying, and I'd never seen such "ugly tears" before. A pile of used tissues sat beside her elbow while she crushed one against her face.

I guess she knows she isn't anywhere close to perfect.

Again, I heard a laugh behind me and jumped, clutching my cup of water to stop the liquid from sloshing over the rim.

If she isn't "anywhere close to perfect," then what does that make you? A devil?

My insides boiled at the internal accusation, and I backed up a few paces before turning and scurrying into my room, setting the cup down on my bedside table so I could cover my ears with my hands.

"Shut up!" I'd said it too loudly and gulped as I glanced back at my open door.

"Please don't hear me, please don't hear me," was my mumbled prayer.

Three

My mind couldn't reconcile the image of my dejected mother, weeping into a tissue, with the cold eyes she rolled over me at breakfast. Did I dream seeing her like that?

No, I'd spied the pile of tissues now lining the waste basket.

"I'm driving you to school this morning," Mom stated in her matter-of-fact tone as I stirred my cereal.

My answer had been a silent nod as I drank my slightly watered orange juice. Sleep had only come in brief spurts for me as my fingers itched for my phone, and my mind screamed taunts and hate behind the shield of my eyelids.

I didn't wear as much mascara as I usually did. Nor did I pick my usual red or pink lipstick either but chose only my hydrating gloss. I brushed and braided my curls in silence, not wanting them bouncing about my tired eyes. I chose my brown tuque instead of my usual pink with black stars. Perhaps if I signalled to the other girls in this way, they would let me have a day of silence before bombarding me with questions about my online absence.

My feet pulled my winter boots through the thin layers of new snow that greeted us as we walked out the door. The motion left distorted tracks through the fresh white landscape. It was crisp, but the sun shone brightly and threatened to lift my buried spirits. I rejected it by sliding on a pair of sunglasses I always carried in my winter coat. The dark lenses hid the sparkles that flashed across the snow's surface. I caught Mom lifting her eyebrows at me as she slid into the driver's seat.

The drive to school wasn't too far, and on bright mornings like this, it almost felt wrong to not be walking. But I knew how fast the chill could creep into someone's bones even when the sun shone with a brilliant, deceptive face. I was grateful to be able to stretch my legs out and lean back instead of scrunching them into the cramped space of the school bus bench.

Mom cleared her throat when we stopped at a red light.

"I have your phone." That caught my attention, and with a flutter of my heart, I looked over at her. "I'll visit the school office this morning before heading over to the church. You'll have the perfect opportunity to apologize as the rest of the kids get off the bus."

"I seriously don't understand what the big deal is." My eyes rolled behind my shades.

"And therein lies one of your problems, Amy." The sigh that escaped as Mom shook her head at me was pure disgust. "Well, the choice is yours. Apologize and get your phone back. Refuse and lose it. It's up to you."

I honestly didn't know what I was going to do. Just the mention of my phone sent my fingers tingling and my brain begging for a look at the lock screen. Things would have been different if I were riding the bus instead of being carted around like a child.

It was early as we pulled into the school parking lot. The first busload of kids was still a ways down the street. Hope is Here Christian School was the name stretched across the small carport protecting the school entrance. The iron letters glimmered in the sun, sporting layers of fresh snow in every curve. It shared the name of our church just a few blocks away, and as the first bus pulled into the drop-off loop, I saw faces of all ages who shared Sunday mornings with me.

I wrinkled my nose at all of them, and I watched the kids split as the high schoolers entered through a separate door, the door I should be using. The elementary kids headed out to the snow-covered playing field to wait for the bell as orange-vested volunteers ushered the kindergarteners through the main entrance. A second bus pulled in and poured out its human cargo, then a third pulled behind it, and a line formed, small faces plastered to cold windows, waiting to be released. The parking lot was also filling up with those who drove to school and those who walked from nearby homes.

"Come on, Amy, your regular bus is in the lineup now."

I skirted around a large patch of ice as I followed her, my backpack slipped onto one shoulder, glaring a silent warning at the first older kids who waved hello to me. Now was not the time for their banter.

I watched my regular group of friends exit the bus. Iris, who was a year younger than me, waved as I walked towards the now undulating mass of kids all dressed in snow clothing until they looked like brightly coloured stuffed animals. Then I spied *her* ducking behind the crowd.

The red behind my eyes rose like a slowly filling pool until I was looking through red waves at her pink and blue tuque, its pom-pom waving hello. One of the other younger girls pointed at me, her breath coming out in puffs of crystallized droplets. I watched as Harmony looked up, her own eyes losing their lustre when she saw me.

Mom pushed me forward as I tried to stop in the middle of the tide of children. I shrugged her off and raised a warning finger to my friend Sarah, who had just opened her mouth, a question peeking out from behind her long eyelashes.

"Now, Amy," Mom whispered from behind me.

I gritted my teeth. This wasn't fair. I shouldn't have to do this in front of everyone else. I shouldn't have to do this at *all*. Now that I was looking at Harmony herself, I wasn't one bit sorry.

"If you want your phone back, do this." Mom's words stabbed the back of my head. My fingers itched, and I slid my hands out of my woolen mittens to rub each finger, an attempt to stop the tingling. Harmony could tell it was her I was looking for, and she grabbed her little friend's hand. Was she afraid of me? If so, good. I knew this would lose me power points in the popularity game, but if she was shaking in her boots, the damage could be mitigated.

She took me by surprise as she let go of her friend's hand and dashed up to me, shifting from side to side as she dug something out of her coat pocket. She didn't look at my face but shoved a mass of cold plastic and metal at me.

"Here, Amy. Thank you, but I don't want this anymore." It was my old phone.

Her abruptness shocked me for a second.

Gutsy, kid, very gutsy.

"Oh, well, thank you for giving it back," I sputtered.

It seemed like everyone was watching us.

Do something, stupid.

"I'm sorry it didn't work out. Maybe when you're older." I looked down my nose at her and watched as a spark came back into her eyes.

"Actually, I'm not interested anymore."

My jaw dropped. Where on earth did this spunk come from?

I felt my mother prodding my back.

"Amy!" Her harsh whisper rippled past me.

"Give me a minute!" I snapped back.

She is making you look like an idiot.

I crossed my arms over my chest and cleared my throat to let everyone know it was my turn to talk.

"I'm sorry too, Harmony. I didn't mean for my *gift* to hurt you. We'll all try to be more careful from now on."

There, I'd maintained my power stance. I could tell by the looks on the other girls' faces I hadn't lost too many points with them over this little one's insecurities.

Harmony simply nodded at me and walked away, her friend whispering into her ear as they went.

The bell rang, and I turned to Mom as the last few kids rushed past.

"Happy now?"

She definitely wasn't. Her eyes felt like claws trying to rip past my red haze.

"That was barely an apology, and you know it."

But I had won in her eyes, and she handed me my prize. The itching in my fingers calmed as I hit the power button and groaned at the high notification number blinking at me.

"Put it away, Amy, you don't have time for it now."

I smirked at her back as she absently waved me into the high school entrance, her own steps taking her back to the main doors. I would be a few minutes late to class, but everyone knew my Mom was here now, so I didn't expect any problems from my teachers. As I scrolled through them, I cancelled the notifications.

"Oh my God. I can't leave these people alone for a minute without *drama*." I giggled.

The red hung at the corner of my vision, but I hardly noticed it as I stowed my backpack in my locker, deposited my coat beside it, and headed to first period.

Four

"Twice a week? Are you kidding me?"

"No, I'm not kidding you," Mom replied.

The table was set for four, but again, Ashley was absent. Her empty seat threatened to suck me in like a black hole from space. I didn't know why it affected me so much, except maybe the fact I was jealous. Why did she get to visit whoever she wanted on a whim these days? The shifting of family rules felt like an earthquake in my heart.

"For how long?" I asked.

"At least the next six weeks. Then the counsellor will assess how you're doing and change the schedule."

"This is ridiculous ..." The sound of my whining made me wince. I knew I was acting like a spoiled brat, but I couldn't keep my mouth shut.

"I apologized to the kid already, in front of practically the whole school, I might add! This is unfair. I don't need to see an F-ing counsellor."

"Amy! That language isn't allowed in this house. I never want to hear you use it in front of me again." My father's voice rumbled as he spoke.

I couldn't stand it anymore. I grabbed my dinner plate and stomped off to my room. No way was I going hungry overnight because of *them* again.

Peas slid around my plate, and I lost a few down the hallway. When one found its way under my bare feet and turned into a slippery mass between my toes, I swore again.

I heard chair legs scraping on the floor and my mother's strained voice.

"Arthur, let her go. Yelling at her won't help."

Well, she's right ...

I was a few minutes late for my appointment, but my feet had rooted to the hallway floor. A full-length glass door stood between me and my destination. "Hope is Here, Counsellors" was painted across the glass at eye level.

My fingers itched again, but this time it wasn't with a longing to flip through my phone. No, I wished I could pick the cuticles off my nails and then chew them to pieces rather than go through that door. The only good part of this situation was the silence of the hallways. Everyone else was in class, so I was free of their prying eyes.

As soon as you step through that door, you will wear a new label.

One far worse than "Preacher's Kid."

Everyone will find out eventually.

But did it really matter if everyone knew? They'd already witnessed my outbursts and humiliation at the hands of Harmony Cooper. Just the thought of her raised red waves through my vision.

"Hello. Are you Amy?"

I blinked and looked into a set of deep brown eyes.

"Yeah, I guess," I replied.

She'd come to the door as I stood in a daze, pushing it open wide, inviting me inside. Her hair was tied in two long braids that draped over her shoulders touching her belt, each fastened at the ends with bands of intricate beadwork.

"Welcome, Amy. My name's Carla. I'm happy you made it, and I'm looking forward to getting to know you."

"I don't remember seeing you around school before." My bluntness slid past her as she ushered me inside and closed the door behind me.

"This is my first year working at 'Hope is Here,' and I'm kept pretty busy. How has your morning been so far?"

I shrugged.

A rug with warm shades of brown lay over the cold concrete floor, and shelves with books and toys lined the walls. Two oversized chairs faced each other, and just behind them, an enormous desk overflowed with papers and pens.

"Are you thirsty? I've water, or would you like some warm tea?"

"I don't care for tea."

Carla patted the back of one of the big brown chairs as she walked to a table against the wall. The sound of pouring water was loud in the awkward silence around me. My eyes darted around the room, taking in all the new colours and textures.

"I've never been in here before."

Carla looked over her shoulder at me, a hot water kettle in her hand.

"I've tried to make my office warm and welcoming. What do you think of it?" she asked as she walked to the centre of the area rug and handed me a paper cup.

I could feel the chill of the water through the thin paper and noticed how dry my throat was. I sipped at the cool liquid before sitting down and saying, "Looks okay to me." The chair's cushion welcomed me like a hug.

"Good!" Carla sipped from her own steaming cup as she sat across from me. "Now, Amy, tell me a little about yourself and why you're here today."

"You mean my mother didn't tell you all about it already?"

Carla chuckled, her eyes twinkling with a soft inner light.

"Of course she did. But that's her side of the story, not yours. I very much want to hear what you think about being here and why your Mom felt you needed to talk with me."

I cocked my head to the side and thought before I answered.

I don't think I've ever been asked what I think by an adult before.

"You're really different from what I was expecting."

"I hope it's a 'good' different."

"Maybe, we'll have to see how all this goes." I waved my hand in a circle while arching my eyebrows at her.

She met my challenge with a smile, and the red that had risen in my vision in the hall parted in front of me like the red sea.

Broken China

Rose

One

THE CARVED SEAT OF the dining room chair cradled me as I sank into its gentle curves. I'd just turned off the lights throughout the house except in the kitchen. Here I'd dimmed them, a relief from the stimulation of the day and the turmoil of confronting our daughter, Amy. Her hate-filled whisper had thrown a bucket of water over my heart. I felt as if I were sitting in its puddle unable to find the plug to pull and open the drain of relief.

"Oh, God, why did you give me a daughter who hates me so much?" I asked as the tissue in my hands soaked in my tears.

I waited, listening to the sounds of the house amplified by human silence. The clock ticked, my watch a backup to its chorus; the refrigerator hummed, a side melody; my heart pounded, its accompanying metronome. Was I missing something? It still all seemed so loud.

God, are you there?

Omniscient.

Omnipresent.

Omnipotent.

These three words whispered through the song grating in my brain. I knew them well. I'd listened to so many lessons, sermons, and conversations about their meaning.

All-knowing.

Present everywhere.

All powerful.

That is who I knew God to be, that is the Being who I was speaking to. He couldn't help but be here, but did He care?

"It hurts my heart when she speaks to me like that. I don't understand where this hate has come from. What did I do wrong, God?"

Again, I listened, hoping to hear that faint whisper I'd been taught was His voice. Instead of the reassurance I longed for, I heard the pat of footsteps in the hall that stopped just before the kitchen. I knew who I would see if I looked up. I wasn't ready.

Go back to bed, Amy. You have school in the morning.

More tears soaked into the disintegrating tissue in my hands, so I threw it on top of the growing pile beside me and grabbed a fresh one. The used tissues had become a disgusting mountain that mirrored my inner turmoil. I pressed the clean one to my nose to catch the steady drips.

"God, please, help me be strong." My shoulders sank with this halfhearted plea.

The sounds of bare feet retreated down the hall, and again I knew I was alone. Yet the silence I longed for remained elusive. I lifted my hands to guard my ears from the evasive ticking, feeling a scream rising in my throat. I caught it between my teeth, and I let it out in a slow, muffled groan as my tears added to the invisible yet chilling water around my feet.

Failure.

I knew that was exactly what I was as a mother. Even so, I had no choice but to go on.

"God, I need strength. Fortify my heart for tomorrow morning. Open doors of help for my daughter."

Again I waited. The air hanging around me felt dead.

"Rose? Are you coming to bed?" Arthur's voice broke my internal guard with a crack. The shock snapped above me, and I lifted my head, gulping air. The strain tightened my throat.

"Yes," I croaked.

"Oh, Rose. Come."

Stepping across the kitchen, he placed his large hands on the sides of my shoulders, lifting me gently to my feet. His height dwarfed mine, but his natural gentleness lifted me above the water puddled in my heart.

He was dressed for bed, and his bare chest sporting curling grey and black hairs welcomed my cheek as we embraced. His kiss was warm on my forehead.

"We both need a good sleep. Things will look up in the morning. Don't they always?"

I longed to rest there in his embrace. But he broke contact, yawned, and grabbed a glass from the kitchen cabinet.

"You're a trooper, Rose," he said.

The creases between his eyebrows told me he wasn't untouched by the day's stress. But he brushed most of it off his large shoulders, unaware that when he did so, it dusted his "little wife" with an extra share.

I smiled up at him. "Yes, to bed. There are appointments to be made in the morning."

The morning. It meant a drive to "Hope is Here School" and a chat with the principal.

Evlin, the principal at Hope is Here, leaned over the desk, holding me with her almost black eyes.

"I know you and Arthur have large responsibilities at home and church, but Amy's behaviour is becoming more erratic. When these things leak over into school life, it sends me a red flag. Something's not right."

"She refuses to open up to us, Evlin. If she won't tell me what's wrong, how can I change anything?"

Evlin shook her head, her eyes dropping down to the desk in between us and the papers strewn across its face. "You might not be able to do anything, Rose. Amy has to make her own decisions when it comes to her behaviour. If she won't talk to you, maybe she'll open up to a counsellor …"

I watched as she shuffled papers on her desk before turning to the large monitor that took up most of the left side of her workspace. "Yes, maybe … She's new, you know, but I think she's very good."

I blinked as the woman chatted to herself and clicked through the windows on the monitor while her eyes danced from place to place. She was a strange woman, but her organizational skills were phenomenal. I didn't know who she was talking about, but through experience I knew if I sat silent, she would eventually share her thoughts.

Evlin let an irritated sound ease out of her throat and glanced at me before pursuing her lips. "I will ask her to make room for Amy. I hope she can fit her in this week. Since she is new, her schedule is fresh and more flexible. But, Rose, you and Arthur need to come up with a plan."

"Who? What kind of a plan?"

"Your daughter needs you."

As Evlin explained about the new school counsellor and what therapy sessions the school was able to offer and not offer, I felt my unshed tears adding to the rising water line around my ankles. The principal wondered if it wasn't time to involve our doctor and if maybe family sessions would be needed as well.

This is for Amy, Rose. I told myself, *Evlin is helping. She cares. It doesn't matter if you're the pastor's wife or not.*

Why did I have to care so much? I signed permission papers, and Evlin started laying pamphlets out on the desk in front of me. They contained reading material about mental health and psychotherapy for kids, as well as questions I needed to ask our doctor and strategies for communicating with difficult teenagers. The water line around me rose with each added paper until I felt it as a pressure around my ribs.

"Don't wait too long to start the process, Rose." Again Evlin pinned me with her dark eyes. I felt like a naughty child, brought before her for a scolding. I should have done better. I shouldn't have let things get this far with Amy. If only ...

"Call me if you have any more questions, Rose. And don't worry, we have resources to help kids like Amy."

I nodded and thanked her for her time before escaping her cramped office and unsettling gaze.

She is there to help, Rose.

But if that were true, why did the pamphlets I carried out with me feel so heavy?

The puddle around me had turned into a lake with waves that crashed against my chest as I walked to the car. I had so much left to do today, and it was barely nine-thirty a.m.

"Breathe, Rose. You can take time to sort through this mess of information tonight." I ignored the sudden cramping in my right hand as I grasped the steering wheel and placed the car in reverse.

Two

The chinking of china sang as I entered the church office. I felt weak after the intense discussion with the school's principal, and my neck felt as if it was made of rubber. A strange pins-and-needles sensation was spreading through my gut, but I ignored it while grimacing against the clattering noise.

"Is everything alright, Rose?" Gail's voice was a little too loud for my overwhelmed senses.

"Yes! A stressful morning," I replied. I hung my winter jacket on the coat tree by the doorway as my stomach gurgled in protest against this new sensation. "Is Arthur's office door open?"

"Sorry, no," Gail answered. "He just closed it for an early morning phone call."

"That's okay. I'll catch him later."

"Speaking of coffee ..." Gail offered me a white cup and saucer from the side cupboard where she stood.

"You're amazing, Gail."

Her gentle smile warmed my heart. She'd already stirred the cream in for me, so I found myself walking down the left hall to my little office tucked at the back of the church. It was kind of my husband and the rest of the team to make this space for me. After all, my position was voluntary, even if it gave me a large workload to balance.

After both our girls had started school full-time, I'd accepted the title of Sunday School Coordinator, and things had snowballed from there. It was only natural, right? I was the pastor's wife, and everyone wanted a piece of my time. Women's conferences, Bible studies, and VBS didn't plan themselves. Jim, our youth pastor, was young, so he'd often pop his head into the little back room, asking questions or organizational favours.

People were waiting for my phone calls and visits today as I was also head of the Compassionate Ministries, and several seniors in our church needed regular visits. I needed to check the schedule and call the other volunteers to make sure this week's appointments were going well. But first, I had emails and messages to read to see if anyone needed to be added.

Get ready for a rough day, Rose.

The light on my answering machine blinked. I pressed play and listened to the two messages recorded there sometime last night. "Rose, I'm afraid I won't be able to finish my Compassionate visits this week or help with the nursery during Bible study. I've caught some kind of nasty cold." The voice recording wasn't very clear. But I still knew immediately who it was: Hillary.

"The poor dear," I whispered while jotting down a note to bring her some hot soup for lunch.

The second message was a request for a visit. I added it to the list and counted out how many volunteers I still had. Three plus me made four. We each had four people we regularly visited. I checked the log for who was left on Hillary's list this week and groaned when I read three more names. With four individuals on our schedules already and just three days to fit the rest in, could we make it work? I added one name to Gail's list, since I knew she wouldn't mind, and took the last two on myself.

"Six people? Next week I'm going to have to ask someone for help. But who?"

I pulled out the old laptop the church had bought me, booted it up, and started plunking out emails with directions for the rest of the week. The last gulp of coffee sat in my cup, cold.

A soft *ting-ting* sound disturbed my concentration, and I looked up to see Arthur smiling at me. A miniature spoon stirred his gigantic mug.

"How did it go at school?" His question landed in the waves still surrounding my chest, threatening to constrict my breathing, chilling me, flooding my body with uncomfortable numbness.

"She's pulling some strings for us and put in a request for immediate help with the new counsellor. I should get a phone call by the end of the day about when they can squeeze Amy in."

He nodded while I talked, looking into his cup, alternating a sip then a stir. "Are you okay?"

"Yes, why wouldn't I be?"

"You look tired."

I sighed. "I'd rather not talk about this with the door open, Arthur."

His nod was slow. "It can wait for tonight. I love you."

Our eyes met, and I saw a shadow of my weariness reflected at me. "I love you too."

He stalled before turning away to walk back down the hall. "Would you like to eat lunch together?"

"I would, but after Bible study this morning, I have six Compassionate visits to start fitting in this week, and Hillary needs some attention as well. The poor woman is sick and can't help. I thought I would take her lunch." Disappointment scrawled all over Arthur's face. "Tomorrow?" I asked, to soften it.

"It's a date!" His smile reached his eyes, and I watched the weariness wash away. His relief was a stark contrast to the growing sensations of rising waves around me.

"Don't forget to write it down, or you might forget," I teased.

"Yes, dear! Good idea ..." As he walked away, his hand was busy typing into his phone.

I swallowed down the lump of jealousy that had risen in my throat while I'd watched Arthur's eyes. *How can he brush it all away so fast?*

I knew the stress, disappointments, and constant drain pulled at him just as much, if not more, than it did with me. How could it not when you lived a life of give, give, give? But how could he brush it aside in a matter of seconds?

Enough brooding, Rose. Get it together and get your work done. People are waiting. But the pep talk seemed hollow to my inner ears.

Chills from my toes crept up my legs, and I hugged myself, wishing I hadn't hung my coat in the entryway. Still, emails flew from my laptop into cyberspace and between every "send," I glanced at my watch. Weekly Bible study happened on Wednesday mornings, and I led a small group there as well. Thankfully, yesterday I finished my read-through of the leader's guide for today's topic. I had just enough time to finish here before walking over to the fellowship hall.

I thanked God for a smaller group of women than normal that morning as I grabbed my purse and headed out to the crisp Canadian air. With Bible study done, my thoughts turned towards Hillary and all the people I needed to squeeze into the day before picking Amy up from school. As I climbed into my car, I prayed that I wouldn't forget that added responsibility.

I took a deep breath of the chilled air and the scent of fresh snow that lingered despite the bright sunshine. February in Canada could be like that—deceitfully bright and achingly cold. With the close of February right around the corner, the bright sun could mean spring was coming early. Or a false spring. I longed for spring as the invisible water around me started to ice over in the cold, slowing down my movements while chilling my resolve to push on.

The car stereo blinked the time at me as I started the engine. There wasn't much time to grab lunch for Hillary and make it over to my first Compassionate Ministry visit appointment, but I should be able to just do it. My body resisted as I twisted to look over my shoulder and check that the space around the car was clear, but I ignored the aches and flutters. I had more important things to deal with right now.

After grabbing a ham and cheddar soup complete with croutons and a small bagged salad from the grocers, I dashed into Hillary's apartment building and triple pressed the open button at the elevator. The warmth of the Styrofoam carton filled to the brim with soup that just touched the plastic lid felt good in my cold hands. I could have stopped right there, ripped the lid off, and drank the rich goodness while standing in the hall. But I shook my head and pressed on.

Hillary answered her door wrapped in a thick pink house coat, her dark auburn dyed hair clashing with her pale skin speckled with age spots. "My dear, you are so thoughtful. Thank you." She wrung her hands as her gratitude bubbled out, and I had to refuse the invitation to join her.

"Call me next week, Hillary, and we'll set a proper date. I'm sorry, I've got to run!"

Before I knew it, I was speed-walking back down the hall. As I reached the main floor and faced the entryway, the chill that had frozen my resolve began to dissipate. The invisible waves of all I had left to do that day began to churn as I walked towards the wide glass doors. I started to sink below the thoughts that surged around me as the cold winter air and bright sunshine hit my face.

Visits, people, paperwork, Amy, *paperwork,* Amy, *people, church, organize. Something is wrong.* It was all too much. I was drowning. I broke as my rear hit the driver's seat, and the door slammed shut behind me. The strange flutters in my gut became painful, and I leaned against the steering wheel sobbing, the cold air threatening to freeze my tears in place. I gasped for breath as waves of shame, guilt, and frustration battered me. Crystallized puffs of my own breath escaped into the air.

"Oh, God, I can't do this anymore!"

I somehow managed to get the car key into the ignition and start the engine. Hot air began to blow onto my shoulders from the vents on either side of the steering wheel, but despite that, my body shook with chills.

"Jesus, please help me." As the words left my mouth, my mind was screaming, *Where are you?*

I didn't understand why my control was slipping. I'd helped shoulder the busyness of my husband's ministry for years. Why were my body and mind rebelling? I wasn't expected to carry any more than I had in the past. I should be able to do this. What was wrong with me?

That was it. The realization struck the water flowing above my head like lightning, sending electric splinters through me. There was something wrong with me. It wasn't just stress, it wasn't just Amy. It was me.

"So what do I do, God?"

Gentle notes reached my ear as a song from the radio broke through my inner turmoil. It opened the waves enough to let a breath enter my lungs. Then I gulped down a second and closed my eyes to listen.

> *... but they who wait for the Lord*
> *shall renew their strength;*
> *they shall mount up with wings like eagles;*

they shall run and not be weary;
they shall walk and not faint.
- Isaiah 40:31 ESV -

The artist had set such well-known words to music. The notes entered the waters around me and flowed through the overwhelming thoughts, silencing them. The engine purred, and I straightened my shoulders. *Wait on the Lord.* I could do this if I waited for His direction.

One day at a time, Rose, one task at a time. And maybe God would bring in help along the way. I thanked Him for words I'd forgotten in the busyness of life. I may have just been leading a Bible study, but I realized I hadn't been listening to God's words as much as I urged the women around me to.

"Alright, God." I prayed as my returning calm stilled the flutters in my gut and the tingling that had spread through my limbs lessened to dull aches. "Help me be patient. Please, give me eyes to see and wisdom to know when it's time to act."

My day flew by as I jumped from task to task. I held people's hands while they talked. I reassured the worried and shuffled papers from one folder to another. At 3:15 my phone alarm sounded, sending my heart into unsure flutters. What had I forgotten?

Pick up Amy.

School would let out at 3:24. There wasn't time to make it back to church to drop off the notes I'd made while visiting people today. I would have to take them home with me and file them in the morning.

Breath, Rose. The water around me hadn't drained, but it felt as if I could now lift my head above the waterline. With the thoughts stilled, I could see ahead to my next task.

Three

She was waiting for me as I pulled into the school parking lot, her head turned towards the school buses. The sun flashed off the rim of the sunglasses she sported in the middle of winter. *Really, Amy?* I couldn't understand how she could stand sitting on the cement bench. Cold would surely have bitten through her jeans as she refused to wear snow pants. She only turned to scan the parking lot when I pulled up beside her, the snow crunching under the slow wheels of the car.

"Is Ashley coming with us, too?" Amy asked as she pulled open the passenger's seat door.

"Not today."

"So she is going to ride the bus even though you're already here?" Her eyebrows drifted up to hide behind her brown tuque.

"Again, no. She asked Dad if she could spend a few nights with a friend. Apparently, 'the fighting upsets her.'"

"Spending *school* nights with a friend? He said yes?" Amy's voice crawled up a few decimals, and I closed my eyes for a second against the stab of sound before checking my mirrors and slowly rolling past the last few cars parked in the lot.

"It's hard to study when your sister is screaming down the hall."

"I don't scream."

I ignored her muttering and turned up the radio. Amy took the hint and stopped arguing.

The rest of the drive home was uneventful, and soon we were pulling into our driveway.

"Well, thanks for nothing, Mom." Amy's insult dropped on me as she bolted for the house, forgetting to shut the car door. It felt like a heavy brick that crushed me under its weight and plunged me again under the overwhelming waves of my own thoughts. My vision swam. Instinctively, my fingers pinched the bridge of my nose, my lungs sucking in cold, crisp air from the open passenger door. The cold burned my fingers, turning them a bright red. But I couldn't bring myself to exit the car and enter that house, where she was, to be alone with her.

I knew the routine well. She would have dumped her bag near the door and made her way to the kitchen for an after-school snack. Did kids ever grow out of after-school snacks? She would complain if she found we were not stocked on the item she wanted. She would yell, ask favours, and be rude when I tried a firm "no," and then she would explode.

Tears welled as my throat constricted. How had this happened? How had I failed so miserably as a mother? My daughter had turned into a monster right under my nose, and I'd missed the warning signs. I could barely stand to be around her. She oozed darkness, and as I resisted the waves around me, the darkness she spread was too much for me to bear. I didn't blame Ashley for not wanting to be at home.

Amy hates you.

You hate her.

"No, I do not! I don't hate my baby."

But you do, and she knows it.

I squeezed the bridge of my nose harder—an attempt to keep myself in the present and ignore the overwhelming, crushing weight of our situation.

"God, I can't do this anymore. I don't hate her. I love her! But I don't know what to do with her."

The radio was still playing in the background. I was wasting battery. Amy's door should be closed. I should …

Have you not known? Have you not heard?
The Lord is the everlasting God,
the Creator of the ends of the earth.
He does not faint or grow weary;
his understanding is unsearchable.
He gives power to the faint,
and to him who has no might he increases strength.
Even youths shall faint and be weary,
and young men shall fall exhausted;
but they who wait for the Lord shall renew their strength;
they shall mount up with wings like eagles;
they shall run and not be weary;
they shall walk and not faint.
- Isaiah 40:28 – 31 ESV -

The radio had switched away from music as one of the announcers read the Bible passage. His voice was deep and peaceful, perfect for scripture reading. As the words flowed over me, the cold, churning waves began to slowly drop. I was crying again, but this time my tears fell away, draining.

"I still don't know what to do."

But maybe that was okay?

I jumped at the sudden buzzing from my pocket, followed by the singsong ring of my cell phone. Fumbling, I fished it out and pressed the glass screen to my ear.

"This is Rose Grill."

"Hello, Rose. This is Hope is Here Christian School. We've an appointment notification for your daughter, Amy." My chest shook as it released a heavy sigh of relief. "The school counsellor will see her Friday morning at ten. She'll have to miss one of her classes, but I'm sure she won't mind that."

"That is wonderfully fast!" I exclaimed.

"Yes, oh, and lastly, she told me to tell you she will set up meetings for twice a week and plans to send the schedule home with Amy after her first visit."

"Thank you so much. We appreciate it."

"No problem, Mrs. Grill."

Amy wouldn't be happy, but maybe this new counsellor could reach her since her own parents couldn't.

I pulled myself upright and made my way into the house. The cold had seeped into my bones, as I'd given myself over to overwhelming emotions. But now I needed to get with it. Dinner wouldn't cook itself.

I heard the TV blaring in the living room and steered clear of Amy. I couldn't believe myself. Was I afraid of my daughter? Maybe not of her directly, but I had to admit I *was* afraid of what she was capable of. I wasn't a naturally fearful person, and the realization stopped me in my tracks as I bent over to open the low freezer drawer on the refrigerator.

"Thank You for the appointment with the counsellor," I whispered, breathing in the cold bloom of air that escaped from the freezer drawer. I dug around for frozen fish, too tired to make much effort today. I hoped Arthur wouldn't mind.

"Salmon and fish sticks it is."

As I puttered around the kitchen, the warmth returned to my icy fingers, and my core relaxed. Soon the rice cooker held a healthy portion of grains for three, and frozen green beans began their date with boiling water on the stove. I could almost have hummed, held in the growing warmth of my kitchen. This was one of my sacred places. Mundane busyness was a refuge. It kept my heartbeat pumping but let me turn off the stress of people and concentrate on the salad greens I laid out across the counter. Each had a space, a placement in the salad. I knew just the right amount without needing to measure. If only working with people could be this easy

...

"Rose! Rose? I'm home."

Arthur peeked into my sanctuary, sniffing the air like a hungry teenager. I'd missed the sound of the front door opening, but then the TV was still blaring from the living room.

"How did your day go?" he asked as he walked up from behind to place warm hands on my shoulders.

"It went."

"We still need to talk," he reminded me.

"I thought we'd made a date for tomorrow at lunch?"

"We did, and I'm still taking you out. But I think we need to talk tonight, Rose."

"After dinner, Arthur."

I looked back at him over my shoulder. His face moved close as his arms wrapped around me. His warm breath, slightly sour from a long day at work, made me wrinkle my nose, but I still smiled up into his eyes.

"You need a breath mint, dear," I teased.

I felt his chest shaking with silent laughter against my back as he squeezed me.

"Alright!" He released me but not before planting a kiss on my cheek.

As he walked from the room, I felt invisible waves rise to slosh against my waist. Did I deserve his love? He counted on me to keep the family in line and the household running while he did the work of Christ. I felt like I was failing him, in more ways than one. A dampness hidden from the rest of the world crept up my legs and back. I tried to tamp down the swirl of thoughts that threatened to churn the waters back into a dangerous tempest as my hands rhythmically chopped vegetables.

Four

Amy was furious when we told her about her Friday morning appointment. I watched her storm off from the dinner table, my hand on Arthur's arm.

"Let her go, Arthur. Yelling at her won't help."

I felt worn through, like an old hand towel ready for the rag pile. The lines around Arthur's eyes told me he felt the strain as well.

"She never used to speak like that, Rose. What's going on?"

"I don't know," I replied. "I feel like we're losing her."

"She's going to a Christian School. It can't be her friends."

My eyebrows rose at his comment. "That label of 'Christian' doesn't mean perfect, Arthur. We should know that well." My hands became very interesting as I folded them together on the table in front of me. Are those new blue veins I spied underneath my pale skin?

"You look tired, Rose."

"I am."

He covered my petite fingers with his large hand. "Maybe you're working too much." He finished by clearing his throat and sipping from his water glass.

"Working? I volunteer. I don't work."

"Rose, it's still work and a lot of it. Maybe you should step back for a while."

"And let the church down? Let you down?"

"It's not letting me down. We can find someone else."

He meant well, but it stung to hear I was replaceable.

"What about what people will say?"

"What about it?" he asked, his eyebrow lifting in the same way Amy's always did.

"I'm the pastor's wife. Things are expected ... I just need more help. If we found more volunteers ..."

Arthur sighed and pulled his hand back from mine while also pushing his chair back from the table, as if to take in the full picture of his wife.

"Amy needs you."

"What do you mean?"

"I think Amy needs you to be at home again." A lump formed in my throat as he continued. "I think you need you to be at home again. You're worn thin, Rose ... I need you at home again."

I couldn't stop the tears from spilling over the rim of my eyes. It felt like my identity was being threatened as someone teased me with the candy of hope: a way out. But leaving the ministry wouldn't solve our biggest problems. I couldn't run away from myself or my daughter.

"I need you to take care of Amy first."

"But, Arthur, I don't know what to do with her! She hates me. She can't stand to be in the same room as me." It filled me with shame, but I couldn't stop myself from blurting out, "I can hardly stand to be around her either."

"Rose!"

"What do you want me to do, Arthur? Lie? It's how I feel ... She's not just a black storm cloud putting a damper on our family, she's thunder and lightning. She's frightening and hurting everyone around her, and–and I don't know how to help her." I grabbed my water glass. The cool liquid still wasn't enough to dislodge the lump quickly turning to a sharp pain in my throat. "I've failed as her mother. I can't fix her."

Arthur just stared at me, his eyes roving over my now dishevelled, whimpering form. I needed a tissue badly and got up from the table to look for one, leaving him silently to question my hunched back.

"It's time to let the professionals do their job, Arthur. This goes beyond normal teenager trials. I've seen it in her eyes. She scares me." My voice caught as the truth dripped out on the tail of my words.

"Rose ... I ... This tells me you *need* to stay home." His voice was soft like cotton and hardly reached me with my back turned.

"But I told you! People expect me to be there, with you, beside you. What will they say when I'm not?"

An edge slipped into his voice as he answered. "It's time we stop thinking about what other people 'think' of us."

He was right, and I knew it. Deep down in my sodden heart, I knew I couldn't handle all the "things" anymore. That night silence hung between us. It was painful, but I couldn't find any more words to dissuade him. When we crawled into bed, his hand found mine, and I knew we were okay. He held my fingers instead of tripping over more words.

I let a week pass as I slowly organized my tiny office, labelling papers and writing out instructions on how I did things. But who would that person be? We didn't know. Gail was the first friend I told about my plans.

"Oh, Rose, why? Are you doing okay? I've noticed you looking pale and drawn the last few weeks especially. Is there anything I can do?"

"No, Gail, I assure you. But thank you for your concern."

Soon the whispers started, and I knew I was going to have to make some kind of announcement. People in the church office tiptoed around me as if I were a china cup sitting on the edge of the table. Finally, Wednesday's women's Bible study came, and I was prepared. Or I thought I was.

I was one of the last women to use the bathroom after the study, and the commotion from the foyer and the hall outside slid under the bathroom door as I stared into the mirror.

"You can do this, Rose."

Can you? What will you tell them?

How badly you've failed?

How weak you are?

The overwhelming waters around my mind had receded while I led my small group, but standing in front of the mirror, looking into my own face ... The churning started down at my feet and slowly rose to my ankles before splashing its way up my legs.

I splayed my fingers out across the cold washstand and leaned closer to the mirror, taking in the lines around my eyes. Was that red behind my pupils? As I leaned back, my hand brushed a card that had been standing beside the faucet. I watched it tumble to the ground in slow motion.

Why not just leave it?

No, I couldn't leave it there. The bright flowers on the face of it caught my eye as I leaned down to grab it. Hand-drawn words had been penned in between them.

Are you tired or lonely?

What a strange thing to write on a card. I flipped it open and found more handwritten words, each carefully gone over a second time in a dark black pen to help them stand out. I could see places where a misspelling had been rubbed out behind it.

Come to me, all who labour and are heavy laden,
and I will give you rest.
Take my yoke upon you, and learn from me,
for I am gentle and lowly in heart,
and you will find rest for your souls.
For my yoke is easy, and my burden is light."
- Matthew 11:28-30 ESV -

But really, was God's burden light? It didn't feel that way to me ... Caring for his people was hard work. Caring for the family he'd given me on top of it was even harder. Then there was taking care of myself.

I held that card in my hand as the seconds on the clock over the mirror ticked away.

Stalling will do you no good, Rose.

My battle of thought was interrupted as the door behind me squeaked open and a group of chatting women entered the room. I nodded politely at their greetings and bowed out the door as my heart fluttered.

Coffee, that's what I need, I told myself. The tall forty-cup pot was ready and steaming as I walked up to the line forming in front of it. A volunteer had stacked the matching cups and saucers and placed them in easy reach of the Bible study participants.

"Hello, Rose."

"Good morning, Rose."

"Lovely morning, isn't it, Rose?"

The barrage of greetings was nonstop as woman after woman passed me or stopped to seek a moment of my time.

"How are the girls doing, Rose?"

I kept my answers to as few words as I could and reached for a cup with shaking hands. Just as I curled my finger around the handle of a cup, I spied another card like the one in the bathroom. This one was decorated with darker flowers surrounded by greenery and read:

Are you afraid?

The waters at my knees churned. I knew I should move on, get out of people's way as they waited patiently behind me, but I stopped and turned the little card up.

... fear not, for I am with you;
be not dismayed, for I am your God;
I will strengthen you, I will help you,
I will uphold you with my righteous right hand.
- Isaiah 41:10 ESV -

Tears teemed against my lashes, and I blinked, a feeble attempt to hold them there.

"Look what Rose found!" Debora squealed from behind me. "Did any of you see the other card in the bathroom? Or the ones on the tables? Rose, do you know who made them? Aren't they just the sweetest?"

She was pulling on my arm, attempting to look at the card tucked in front of me. As she jostled for a look, I heard the squeal of her shoes against the smooth floor and her body pushed against me in a half trip. My elbow stuck out.

"Debora!"

"Rose!"

We both grasped at each other as my elbow connected with the neatly stacked coffee cups. The waterfall of porcelain hit the floor and sent up shards like the mist from Niagara Falls.

"Oh, no, Rose! I'm so sorry. Are you hurt?" Debora's face had flushed, and as we held each other's sleeves, I felt her trembling.

The next waterfall imitation was actual water as it fell over the dam of my lashes, free.

"Rose, I am so sorry!"

"I'm okay, Debora. I'm okay! But don't move. Wait for help."

I held her in place as a crowd of eyes surrounded us. Some looked shocked, some concerned, others as if they wanted to laugh but turned away before anyone could see.

"Stand back, ladies! Is anyone hurt? Rose, are you and Debora hurt?" I shook my head no to Gail as she parted the crowd and produced a set of brooms.

I raised my voice above the hum of sound. "I'm sorry, ladies. I guess I'm all thumbs today." I gave the card still in my hand to Debora. "Put it away, dear. It's okay."

Debora was in a daze as Gail and a helper cleared a safe space around us, allowing us to walk away from the mess and sit at a table.

"Are you alright, Debora?" My tears were still flowing. The hem of my sleeve soaked up the drops before someone handed me a tissue.

Debora only nodded. Her face had gone white as a ghost.

"Sit with me?" I asked her.

She didn't protest as I thanked the ladies around us for their concern and told them we were okay and wasn't Gail wonderful for cleaning up my disaster. They all nodded yes and agreed Gail was the greatest.

One of the other ladies took charge as the room settled, and Gail swept away the broken pieces of porcelain. I wondered how many we'd broken. How much money would it cost to replace them? I should ask Gail how many she thought were gone.

The accident had snapped me back to reality, and I sucked in a long breath and released it through my nose. My eyes roved over the many faces in the room. How could I tell them all I was stepping back from my responsibilities, without knowing who should or could step in behind me?

It's time, Rose.

But who will help me?

It's time, Rose. Trust me.

I felt an assurance in my heart as I looked out across the tables filled with mothers, sisters, and grandmas. It was time to tell them and let God fill in the gap.

Abigails Prayers: Three

Dear Heavenly Father,

I saw her crying in church today.

She was hiding it, but I noticed her wiping tears during prayer
time. I never thought I'd see her cry. It was wrong of me to judge
that, even for a second. Please forgive me.

The seat beside her was empty, her children missing.

Is that why she was sad?

I should have asked her.

I should have been brave and told her I was thinking of her.

But she's so important ... not like me. How can someone like me
comfort someone like her?

Would she even let me?

I'm still not brave enough to ask if she's okay.

Next time, make me brave.

Amen

Just Forget It

Beth

One

THE NURSERY WAS PACKED full of tiny people, just the way I loved it. Each little smiling face gave me joy while each tear tugged at my heart. Gloria was holding my hand as I rocked James in my lap.

"Jesus loves me. This I know," we sang together.

My aging voice crackled on the "know," and Gloria drew out her words behind the tempo.

"Well done, Gloria," I said.

"James, you sing with us now?" she asked him.

His little shoulders shook with a half sob, but the tears didn't flow like I feared they would. His back was warm as I stroked my hand up and down, up and down. He looked at me then over at Gloria.

"No," he replied.

"It's okay, James. You don't have to sing if you don't want to," I assured him.

Gloria crossed her arms over her chest and glared at him, her pigtails bouncing with cross motherly energy.

"You should sing, James."

"Come on, Gloria. It's okay if he isn't ready yet. Maybe he'll sing with you next time," I told her. "How about you go find the train pieces in the toy bin? Maybe James would like to play with you once he sees you put the track together."

"No!" was all she said to my suggestion. She turned away and stomped off.

"Oh, my. Someone is in a mood this morning," I remarked as James and I watched her go.

We sat there for a moment. His breathing slowed and then shuddered again in a rhythmic dance.

"Hello, James," I said. "How are you this morning? Are you still tired? Would you like to sing?"

He shook his head no but didn't speak. I could tell it was a fight to hold in the tears.

The other children in the room were busy driving toy cars, building with blocks, and chatting to the other nursery workers.

Then I spied Gloria, her frustration plain as she dug through an open toy bin, unable to find what she was in search of.

"Gloria? Dear, would you like to sing with James and I? Maybe it would cheer him up, and he would decide to play with you."

"No!" she shouted at me. "James doesn't want to."

Her little face was angry, and I saw the tip of a tongue try to escape from in between pursed lips. But then it darted back into its home, unsure if it was safe to come out and play. The child's anger gave me pause. Had I forgotten something?

I looked around the room. I was supposed to do something when I felt this blankness in my mind. I'd promised myself I would do it, but what was it?

"Never mind, James. It will come to me when I need it again. I hope ..."

He looked up at me with sad, tired eyes before laying a cheek on my withered chest.

"You are a sweet boy. But my, you are extra tired today, aren't you? Well, no worries. Let's just take a nap together."

I noticed for the first time that the chair I sat in was a rocking chair, and soon James' eyes had closed as I squeaked out a song for him against the vinyl floor, the wooden rockers my instrument.

What a gift little people are to an old soul.

"Yes, they are," I answered the voice in my head.

"What was that, Beth?" Hillary asked from across the room. "Did you say something?"

"Oh." I had to think about it for a minute. "I must have. But isn't it funny? It just slipped from my brain."

Hillary eyed me for a moment. Her dark auburn hair was a stark contrast to her pale aging complexion, but it suited her blunt personality well. For as long as I'd known her, she'd always sported a high contrast and freshly painted look. I shrugged and smiled as I gently rubbed the back of the little one in my arms, brushing off her piercing attention.

"The nursery is so full today, isn't it? I just love all these little dears. What a gift."

She was still looking me up and down. "Yes, they are. Signs of a healthy, growing church."

"Healthy and growing!" I flashed an extra bright smile as I continued rocking the child on my lap. His breathing was so peaceful, I didn't want to disturb him.

My foot slowed the rocking as I looked down at his little head. Whose child was I holding again?

It's James, Beth. Mary Cooper's son. You've been holding him for the whole nursery hour so far.

"Oh, yes," I whispered to myself, realizing I'd forgotten.

Forgotten? I carefully reached into the pocket of my favourite cardigan, the yellow one with daisy buttons I rarely closed but still loved. There it was: my notebook with my half-size black pen hooked within the spiral binding for safekeeping.

I gently wiggled the cap with one finger and smiled as the pen lifted out of place. The pages whispered to me as I opened the little book, glancing at my own well-known handwriting.

"Yes, yes, that's right." I found the last used page and read my note from this morning.

Beth, this is you reminding yourself,

you have Bible study this morning.
Help in the nursery!
Make a note if you notice you have forgotten something.

I was quite kind to myself, I thought. The gentle words made me smile. Was it appropriate to thank this woman of the past? Yes, yes, it was.

Dear me,
Thank you for the kind reminder.
I believe I've forgotten conversations in the middle of nursery time.
I forgot who the little boy I was rocking was.
It was James! I love James.
I've forgotten something else as well, but it won't come back to me yet.
I'll try harder to remember.

Writing the words as I balanced the little book on the arm of the chair was difficult, and the muscles in my arm stained as I scratched out the words.

"Relax, Beth. There is nothing to be afraid or ashamed of. You are among friends in this place," I reassured myself.

My forgetfulness had grown in the last few months. It was something I'd been expecting for some time. The memories of watching my mother whither before my eyes were still fresh, as well as the pain as her fearful words lashed out while she lost pieces of herself every day. My sister Dorothy had suffered the same fate. Just now, I struggled to remember how long it had been since she was gone, but I still remembered her desperate old hands batting at the nurses trying to care for her, convinced they were there to do her harm.

As I put my little notebook away, I closed my eyes. *Dear Lord, please, help me stay kind, no matter what happens. Help me remember what love is.* I must have prayed a similar prayer thousands of times over the last few weeks.

A tear grew at the edge of my closed lashes. My hand trembled as I wiped it away.

"Time for a breather, Beth," I told myself.

I stood and asked Hillary, who was sitting across the room from me, if she wouldn't mind taking the precious little one while I used the restroom.

"Beth, are you alright?" she asked. I recognized the suspicious glint in her eye. She was a sharp woman. I needed to be careful.

"Oh, yes. I'll be right back."

The little boy stirred while I shifted him into Hillary's arms, but he settled again before I turned to walk out to the hall. I stepped over car tracks and dodged a bouncy ball as a blonde-headed toddler waddled after its fast retreat.

"What a cutie," I exclaimed.

They filled the church nursery with child safety gadgets, and on reaching the door, I paused, studying the funny white cover guarding the knob.

I didn't remember it. Had it been there before?

Deep breath, Beth, slow down.

I listened and noticed the thumb-shaped indents on both sides of the strange device.

"Oh, yes!"

I grasped the white door knob, pressing the plastic against the metal underneath and felt the rubber grips inside holding fast. Then I twisted, and the door opened.

The relief of success sent a fresh tear to the corner of my eye, but I blinked it away and smiled.

"Thank you, God."

Two

The halls of the church were empty. As I walked towards the women's bathroom, I glimpsed heated discussions, nodding heads, and turned backs through the small glass windows on each door. The greeting hall was wide open, the lights still bright as it waited for the small groups to conclude, the smell of percolating coffee wafting on the breeze from the overhead fans that were left on low to push the heat around the large room during winter.

It all looked so welcoming, and I sighed in contentment. Just being in this place of gathering was a blessing, even if everyone else was busy. The ladies' room welcomed me, and I laughed at my reflection as I passed the mirror over the twin sinks.

"Beth, you need a haircut," I told myself as I tucked a stray wisp behind my ears. "A cut and curl."

It had been a long time since those stray wisps of hair had been straw-brown. Now they were white, and if I stood just right behind a lamp, it looked like I had a translucent angel's halo. I didn't know if people became some kind of angel once they died and entered heaven. But back in my younger days, it was a thought we used to comfort ourselves. I didn't mind the thought. I also figured my white hair was just a step away from glowing glory.

I finished my business and stepped up to the washstand. The soap dispenser gifted me with pink-tinged foam, and I massaged it carefully into the wrinkles around my fingers. I never used hot water for washing hands as my skin was sensitive, and the cool liquid that I let run over my skin was refreshing. I even patted my cheeks with a splash.

"Wake up, Beth! Now, time to get back at it."

Before I turned away, I spied a small card set up by the mirror. The hand-coloured flowers gave it a homey touch.

"Now, how sweet is that?"

The front of the little card read:

Are you tired or lonely?

The question gave me pause, and I looked up into the mirror. My face was a map of wrinkles, my hair white, but my eyes were bright.

"No, I'm not tired. Sometimes lonely, but not right now."

I turned away, ready to continue.

"Wait," I said out loud. "What was I supposed to be doing?"

My fingers tingled with cold as I held the metal door handle, ready to pull it open. I looked around. I was in the church bathroom and knew this place well, but what was I doing here today?

I pulled open the door, and the hall was silent. My heart sank. A cloud had filled my brain. I closed my eyes and tried to push through the fog to find the answer I needed. Why was I at church?

The cotton heaviness wrapped itself around me, and it didn't matter where I turned, I couldn't see past it.

Beth, take a deep breath.

I did. It was something I'd often told my mother as she battled the fog and later my sister as well. They had handled the isolation differently. I silently asked myself, "How will you handle it, Beth?"

"The church is where I help people. I love to help people. I love people."

Helping is what I knew, so I would help even if I couldn't remember exactly what I was supposed to be doing.

Beth, this fog is getting worse.

You need to tell someone.

I walked past the coffeemaker in the greeting hall and noticed it was full and ready.

"Cups! No one has put out the cups yet. Or … Maybe cleared already?"

I didn't want to make a mistake. So I stood there, staring at the coffee pot, trying to think.

"Hello, Beth."

"Hello!" I said without turning to look, intent on trying to put the puzzle pieces together.

"Is everything okay?"

I blinked. *Ask, Beth. Ask her what you should help with.*

I turned and saw Abigail. Her bright red hair and freckles always made me happy. Her wheelchair was one of those new electric ones with a small joystick control beside the right hand. I marvelled at how quiet it was as she manoeuvred around me.

"I am just wondering what I should do to help this morning," I told her.

"Well, I was just about to set out the cups and saucers before Bible study lets out."

"And I just noticed there is something missing from the table. Should I help you, Abigail?"

Her blue eyes sparkled at me as she smiled. "Yes! But I can get the cups. Would you like to set out some cookies? You're so good at organizing the dainty platters. I know there are three or four varieties of goodies today."

I busied myself in the kitchen with a large plate and a few plastic bins from the fridge and counter, each brimming with goodies. A wave of peanut butter scent met my nose as I pulled the lid off one of the containers. "Oh, my! Someone has been busy."

Each cookie was exactly the same size, and the dainty circles were each pressed with the imprint of forked tongs. I heard a giggle behind me.

"Beth, you brought those, didn't you?"

I lifted the container up and peered at the bottom. Sure enough, my name was printed across the plastic in dark permanent marker.

"Oh, my goodness! I can't believe I forgot about my own cookies."

Abigail and I both laughed as she pulled cups out from a lower cupboard. Her fancy chair lifted her just high enough to reach the first row, and she made her way along the line until she had them all resting on the countertop before filling a large plastic tray that she balanced on her knees. I walked out into the greeting hall right behind her and placed my own tray on the far side of the coffeemaker as she unloaded the first few cups from her lap.

"Now, Beth, why don't you get yourself a coffee and a cookie and sit down? We have about two minutes before the study is over."

"Thank you, I will." With that, I helped myself to the cookies I'd brought then turned to find a seat at one of the large tables ready to hold eager coffee drinkers and cookie eaters.

I always loved this time right after studying. The little ones were let out of the nursery and soon came running for the cookie tray, dragging their mothers by the hands. The fellowship was so good for us. I waved at the little people, trying to put names to faces as the coffee line grew longer.

"Beth! There you are. What happened to you? Why didn't you come back to nursery?" Hillary's sharp words came from my left as she found a free chair beside me. "I had to hold James the whole rest of the hour, and now my joints are aching. You know how bad my arthritis gets in the winter."

She was wringing her hands, rubbing the finger joints as she sat beside me. Her eyes clouded over as she stared at the coffee line.

"Oh, I'm sorry, Hillary." I stopped to think and sipped my coffee. My hands shook, and I almost spilled it all over my yellow sweater. "Oh! Oh, dear. I am sorry."

"Well," said Hillary, sitting back a bit as she let her shrewd eyes travel over my face. "Just try not to forget next time."

She left, still wringing her sore hands, and joined the coffee line as it shrank. Before I could turn back to my drink, a loud crash rang out, and an audible intake of breath ran through the entire crowd. I couldn't see what was happening clearly as people moved towards the coffee table and blocked my view. But I spied bits and pieces of broken cups all over the floor.

The noise sent my heart racing, and I couldn't help but hold a hand against my chest.

"I think it's time to go home, Beth," I told myself as I blinked back a tear.

Home—it was the single thought I held in my mind as I grabbed my coat hanging in the church entryway. As I slipped into its warmth and pulled a hat over my white curls, the gathered women started singing, the broken coffee cup incident cleaned away and almost forgotten.

Home, Beth.

I wouldn't let myself get distracted.

"One finger after the other," I said as I slipped my hands into my gloves. They were my purple ones, the ones my sister made for me years ago. A hole had opened between the thumb and pointer finger once, but I'd mended it. The yarn I'd used was a shade or two different from the original but still worked, and the visible patch helped me hold the memory. I missed her, my sister.

Soon my handbag was resting in the crook of my elbow, and I was ready to push the entryway doors open when I felt a tug on the hem of my coat.

"Church Grandma?" Gloria's little fingers were curled around the hem of my coat. "Church Grandma, I love you."

She waved a little card with hand-drawn flowers in my face as I bent down to give her a hug. I remembered her, all the many times I'd watched her in the nursery. How she had grown over the last four years into a precious bundle of sparks.

"Thank you, Gloria. I love you too. What is that you have? How pretty! Did you make it?"

She shook her head no as I took the card.

"Was on the tables, Church Grandma. You take it home, okay? Mama said it says 'love' on it."

It did, but as a question.

Do you feel loved?

> *"For God so loved the world,*
> *that he gave his only Son,*
> *that whoever believes in him should not perish*
> *but have eternal life.*
> *- John 3:16 ESV -*

How many years ago had I first memorized this verse? Many ... But still the words seemed to sing in my ears with the voice of my mother as she hummed while stirring a soup pot, or the steady thumping of my father's thumb against a fence post. He used to stand looking out at the field cows in the mornings. Sometimes I stood there with him.

My hair might be whiter than his ever became, but I could remember the weight of his hand on my head as he looked down at me once and said, "God's love is in the sunrise and the cow pastures, Beth. Just as much as it is on the cross."

As I looked into Gloria's eyes, I knew it was there too, even if she didn't know it yet.

"Thank you. What a beautiful gift."

She walked away as a group of other little ones ran past, and I pushed my way out the door into the cold winter air.

Three

My walk home was uneventful. As I opened the front door, a hug of scent enveloped me. Home—it was a mix of potpourri in the bowl on the living room coffee table, the lemon and vinegar I used to clean the kitchen, and today the smell of peanut butter cookies lingered in the corners. As I hung the house keys on the labelled hook by the door, I felt tension drip down my neck and shoulders and puddle at my feet.

"Hm, like melting snow," I said as I dusted a few real flakes from my shoulders before hanging my outer clothes on the hall tree.

The smells, the relief, home—it brought back my memories in gentle trickles as I walked down the hall to the kitchen. The kettle was right where it always was. My chair was half pulled out, ready for me, my favourite tea packets resting in a cracked mug I didn't want to throw away. It was old but still useful. Like me. Or ...

I pulled out my little notebook and read the last lines I'd written while still at church.

I will try harder to remember.

I added to them, now confident in my home.

I forgot to go back to the nursery after needing a bathroom break. Hillary was upset with me afterwards, but I didn't remember my mistake until getting home.

I helped Abigail lay out cookies instead and left James in Hillary's arms.

Remember to pray for her. Her hands looked like they were hurting again.

Maybe I should phone her to apologize?

Pray about it.

I'm exhausted after Bible study.

My memory loss is getting worse.

I'd brought home the little card Gloria had handed me and laid it out on the table to read the verse again.

"What a sweet child."

Making a note on the back about who had given it to me and where it had come from, I tucked the card into my notebook. I didn't want to forget it.

Beth, you can't hide this for much longer.

It's affecting other people.

Tea. I needed tea. I ran the water to fill the kettle and looked out past the snow built up around the windowsill. The layers of crisp white were too deep for me this time of year. The untouched snow glittered in the noon hour light, and my stomach gurgled, telling me lunch was also in order.

My little two-bedroom house was a nest of warmth in more ways than temperature. Everywhere I looked was a treasure trove of memories. Pictures of Gregory, my late husband, lined the hall. As I sat eating a ham sandwich, I could look up to see our wedding picture. The old photo captured our deep smiles, and I remembered they had taken it right after a particularly good kiss.

We'd bought this little house together and readied the second bedroom for children who never came. Instead, it had housed my mother and then, for a short time, my sister.

"Gregory, I wish you were here."

A deep hole formed in my heart. My hand shook, and bits of ham fell from my sandwich.

"God, I don't want to forget him."

I felt no tears, just shaking hands and a black, ominous feeling deep inside. I'd watched my mother lose bits of herself, and it had been horrible. She'd fought it in her own way and lost. Now …

I knew how these things went. One day I would look up at that photo and say, "Oh, those people look so happy. I wonder who they are."

How long would it take before I lost my house? My safe place …

Beth, I am with you always.

Would I lose my joy as the black hole grew bigger? I always used to have the knack of seeing the sunshine in every situation. What now?

Beth, call someone.

I knew I needed to tell someone before it got too late. It was time to make a call to the clinic, and then I needed someone to help take me there.

Call Hillary.

"She won't want to talk to me again today."

Call her.

The black hole shrunk within me, and I walked over to my familiar white wall phone with the large digits. I had a list of names and numbers taped to the wall, ready for when I needed them but might not remember.

I dialed and listened to the half-ring connection then the next two full rings.

"Hello, this is Hillary."

"Hillary? This is Beth ... I need your help."

Four

I was waiting for someone, but couldn't remember who. I'd buttoned my coat against the cold and pulled my hat down over my ears. It wasn't too chilly today, but it was damp. Grey, heavy clouds hung low in the sky, blocking the sun, ready to dust the earth with yet another layer of snow.

I stood on the front step, holding my purse, looking down the street.

"It's okay, Beth," I told myself. "Just wait, and when that someone comes, you'll remember."

Or that's what I hoped.

I shifted my toes in my boots as I waited. Damp cold had a way of finding every crack, every loose stitch, and wiggling its way into clothes, boots, and even the house. But movement had the power to keep winter's chill at bay. At least for a time. So I kept wiggling my toes then shifted from one foot to the next.

Was that them? A red car turned onto my street, and I watched it slow down but then felt my heart sink as it passed me.

"Patience is a virtue," I recited the old saying to myself.

It was true, but I felt the dark hole in my heart growing slightly. Deep breaths and keeping calm helped shrink it, but I knew it was here to stay, unlike my memories.

I watched a blue car pass, and then a black one pulled in front of my walkway. I hesitated. What if they were just parking there and visiting a neighbouring house? I would wait to be acknowledged

... it was safer. Then the window rolled down, and a brown mitten waved at me.

My cold feet shuffled down the walk.

"Oh, my! My poor old brain must have frozen for a moment along with my toes."

The woman in the driver's seat raised her eyebrows at me. "It's like you didn't recognize my car, Beth."

I looked at her as the black hole grew again.

Be honest, Beth.

"Well." I took a deep breath. "I didn't, actually."

I knew that I knew this person. Her arched eyebrows were familiar as well as her voice. But I couldn't dig her name out of the back of my mind. It was like it kept jumping away from me.

"Can you remind me of your name? I know I know it. But I can't catch it with my mind and say it."

Her arched eyebrows lowered. "My name is Hillary. You asked me last week if I could drive you to a clinic appointment today."

"Thank you, Hillary," I breathed. "I knew it was you. I really did. But for a moment, I lost you."

Hillary's eyes darkened with concern as laughter bubbled out of me. The black hole shrunk a bit again, and I patted her arm reassuringly. She didn't seem to share in the humour of the situation but kept her silence as we pulled away from the curb.

"It's a good thing you needed a ride. I need to talk to the nurses about refilling one of my prescriptions early."

The Pill Cabinet

Hillary

One

"Good morning, Amber," I greeted the young receptionist behind the counter. "Can you leave a note with Dr. Ivan? I need refills for a few of my prescriptions."

"I sure can, Hillary, but didn't you just ask for refills a few weeks ago? Are you sure you don't have enough?"

I usually loved how close and familiar I could get with the staff at this small clinic, but today I could have gone without the questions. I watched her flip through a binder as she spoke before shifting over to the computer screen. The *click* of a computer mouse and the *tick* of the wall clock were the only sounds in the clinic's empty waiting room.

"Yes, I'm sure."

After a pause, she looked up at me, a question in her eyes.

"Have you been using more than the prescribed amount, Hillary?" she asked softly. Her eyes searched my face for something.

I stared back then blinked in my no-nonsense way. "Of course not!" I replied as bubbles of offence gurgled in my gut.

After another moment of electronic clicking, she grabbed an appointment card and scribbled out a note.

"Do you have enough left to get you through the next week?" she asked.

"Yes, I think so," I replied while fiddling with my brown mitts. I hadn't expected these questions.

"Don't worry, Hillary," she said as she handed me the card. "Maybe you need a stronger dose. But if you're running out this fast, it's best to come in and have a chat with Dr. Ivan."

"You're absolutely right, I'm sure," I replied as I slipped the appointment card into my pocket.

Next Monday? A whole seven days' wait? Well, I had little choice but to get through the next week on pure grit, I told myself.

I flexed my hands as I found a seat and waited for my friend, Beth. She was the reason I was here. Good thing she'd asked for help. My wait for a refill could have been much longer.

Should I count out the pills left once I got home? Maybe I should stop at the drugstore for a calendar so I could map out exactly what I needed and how much I had. I could always grab something over the counter, just in case I ran out of my prescription. But nothing helped like the painkillers from the doctor. What if I was left with nothing for a few days?

My joints ached. I didn't want to think what a day would be like without that buffer. The pain radiated from each knuckle, and I gave in to the urge to massage them. I felt Amber's eyes on me as she typed out notes on the keyboard hidden behind the counter. What was she thinking?

It didn't matter.

I ignored her interest, closed my eyes, and listened to my heartbeat. The ticking of the wall clock grew louder. I heard shuffling from down the hall as nurses and doctors moved around.

"Good morning, Amber!" I opened one eye and looked over at the reception desk. A woman holding the hand of a red-nosed child waved as they entered the waiting room.

"Good morning. I'll let them know you're here, Ester. No change in your information, right?"

"No changes, thank you," the woman replied as she pulled the child along and sat down beside the small bookshelf against the right-hand wall.

I heard the door open again, and more greetings rang out. Thank goodness Beth and I had arrived when we had. The waiting room filled, and I clutched my handbag along with my mittens securely on my lap.

I had my eyes closed again when I heard my name called from the hallway.

"Hillary? Hillary Shear?"

"Yes?" I answered. "Is everything alright? I don't have an appointment this morning."

"Yes ..." She paused. "You brought Beth Daily to her appointment this morning, right?"

"Right."

"Could you come back with me? She needs you for a moment."

The nurse's sneakers squeaked against the smooth floor as she guided me to a small room with the number three painted in bold black over the lintel. I noticed the trim also held a layer of dust and rolled my eyes at no one in particular.

"Beth, is everything alright?" I asked as the nurse held the door open for me.

My friend sat with a small notebook in her lap, eyes glued to the pages, finger tapping against lips as the old gears behind her light grey eyes turned. A middle-aged man dressed in a button-down shirt and black trousers with a stethoscope draped over his neck sat on a stool in front of her.

"Hello, Hillary. How are you today?" Dr. Ivan asked as I and the nurse entered the room together.

"Sore today, Doctor. Oh! I left a note for you at the desk."

He held up a finger to silence me but smiled and then motioned to the metal chair beside my friend.

"I'll check your message as soon as we're done here, Hillary. But first, we need your help."

Immediately, I smelled trouble and sat down beside Beth.

"Is everything alright, Beth?" I asked again, placing a hand on her arm as she continued to stare at the notebook in her lap.

She turned a page before looking at me and smiling, grey eyes sparkling.

"Oh, yes, dear. Everything is fine. I'm just having one of my 'moments.'"

"Moments?" I asked.

"Hillary ... Have you noticed Beth acting differently? Maybe being more forgetful than usual or withdrawn?" Dr. Ivan asked. I noticed he used his extra gentle tone as he spoke. He rarely used that tone with me.

"Well, now that you mention it, yes. Why, just the other day, she left the nursery at church and completely forgot to come back. And this morning, when I picked her up, it was like she'd forgotten we were coming to the clinic."

"And you're close friends, yes?"

"Yes, yes, we are. We've known each other for over forty years."

"Beth," Dr. Ivan addressed her directly. "Can you tell me who Hillary is?"

"Hillary? Oh, yes!" Beth looked at me and then over at Dr. Ivan. "Hillary is my dear friend. We go to church together."

"And do you remember why she's here with you today?"

She paused and looked back down at the notebook in her lap, turning to the half-filled page in the middle.

"She was to bring me to the clinic this morning. See here?" She pointed to a few lines at the top of the page. "I wrote it down so I wouldn't forget."

"I see, and well done, Beth. That was wise of you," Dr. Ivan assured her. "And do you trust Hillary? Are you okay with me talking to her about your health?"

"Oh, yes. She is a great friend."

"Alright."

I read the concern written all over Dr. Ivan's face but kept my silence as he began.

"Beth, after what you have shown me from your book, I believe you have developed some kind of dementia."

I watched as the twinkle vanished from Beth's eyes and was replaced with shadows like heavy rain clouds.

"Yes, I've been waiting for it. Just like my mother and sister. Has my turn come for sure?"

The sadness in her voice shocked me, and I saw Dr. Ivan blink back a tear.

"Yes, Beth. I would like you to write what I say to you in your notebook. You will need help from your friends from now on."

He handed her his own pen and gently dictated a few lines of explanation for her to scribble down.

At first, I didn't know what to think. I'd snapped at her at church for forgetting her nursery duty. Shame crawled into my heart as I remembered my tone. I'd watched Beth as she upheld her mother and sister through their last battles. Now it was her turn, but she didn't have her own Beth to guide her.

"Hillary, Beth lives alone and is childless?"

"Yes, yes, she is."

"She will need you and the help of other friends."

"Of course." I sat up straight.

Helping, yes. Beth might not have her own sister, but she had me. I would need to be strong for her.

"I will have her name added to the waiting list for Esther Manor immediately. Unfortunately, she has no one documented as a health advocate. We need to find someone who will step into this role." He shook his head. "I'm very upset we missed this. But it looks like Beth has been monitoring her own memory for some time. We may need to find someone to visit her regularly, or even live with her, before space becomes available at the group home. Does she have other close friends? You may all need to have a meeting about how best we can help her. This small town's facilities are at capacity."

"Of course. She has been an active member of Hope is Here Church for many years. We will make sure she is taken care of."

Dr. Ivan nodded as he went over what Beth had written out for herself.

"Kelly. Can you take Beth and Hillary to the front and help them make appointments for proper dementia testing for Beth? The fact she could take down what I asked her to write is good. But we need to know exactly how far this has progressed."

As Dr. Ivan rose to leave, I reminded him, "Don't forget about my note."

"I won't, Hillary."

He gave me a tired smile as he left the room and accepted a new file from a waiting nurse. I resisted the urge to remind him the note was at the front desk.

"Are you ladies ready?" Kelly asked.

"Come, Beth, there's some paperwork we need to fill out and gather before we leave today," I said.

"Oh? Remind me what kind of paperwork, Hillary. I was reading my notebook and seem to have forgotten," Beth replied.

Two

My mittens clearly weren't enough to keep the damp cold at bay. I felt a turning in the air. The deep freeze of a Canadian winter was shifting to a snowy spring.

"I hope Dr. Ivan has time for my note today," I said as I grasped the steering wheel and slowly eased up on the brake pedal under my boot.

Beth nodded as she watched snow falling from the dark sky through the car window.

"Doesn't the snow always make everything look so new? I love the snow," she said.

"I don't," I muttered as we pulled out into the street to join the traffic. "How are you feeling, Beth?"

"Oh, just fine, thank you. Where are we going?"

"Home. We've just been at the clinic, and you had a chat with Dr. Ivan."

"Oh yes! Yes." Her voice dropped in tone. "It's my turn now."

"I'll take care of you. You won't be alone."

"Thank you, Hillary."

We lagged into silence as the streets passed by. My knuckles ached as they pulled the steering wheel, turning the car down Beth's street. Did I bring my pills this morning? For a moment, I couldn't remember, and my heart skipped at the thought of being unable to drive home because of the pain in my hands. The ache had already moved up my wrists into my arms.

"Beth, I'm sorry for being angry with you after Bible study."

"Did you get angry?"

I glanced at her for a brief second. Her eyes held that soft grey shimmer again.

"Don't worry about it, dear. I don't even remember."

"I still need to apologize."

I caught sight of her head bobbing a yes as we pulled up in front of her house.

"Yes, apologies are important. Hillary ... I'm going to be forgetting a lot of things in the next few months. You'll have to forgive me for that."

"Health issues are not something you need to apologize for."

"I know. But ..." I watched her falter, lost for words as hidden fear bubbled into her eyes as tears. "I know what people with dementia can be like. I'll apologize now. Before ... Before I can't."

Before unbuckling the seat belts, we both just stared at each other, letting the weight of her words hold us in place.

"It's okay, Beth. I forgive you. Will you forgive me?"

"Of course. Would you like some tea? I must also have fresh cookies in the house. I love cookies, you know."

"I would love some tea."

Beth's house was warm and cozy. I always loved how the moss-green hallways invited you in and asked you to stay without words.

"What kind of tea would you like?" she asked as she hung her house keys on the peg labeled "house key."

"Just plain tea is fine, Beth," I called to her as she entered the kitchen, leaving me to hang my coat on the hall tree.

I didn't remember labels on the pegs beside the door the last time I visited. The next peg read "mail key" and the last one "shed key." I noted how she added the word "key" to each label despite it being very apparent they were all key hooks.

The pain in my hands had eased up in the warmth of the house, but I still rubbed them before joining my friend at her kitchen table. The kettle soon bubbled, and we poured the hot water.

I watched her pause for a moment as she looked at the tea bags nestled in an old mug in the centre of the table.

"Plain tea, right, Hillary?"

"Yes, that's right," I assured her as she ripped open a bag and added it to her small china teapot.

"I've noticed you've labelled the whole house, Beth." My eyes roved around the kitchen.

Yellow stickers hung everywhere, and on each one, a simple word or two described the contents of the cupboards.

"They help me relax."

She seemed more at ease now that we were in her own home.

"It also makes it easier for friends that visit." She smiled at me, the spark of her happy self now firmly back in those grey eyes.

We filled the next hour with tea, peanut butter cookies, and laughter while sharing memories of days spent with our husbands, now both gone. I relayed the latest about my children.

"They are both busy men with equally busy families. But I miss them," I told her.

I could tell her brain had wandered off. She looked around her own kitchen as if seeing it for the first time, the gleam in her eyes shifting but never dimming.

"Do you remember the time the boys painted my back shed? They left purple handprints all over the back."

I remembered the summer she'd paid my boys to do the job her husband had put off, and in frustration, she'd paid them with his cigarette money. As I shared the memory with her, we both laughed in between the last sips of tea. Old memories, aged to bring out the flavours of life, were so sweet.

"Beth, it's time I go home. I've more errands to run today as well."

"Oh, yes, of course. You must be busy with those boys of yours."

I ignored her lapse while sharing in her sunny smile. "I think I'd better use the bathroom before going. All that tea."

"You remember where it is, right?" she asked.

I was already walking down the hall as I called back a yes to her, hiding the tear I wiped from the edge of my smile.

"At least I have those 'boys,' though far away. Beth has only me. I should call Rose when I get home. She'll know how to plan for all this care."

The bathroom mirrored the kitchen with its yellow labels pasted on everything. I had to admit that Beth knew how to be prepared. The sad fact gnawed at my heart as the pain in my joints wore on my energy. It was time for a dose of my meds.

After finishing my business, I dug around in my handbag, propping it up on the washstand as I stirred through the bottom. There it was, the translucent yellow container with a snap lid. I read the white sticker wrapped around it, double-checking to make sure I had grabbed the right one.

"Thank God," I whispered while filling a tiny paper cup from the old-fashioned dispenser stuck to the wall.

I should have just taken them with my tea, but when an aging body has to go, it has to go. I shook the pills out of the yellow container into my palm, then dropped it back into my handbag, and groaned in frustration as the bag tipped over the edge of the sink and slid down into the basin.

I swallowed the stomach-in-my-throat feeling as I pulled the purse back from the drain. Did I lose anything? It didn't look like I had, and my stomach settled back into place until I noticed the pills from my hand were gone.

"Oh, no!"

Had I dropped them on the floor? Down the drain? I didn't see them anywhere. My heart hammered as I set aching hands on the cold washstand. The chill from the porcelain bit into my joints. I needed those pills. I couldn't wait any longer.

I found myself on my hands and knees scanning the floor, moving the wastebasket, and rummaging through towels on a low shelf. Nothing. I couldn't find them. Could the tiny white ovals have rolled off the washstand into a crevice in a door and landed in a basket? In desperation, I started opening them in rapid succession.

Beth had her bathroom organized to a staggering level. Everything that could fit in a small bin was in its place, a yellow label adorning the front of each brown plastic cage. I pushed those baskets around, rearranging things and looking in between them and into the bottom of each nest. Then I lifted each from its place and checked under it, just in case. I grabbed a small basket filled with familiar-looking pill bottles, pushing the over-the-counter pain management around until a white printed label caught my eye. My heart skipped again. Maybe I didn't need to find those lost pills after all.

Three

My mind wrapped itself around that pill bottle, and I could almost feel it jostling around in my handbag as I waved to Beth one last time before climbing into my car. I'd popped several tiny white ovals from the bottle with her sister's name on it into my mouth and washed it down with a good gulp of water before making a hasty exit, fleeing the scene of my crime, like a child who hides from its mother, shame burning in its mind. I told myself Beth didn't even remember those pills were there. If she did, she'd have tossed them a long time ago.

I relaxed as I felt the slow release inside me, and the sharp twinges of pain in my hands dulled again. My feet had started to ache, and the burn had travelled up my legs before I left Beth's, but now it was tamped back down. I filled my lungs with a deep breath and almost closed my eyes as a wave of relaxing ease rushed through me.

"Thank God," I said to myself.

I pulled into the parking lot of my apartment building and made my way up to my small condo. By the time a numbness started creeping into my fingers and toes, I was already sitting in my recliner, eyes closed, muscles relaxed, enjoying the absence of pain. I'd forgotten what it was like to be free of it for any length of time. I relished the floating sensations flowing through me, forgetting about all those things I had told Beth I needed to get done.

Time sped past, but my brain couldn't quite grasp that it was moving. I felt suspended in peace, pain-free peace, until my cell phone rang from inside my handbag, and it forced me to open my eyes, the noise washing through my calm like a finger breaking the surface of water.

As I thumbed the device on, the time flashed at me from the lock screen: 4:00 p.m. Had I really been sitting here that long? How late had it been when I left Beth's? I couldn't remember, but it couldn't have been after lunch. I remembered having tea and cookies. I never ate cookies close to the noon meal. My stomach growled, and I wondered if the person calling could hear it as well.

"Hello, this is Hillary," I said. The syllables of my words dragged out, and it felt like walking through a dream as I listened to the answering voice.

"Hillary, it's Abigail. I've got your weekly Compassionate Ministries visitors list for you."

"Abigail? I thought ... Why isn't Rose calling me?"

"Were you at church this last Wednesday?"

With my brain waves crawling through molasses, I couldn't remember. Wasn't I usually at church when functions were happening? Yes, I was always there.

"Did I miss something?"

"Miss something? Rose is stepping down from her church positions."

How had I not heard that? I knew I'd been upset with Beth for forgetting me in nursery. I'd been in pain.

"She announced it during the closing coffee break."

"Why on earth would she step down?"

"Well ..." Abigail hesitated, her voice dropping an octave. "She said something about ongoing health issues, and things being unsettled at home. She mentioned her daughters needing more of her time. But she didn't go into detail, and really, it's better that way. If she wants us to know what's going on, she'll tell us. I don't think we should talk about it too much."

"Of course ..." I replied.

"Hillary?"

My concentration had wandered away as I pushed myself up from the recliner. I couldn't feel the floor under my feet and stomped at it to see if it was truly there. Then the floor melted away from underneath me.

Four

"Hillary? HILLARY!"

The noise slipped under my front door and bounced across the floor towards me as I sat floating in a bubble of nothingness.

"Unlock it! Hurry! What if she's fallen?"

Someone fumbled at the lock as I turned my head towards the voice.

I sat on the floor, my back against my recliner. Had I slid out of the chair?

"Hillary! Are you hurt? Can you move? Did you break something?"

Two figures burst into the room. One placed a hand on my shoulder, yet the voices felt distant. I knew my reply made no sense, but still I wanted to reassure the red flash of hair that I was alright. I was better than alright. Nothing hurt.

"What's wrong with her? Is she having a stroke?"

"I'm not sure. I've never seen anyone like this before."

My brain registered that the one person beside me was Abigail. I didn't know anyone else with such red curls. I felt her hand anchoring me to reality. She pulled my arm up into her lap as she bent over the front of her wheelchair and moved one hand from my shoulder to my forehead.

"She feels warm."

"Fever?" The second person was a man. But I didn't recognize who he was.

"Hello?" he said. "Yes, this is Edward, the custodian at the 11th Street Apartments. We need an ambulance at apartment 209. I have a senior woman who may have fallen. She is really out of it. I can't tell if she's having a stroke or something."

"I'm fine." I heard the wrongness in my voice as tremors ran through my arms and legs. It scared me.

"It's okay, Hillary. I've got you," Abigail assured me as she squeezed my hand. "They won't take long to get here. You're going to be okay."

Abigail only left my side for the ambulance ride. She'd grabbed my cell phone and purse off the floor before following the paramedics out the door. But as soon as I was being unloaded at the emergency room doors, she was right there behind me, the wheels of her electric chair leaving tracks in the lightly snow-covered cement.

The paramedics had wrapped me in warm blankets, but I still should have felt the winter chill on my cheeks. Strangely, it was absent, though white flakes were gently blowing under the emergency door canopy.

"Are you family?" a nurse asked Abigail as she followed my gurney indoors.

"No. But please, she has no one who lives close. She needs me." The force behind her plea followed me down the hall.

Words flew past me as the paramedics and nurses discussed my case. They placed a plastic clamp on my finger at the same time as a blood pressure cuff was wrapped around my arm.

"She's stable," someone announced, and I heard Abigail breathe a prayer of thanks as she rolled up and took my hand.

It wasn't long before Dr. Ivan was at my side, flashing a tiny but bright light into my eye as he gently held the lid open.

"What did you take, Hillary?"

"What do you mean?" I asked. Now that I was hooked up to fluids through an IV, my faculties were coming back at a steady rate.

"Hillary, I believe you're experiencing some kind of drug overdose. We will test your blood to confirm, but I need to know what you took. Your regular medication wouldn't have done this to you, even if you took double your prescribed amount."

Abigail's wheelchair was pulled right up beside the gurney. She squeezed my hand gently, her fingers laced together with mine. "Hillary, if you took something you shouldn't have ... We can't help you if you don't tell us."

Realization and shame crawled up my chest, carrying heavy chains that bound my lungs. I spluttered, unable to give a coherent reply.

"Hillary." It was Dr. Ivan's turn to lay his hand on mine. His deep brown eyes softened. "Please tell us what happened."

I couldn't. This was ridiculous. Familiar pain crawled its way back into my fingers and toes. I longed again for the numbness and freedom my mistake had given me despite being left drained and weak.

"I'm tired. I just want to sleep," I croaked.

"Nurse? Could you please grab a glass of water for us?" Dr. Ivan asked the quiet woman at his elbow.

Both my companions waited until she returned, a plastic turquoise jug and Styrofoam cup in hand.

"I thought more was better right now," she said as she handed the full cup to the doctor, who handed it to me.

"Hillary, we need to know what you took."

I sipped the cold water from the cup. The wet liquid against my lips was calming, but with the relief came exhaustion. I didn't want to fight but couldn't run. This wasn't fair.

Time to own this mistake, Hillary.

My lips wouldn't move, but I looked at Abigail, and her worried eyes broke me. I pointed to my purse on her lap and then closed my eyes after handing back the cup of water to Dr. Ivan.

Abigail released my fingers so she could open my purse. I ignored the sounds of her rummaging through my things.

"What am I looking for, Hillary?" she asked. I didn't answer.

"It may be best to empty the whole bag," Dr. Ivan stated in a low voice. "She may not be able to intellectually or emotionally direct us right now."

They spilled my things across the foot of the bed. I heard objects rattling against each other and then hitting the thick covers with a dull thud.

"Look for bottles, or plastic bags, containers that hold pills, or even powders." Dr. Ivan's low voice turned my gut. I wouldn't look. I couldn't look.

"Sometimes people grind or liquefy medications to give a better high. If someone on the street gave Hillary something … It might not be in pill form."

"Doctor, you don't really think she would have?"

He didn't answer her, and I heard a rattling sound like pills in a bottle.

"Nurse, is Dr. Andrews on call today?" I opened my eyes to see Dr. Ivan holding a small bottle and squinting to read the faded print on the label.

"He was doing rounds earlier. But it's getting late."

"Go see if he's still around. I need to speak to him right away."

Abigail was lifting papers from the pile and placing them back into my purse as Dr. Ivan left, pill bottle in hand.

"Are you feeling any better?" she asked.

I gave her only a nod as reassurance then let the silence drag out as we waited. All the regular hospital noises filled my senses. It was getting late, and visitors were leaving. Nurses prepared for shift changes with last-minute paperwork and ran around making sure everything was in its place. The silence in my small assessment room amplified the noise outside the door. We heard a second group of paramedics yelling out instructions as doors opened and closed. Abigail said another prayer for whoever they were bringing in. I joined her in a whisper and then closed my eyes again, only to open them when a new nurse entered my room.

"Okay, dear, let's get some blood samples, shall we?"

Her voice felt overly chipper, and I couldn't help wrinkling my nose at her while nodding my assent as she set a carry bin of needles and tubes down beside me.

I winced as her finger probed my arm for a good vein and looked away when she found one and produced a needle.

"Abigail, go home," I told my friend, trying to distract myself from the bright red seeping from my vein into the collection vial attached to the needle.

"No." Her response was quick and forceful. "Not until I know if they're admitting you for the night or longer."

"Your family will want you home," I interjected.

"Ben has already told me to stay." She waved her cell phone at me in emphasis, but then lowered it and stared at her hands. "Unless you don't want me here, Hillary."

We paused as the nurse released the rubber tie she had wound around my arm.

"Just about done here!" she said, her chipper voice ringing in my ear.

"Um, thank you."

The nurse's deft fingers pulled the needle from my arm and placed a cotton ball in its place, all at once.

"I think they'll keep you overnight," she said in a softer tone.

I watched her tip the full vial of my blood upside down once before placing it into her plastic carry bin.

"Here." She placed a piece of medical tape over the cotton and smiled. "Make sure you hold pressure there for a few minutes."

She paused as she got up to leave. "It looks like you have a caring friend. Don't push her away."

My mouth must have hung open at her forwardness because the next thing I knew, Abigail was crossing her arms over her chest and giving me a strange look.

"What?" I said. "That was very bold of her."

"Bold and true."

I looked down at my hands. My knuckles ached.

"It's not a nurse's place to give personal advice unless asked for. It's unprofessional."

"Hillary …" Abigail dropped her hands into her lap as well. The edges of her eyes reddened with unspilled tears. "Hillary Shear, you are sometimes a very hard woman. But I know it's because you are a strong woman, not unkind. Do not push the people who want to help you away."

My throat constricted as I listened to her. I couldn't look at her so instead reached for the cup of water Dr. Ivan had left beside me.

"Do you want me to contact your boys?"

"Good Lord, no!" I almost spit water across the blankets, and panic sent my heart racing.

Abigail raised both her hands to shelter from the few water drops that escaped my mouth. "Okay! Okay …"

"At least ... Not yet," I added, taking a deep breath to settle my nerves.

No, we didn't need to trouble the boys. There's nothing wrong with me, I told myself. Nothing a night in the hospital and a good sleep couldn't fix, anyway. Maybe a good dose of my painkillers on top at the very most.

Are you sure, Hillary?

I squelched my inner voice as I took another slower sip of water. There was *nothing* to worry about.

My nerves had calmed, and my eyes were closed when Dr. Ivan walked back into the room. Abigail's gentle shaking of my hand roused me enough to notice he wasn't alone as he pulled over a stool.

"This is Dr. Andrews, Hillary," he said, pointing to the elderly man at his elbow. "We have some questions for you, but first, we've decided to keep you overnight and possibly for a second. That will be decided tomorrow."

"Two nights? Is that really necessary?" I asked.

"We don't know yet. What we do know is you took some powerful drugs, whether you meant to or not."

"Mrs. Shear, please, I would like to know where you came by these pills." Dr. Andrews' voice was so deep it rumbled as he produced the offending bottle.

"I don't remember," I lied.

"Okay. But do you know the person whose name is on the label? It's not yours." Dr. Andrews slid his glasses off and held the bottle farther from his face while reading it to himself.

"If it's not my name, then, no. I don't know."

"It reads 'Darla Diggory.' I remember Darla well. She hasn't been my patient for some years ... Dr. Ivan has informed me you accompanied Beth Daily, whom I believe is her sister, to the clinic this morning."

Abigail remained silent through this spill of information, but her fingers tightened around mine. "Yes, I drove Beth to her appointment this morning. In fact, it's been a long day. I would like to sleep now."

Dr. Ivan glanced over at Abigail. "Hillary, would you like your friend to leave the room for a moment?" he asked.

"No, she stays."

Abigail's grip on me tightened again. I could hear her whispering something, but it was too soft to make out. I took a deep breath.

Hillary, it's time.

The voice didn't just slip through my thoughts; it resounded in my chest, pulling at the invisible chains that were tightening around me as my panic rose.

"I ... I ..."

They all waited. All three sets of eyes were ready for me to say what had happened.

"I dropped my pills while using the bathroom at Beth's this morning. I must have picked up the wrong bottle."

Dr. Andrews' gaze narrowed. Dr. Ivan squeezed the bridge of his nose as he sighed.

"Alright, Hillary. We'll leave it there for now. But it doesn't change how serious this is. You could have died."

I glanced at Abigail. Her usual rosy cheeks had drained of colour, but she held her silence along with my hand. What must she think of me? Did it matter? Did I care?

"At her end, Darla Diggory was on some powerful stuff. It was a difficult passing. You should know that, Hillary, if you are as good a friend of Beth's as Dr. Ivan has told me. We'll watch you closely tonight ... Now, Dr. Ivan. I take my leave."

Dr. Andrews bowed his way out of the room. I could tell they didn't believe me. But really, what did it matter?

Dr. Ivan again glanced at Abigail before continuing. "Hillary, I read your note from this morning. I went over your chart just a few moments ago. The only way you would need more pain medication is if you've been taking more than I prescribed. We talked about this when you started the prescription. Pain medication isn't something you can experiment with. I believe you've built up a tolerance, and ... You may be on the edge of addiction."

"What?" I couldn't control myself anymore. Angry tears poured down my face as I shifted in bed, trying to sit up higher. "I'm too old for this!"

"Hillary, calm down." Abigail tried to soothe me by pulling my hand clean off the bed and into her lap.

"I won't calm down! This is ridiculous. I accidentally took someone else's medication. Fair enough. That doesn't mean I'm addicted to anything!"

"Not yet, Hillary. But tolerance can lead to addiction if we're not careful. Addiction affects the mind, not just the body—it's sneaky. You may never fall over that edge, but you are dangerously close."

I was lost for words and couldn't believe what had just come out of his mouth.

"And what's more, Hillary ... Beth needs you right now."

"What's wrong with Beth?" the question bubbled out of Abigail. "Oh ... I'm sorry. I shouldn't have asked that."

"It's okay," Dr. Ivan said. "But I can't answer that. You will need to talk to Hillary and Beth herself."

The stool Dr. Ivan sat on swivelled, and he turned to look directly at me.

"Hillary, Beth is no longer the only one who needs the help of others. I'll refer you to a psychiatrist. We need to nip this in the bud, and I'll be reviewing your prescription and the dosage."

As the word "psychiatrist" left the doctor's mouth, I felt the chains inside pull. The wind left my body, and I choked. I tried to pull a breath into my lungs, but they wouldn't open. My chest hurt, my fingers burned, my vision blurred.

"Hillary?" Abigail cried. "Doctor!"

"Nurse! We need help here," Dr. Ivan yelled.

They gave me some kind of sedative to calm me down, and then Dr. Ivan left. Only Abigail stayed to witness my unravelling. Tears and words I knew a woman of my age should never say in public spilled out of me.

They had laid me down flat in bed and turned me on my side while I wrapped one hand around Abigail's and the other around the metal bed rail.

"What's happening, Abigail? Is God punishing me? Good Christian women don't have addictions." I wept into the pillow.

"Hillary ... I wish that were true. I'll stay with you tonight. Do you want me to phone Rose?"

"No." I wanted to yell the word, but it came out only as a gasp for air. "If Rose knows, the whole church will know. No ... no, they can't know. The church is all I have left. Please ... No."

"I'll never leave you or forsake you. God said that to his people in the Bible. You have a battle ... no, a war to fight, Hillary. God won't leave you and neither will I."

Abigail's Prayers: Four

Dear God, how long has she been suffering?

How many more of us are in pain and hide it?

What are we so afraid of?

You?

Each other?

I held her hand as she fell asleep.

I've never seen her look so old ... so worn.

Secret pain introduced to secret sins ...

What am I hiding inside my own heart?

Show me.

You are the only one who sees all.

Please, give me strength to know when to be silent

but also when to speak. For her, to her, and to others.

Amen.

Her Choice

Debora

One

I'D FROZEN AS THE cascade of coffee cups crashed onto the floor. In the aftermath, Rose had taken the blame on herself. I should have thanked her for it. I should have loved her for it. But instead, I shoved the card she'd been looking at into my pocket without reading the words written across its surface. *Why had I wanted to look at that stupid card so badly?* I reminded myself what an idiot I was. *Why couldn't you just keep your mouth shut and your hands to yourself?*

The church parking lot was empty. Gloria had fallen asleep in the back seat to the hum of the car's engine. Still, I sat there, hands on the steering wheel, staring off into space. I knew from experience it wasn't safe to let myself drive while my mind was a tornado of thoughts. So I waited, time slipping by. I didn't feel the cold as it made war with the engine of the car, its battlefield my toes and fingers. It was Gloria's snore as her head slid down onto her chest that pulled me back from the edge of nothingness.

"You're a mother, Debora. It's cold. Take her home." I said the words out loud to punctuate the need to move, trying to wake my soul as it sat inside me, half frozen.

Just a minute longer. I don't want to move, it whined.

"Go home, make soup, get Gloria to eat. Give her a bath. Prepare dinner. Then Paul will come home." Again I said it out loud, giving myself a verbal road map for the rest of the day.

Paul will be home.

I hung on to the last sentence as a lifeline. I only had to do these things, and then he'd be there. If I could just make it to the moment he opened the front door, we'd be okay.

We'll be okay.

I glanced back at Gloria. Her deep breathing rumbled as her chin rested on her chest. I leaned back and carefully pushed her forehead up to lean against the side of her car seat. I knew it wouldn't stay there for long with the turns and bumps of the drive home. Despite that, I was a mother, and it was one of those small things I was supposed to do ... Wasn't it?

I shifted gears and accelerated out of the empty lot.

Home, soup. Soup would be nice ... Eat, bathe, prep dinner.

The list was a beacon guiding me home. As I held that single focus, I barely noticed the jolt as I clipped the frozen curb before pulling out on the street. I never looked back to check on Gloria.

It would have distracted me from the goal: home. The streets flew by. Did I remember to stop at that red light? I must have. My body and mind were on autopilot, my soul half frozen in the darkness.

Home.

I was home but still didn't move. How long did I let the car idle in the driveway? How late was it? The questions all came tumbling in as I realized I'd lost time again. I looked at the stereo clock, and it answered the only question it could.

"One-fifteen. Where did I lose an hour and fifteen minutes?"

"It doesn't really matter," I told myself. Gloria was still asleep and only roused as I carried her into the house. Her hands shook with half-asleep as she held on to my neck.

"Mama?"

"Yes, baby?"

"I'm hungry."

"Good, then you'll eat up all your soup."

"Soup?"

"Yep."

She wrinkled her nose at me as I set her down to peel her out of the winter coat and boots. Those boots stuck like glue, and the insulated insoles popped out, still hanging on to her little foot.

"Oops."

"Silly boots," Gloria giggled.

I let her scamper towards a corner of the open living room filled with toys and sighed while stuffing the insoles back into place. Had I laughed loud enough for her? Did I smile wide enough?

You're home. Now soup, then bath.

"What kind of soup do you want, Gloria? Tomato? Or mushroom?" I called.

She'd stuck her head down into the toy box, her four-year-old feet on tiptoes as she strained to reach something at the bottom.

"Mushroom? Yuck!"

"You're not allowed to change your mind at the last minute."

"NO mushroom." Her hair charged with static on the way back to standing, and I couldn't help laughing as the ends drifted in the air around her round cheeks.

"Excuse me?"

"No mushroom, thank you."

"Better. Tomato it is."

I hung my coat over hers on the first hook on the wall. Paul had bolted a new row up last spring when we thought our family might be growing. They were still empty.

I paused. Did I lock the car? Did I bring everything inside? I didn't want to have to make a trip out into the cold slush once it got dark. During the day, the snow and ice would slowly melt in the sun, collecting in the walkway and drive. Then at night, it would freeze hard in a sheer sheet. But still, the soup sounded better than going out again to double-check.

I pointed my automatic key out of the cracked door and watched the lights on my little white car blink. At least now I knew it was locked. Anything I'd forgotten would be there tomorrow.

The wind pushed against my thin cardigan as I closed the door. It left like icy fingers trying to push their way into the house at the last second, and the satisfying click once it was closed made my heart flutter.

Safe at home.

I released my breath. How long had I been holding it for?

Every step across the hall to our dine-in kitchen leeched my energy away. The sight of the sink stacked with unwashed dishes pushed water into the corners of my eyes. How had I forgotten those? I was home, so I let the tears slowly trickle down my face, wiping them away only to distinguish the can opener from the other odds and ends that lived in the utensil drawer.

"I shouldn't be so tired."

Shouldn't, but I still was. I'd made it through Bible study and should've been proud of myself. Gloria seemed happy after her play time in the nursery, and the nap in the car had done her good. I locked the manual can opener onto the edge of the can of soup. The blade sliced through the metal as I turned the crank, and the gears bumped against each other in uneven friction. When was the last time I washed this thing?

When the can opened, I dropped the tool into the sink. This way, it would be one of the first things I washed. Wait, was there a clean pot? Could I even cook this soup?

My shoulders ached, as if something was sitting on them trying to press me into the floor. I rolled them in an attempt to shake it off before reaching for a pot from the centre of the dirty dishes. I did my best to not disturb the rest of the pile but failed as a bowl slid free.

My fingers grazed its rim as it fell, sending it spinning until it touched the hard flooring and shattered at my feet. My mind flashed back to that morning, the white porcelain cascade, the shards trapping Rose and I in place.

"Mama, are you okay?"

"Yes! I just broke a bowl ... Don't come into the kitchen! You'll get glass in your feet."

I shoved the pot back onto the counter and cast about for the broom. Self-disgust crawled up my legs as I tiptoed through the shards around me when I spotted it beside the fridge. The weight pressing me down grew heavier as I pushed the glass pieces into a pile. I blinked away the mental image of stepping across the floor and finding blood-smeared footprints in my wake.

I spied Gloria watching me from the hallway as I dumped the bowl's remnants into the garbage, telling myself I would take the bag out back as soon as lunch was over.

"What is it, baby?" I asked her.

She waved the TV remote at me as she eyed the kitchen floor suspiciously.

I nodded, and she dashed back towards the living room. Before I had returned the broom to lean against the fridge, the singsong sounds of cartoons floated in the air.

Pot. Clean it.

Why were these little things so hard?

I grabbed the pot again and ran hot water over it while wiping the inside with a damp cloth. It would have to be good enough. Where was the open can? I grimaced at the sound as the condensed mass hit the pan's bottom. For some reason, soup didn't sound as good as it once had. Still, I stirred in water and set the pot on the stove.

The sounds of stomping drew me to the living room as I waited for lunch to heat. Gloria was glued to the flashing pictures on the TV screen as she mimicked the movements of a dancing penguin and moose, their cartoon bodies round balls of colour.

Pinpricks of pain gnawed at my heart as I laughed at her, and the warmth of love threatened to force my soul closer to life and reality. It groaned within me, and I sucked in a ragged breath. My cold fingers found the pockets on my cardigan, and I wrapped my fingers around the edges of the card Rose had handed to me that morning. It felt good to warp it into a tube—the stupid thing—and hold it tightly. I shifted it back and forth, feeling the cardstock give way and form creases. I poured my frustration into its deteriorating fibres.

Settling onto the couch, I glanced at my watch. It would take a few more minutes for the soup to warm, so I stared off into space. My mind flowed past Gloria and her waving arms, past the TV and its ridiculous display. My fingers worked the paper in my pocket, folding it again and again.

I felt ashamed of how tired I was and the weight that pressed me into the couch cushions. It always crawled onto my back while engaging with Gloria, stealing my joy with greedy fingers even while my little sunbeam threw smiles and laughter at me to catch and cherish.

The weight grew heavier as it gobbled down what should have been mine, and with the loss came the cold. I should have fought with it—reached out to snatch those gifts before the invisible thief could steal them—but I was never quite strong enough, fast enough, or willing enough.

You don't really want them, anyway.

You're tired.

"Mothers are supposed to cherish these things."

Then, you're a terrible mother.

Was that why God had changed his mind about letting Paul and me add to our family? I looked over at the hallway and the nearly empty hook rack. I told myself it must be true as painful memories flooded in.

I was so tired.

Two

It was last spring. I'd jumped into Paul's arms as he walked in the door from work, a used pregnancy test clutched in my hand.

"What's going on?" he'd managed before I half-smothered him with a kiss that took his breath away then flashed the pink and blue stick in his face.

"Why are you waving a pee stick at me, Debora?"

"Oh, really, Paul!"

"Well, you did just pee on it, didn't you?" I'd stomped my foot on the entryway carpet in frustration as he gave me a wolfish grin before grabbing the test away from me. "Sorry. Bad joke."

A new kiss had sealed his apology.

"Positive?"

"Positive."

"OH MY GOD!" he'd yelled, lifting me off my feet and dancing me around the living room while Gloria giggle-screamed at our outburst while sitting in her toy corner.

"What do you think of that, Gloria?" Paul had asked while waving the stick in the air.

"Oh, put it down," I'd laughed.

"Daddy, what ya doing?" Gloria had asked in her high-pitched three-year-old voice.

"CELEBRATING!"

Our joy hadn't lasted long. I remembered the day I started bleeding and the fear that turned my soul to ice. That fear lived with me even now, crawling through my veins, stabbing with sharp pricks every day.

"Thank God we waited to tell anyone," Paul had said one night as he sat beside me in bed. I wept into my pillow, knowing it was his personal way of dealing with grief, but the words threw ice waves over my head. "We have a child already. We're still so blessed."

It was all true. We had Gloria, our beautiful little girl. I had so much to be thankful for.

Then why couldn't I shake this darkness?

Two months after our loss, I held a new pregnancy test in my hand but kept the pink lines that showed along the indicator strip a secret from Paul. "Why hurt him if by some chance it happened again?"

He'd found me weeping on the toilet a month later as I lost the light that had been growing inside me. It was nothing more than a few extra days of bleeding, but it shredded my soul.

"Mama?"

Had I felt a cold little hand on my forehead? Was someone calling my name? I heard only muffled words and turned over, curling tightly into a cocoon of protection.

You're cold.

Nothing is protecting you.

My shoulders shook as a shiver from my core travelled up along my limbs.

"Debora? DEBORA!"

It was Paul's voice pulling me out of my chill, his large hand on my forehead.

"Is Mama sick, Gloria?"

"No. But she won't wake up. I tried."

"Debora. It's time to wake up. Debora?"

I sensed the growing frustration in his voice. Or was it worry? My shoulders shook again, his large, warm hand forcing invisible icicles growing along the ridges of my mind to crack and shatter.

"Debora, are you sick?"

"N–No," I stammered.

I rubbed invisible frost from my eyelids. My body trembled with the effort of movement.

"What's cooking in the kitchen? I can smell it from here."

"Cooking? Oh no!"

I hauled myself off the couch and pushed past him to dash towards the kitchen.

"NO!" I yelled as I grabbed the hot smoking pot off the stove. The room smelled of burnt food, but the air was mostly clear, and the smoke alarm hadn't gone off.

"What's wrong?" Paul asked from behind me.

He held Gloria on his hip, her arms wrapped around his neck.

"The soup," I moaned.

The burnt remnants of tomato soup looked like tar at the bottom of the pot. I threw it in the sink and ran cold water into it that sizzled for a second before turning brown.

"I'm sorry. I'll get this cleaned up."

"It's okay, Debora. I'll check that smoke alarm."

It wasn't until I turned towards the pantry to look for something fast for dinner that we noticed the boxes of cereal spilled in a pile beside its door.

"What's this all over the floor?" Paul asked.

Gloria pinched her lips together.

"Did you do that?"

"I was hungry, Daddy."

Paul looked at me, questions in his eyes, but I couldn't face it and turned away.

"I'll just put some rice on, it won't take long. How was work? Did you finish the project you were working on? I know you were up late last night, too. Did you hang up your coat? Can I get you a coffee?" The waterfall of words spilled out of me as I again grabbed the broom from beside the fridge.

"Coffee sounds great."

"Are you sure you want coffee? Maybe I should just get you juice since it's past five. Or maybe you would like a beer. Would you like a beer?"

"Deb! Slow down, baby. Slow down."

"Sorry. I'll make the coffee." I flung the words at him as I scuttled over to the far counter, taking care not to look his way.

I didn't want to see the look of disappointment I imagined him holding against my back.

"Debora, are you okay?"

"I'm fine," I assured him. "Really, I got it."

"Daddy? I'm thirsty," I heard Gloria whisper as he carried her from the room.

You're a bad mother.

I crammed the fabric of my shirt sleeve into my eyes before the water collecting there could drip down and leave stains on my cheeks for Paul to see. Why was I so damn tired? I should never have sat down. How could I forget a pot on the stove? Dinner should have been ready and on the table as Paul walked in the door. I used to be so good at this housewife/mother thing. Why couldn't I just get it together? My life hadn't changed in the years since we'd married. It was a good life. Why was I falling apart?

I grabbed a box of minute rice out of the pantry and hastily rinsed a second pot from the sink, telling myself I was boiling water, so it was clean enough. Once it was on the stove heating, I started making coffee.

I tried to ignore Paul and look busy as he walked into the room and grabbed a cup out of the cupboard for Gloria.

"How was your day?" he asked hesitantly.

"Fine," I said, letting the tone of my voice rise to a cheery ring. "Gloria was so good in the nursery this morning. Oh, yes! Did you know Rose is leaving the ministry? I mean, not leaving the church.

I'm sure she'll still be attending. And of course, Pastor Grill won't be going anywhere. But Rose told us she's 'stepping back' today. What do you think that means? She said 'because of stuff going on at home.' Isn't that strange?"

"Rose? Pastor Grill's wife?"

"Yes, Rose! We don't know any other Rose, do we?" I stopped to catch my breath as I flipped the power button on the coffeemaker. "I hope you don't mind minute rice, dear. I thought it would be fast. Would you like a salad? Do we have a bag left in the fridge? Oh, I should just check. What kind would you like if we have more than one? I went to the grocery store yesterday, so, yes, we should have enough."

"Debora, slow down." Paul shook his head but smiled at me. "A salad sounds great, and either will do."

"Oh, good. Look, we have baby spinach too. I forgot we had that. Just give me a few minutes to throw it all in a bowl and set the table. Or would you like to eat in the living room today? Are you tired? Is there something you would like to watch?"

"The table is fine, Debora."

"Okay, just let me finish here. I'll bring you coffee in a minute."

"Wait!" Paul grabbed my hand as I started throwing bags of greens onto the table. "I love you."

His kiss stopped me in my tracks, and I felt tears welling up as he held me still.

"Debora. Are you okay?"

"I'm fine, Paul. Maybe I'm a bit tired but fine."

I shifted away from the gaze of his soft blue eyes as he tried to look into mine.

"Are you still taking Gloria a drink?" I asked.

"Oh ... OH! Yes, of course."

He backed away from me slowly, holding onto my fingers until the last second before letting my hand drop.

"Careful, or you'll spill that." I arched my brow at him and shooed him from the room.

"Just put the coffee on the table, Deb. No need to bring it to me. Just call us." He looked back at me twice while leaving the room.

Hold it together, Debora, and cool down on that mouth of yours. I bit my tongue.

"Okay, bag of greens, bowl, salad spoons, dressings. Now we need protein." I nodded, my mental list ready and directing me to the cupboards then the fridge.

Once dinner was on the table, Gloria took my place as the chatterbox, telling Paul all about her time in nursery. "James is a crybaby. He didn't want to play today," she stated.

"Oh, come now. James is still very little. Is he three yet?" He turned to me for the answer, and I nodded.

"Barely three," I said.

"See?" Paul said. "He's still little, and you're already four, and just think—after the summer, you'll be in school, and James still has to stay home with his mommy."

"Yes! Because I'm a big girl, and James is still a baby."

"Well, not a baby. But definitely more of a baby than you." Paul laughed.

With Gloria satisfied by her perceived win, she stuffed her face. I watched her, guilt gnawing at me. The burnt pot still lay in the sink swamped with nasty brown water. I didn't think I would ever be able to get it clean.

I pushed the food around my plate. Nothing looked very appetizing. I practised cutting my salad into smaller and smaller bits. As I did, the pile shrank and gave the impression that there was less.

"So, Gloria. Are you all ready to visit James at his house tomorrow?" Paul asked.

"Visiting?" she asked back.

"Yes. Isn't that what you told me yesterday, Debora? You have a play date scheduled?"

"Oh!" I jumped at the question, not remembering. "Did I? I'd forgotten. I should check the calendar to make sure. Silly me!" I continued as I rose and stepped over to the fridge. "Look there. You're right, Paul. I should phone Mary this evening to make sure it still works for her. Maybe we should take some leftovers to help with lunch? What do you think of that, Gloria? Shall we take leftovers?"

Gloria just shrugged at me, not wanting to be distracted from dinner.

"But are you ready, Gloria?" Paul asked. "Did you have a bath today? You don't want to go to a friend's house all smelly and dirty."

"I'm not smelly!" she protested, her eyes shooting up to him and squinting until the edges crinkled.

Paul laughed again at her classic "stink eye" expression. Before he could continue, my hands rose to my cheeks. "I forgot ..."

"Oh?"

"The bath." I closed my eyes as I dug the afternoon's mental list out of the imaginary discard pile. "Home, soup, *bathe Gloria*, dinner prep, then you come home. I spaced again ..."

Paul glanced at his watch and then flashed me a smile. "I got it, baby. There's still plenty of time to get her in the bath."

But I couldn't grasp the reassurance he offered me. It felt like being handed a metal bar covered in butter that slipped away as soon as I tried to take hold of it.

"You go on, call Mary. I'll get this monkey to bed," he added, flashing Gloria with his grin and giving her side a gentle poke that sent her into a fit of giggles.

"Hands to yourself, Daddy!" she squealed.

"Alright, alright," he relented.

They both tumbled from the table in a half run, half tackle, and I watched their glee as if a wall of fog separated us. I'd tried so hard to remember. Usually, my mental lists helped me squeeze through the day, everything important managed, even if just. But today felt like nothing but a series of mistakes and missing moments whose absence weighed on me, crushing the warmth and making shadows where darkness could burrow deeper, growing its frost-covered fingers.

"Put the food away, stack the dirty dishes, wash, wipe the table, call Mary," I muttered the list to myself. What was the point of all this trying?

The hot soapy suds that soon filled the sink only went a short way to warming the chill that gripped me. I felt sweat forming on my forehead as I leaned over the steaming water, but shivers rippled through my legs and up my spine. The scratchy pad I held pricked me as I rubbed it against long-dried food particles, adding to my discomfort.

You're lazy, Debora.

Cleaning this pot would never have been this hard if you had just done it right away.

I wiped the drips from my forehead on my rolled-up sleeve. How long had I been scrubbing? It felt like hours as my shoulders weighed me down. But the kitchen clock told me only fifteen minutes had passed since Paul left the room. Had I really just started?

My feet were too tired to stay still, and I did a shuffle dance in place while filling the drainer with dripping clean dishes. The constant movement didn't help me keep my eyes open, and the last dish I washed was almost dropped in my blind grasping to find it a place.

I searched for the edge of the table behind me, a new dish rag in hand, ready to wipe the residue of our meal away. The smooth wood was cool to the touch, and the drops of hot water on my knuckles soon cooled.

"You look blue, Debora. Do you want some tea?" Paul was standing in the hall doorway watching me.

"Oh? Are you finished already?"

"Yep. Our monkey is freshly dunked and squeezed and watching *one* show before bedtime. Now, tea?"

I nodded, my eyes still veiled by half-closed lashes.

"How about I grab the phone for you, too, so you can call Mary? You still need to call her, right?"

"Yes, please, and don't let me forget to pack the leftovers for tomorrow. I should take them with me, don't you think?"

"Sure thing." He grinned while filling the kettle from the kitchen sink tap.

"Are you sure you're not coming down with something?" His voice dropped to a soft tone as he set the kettle back on its electric stand and flipped the power button on.

"I'm sure. Just tired, Paul. Not sure *why* I'm tired. But still, tired."

"Um ... Are you ... are you late this month?"

His question stole the breath from my lungs. Was I?

I stole a look at the calendar again, noting that the last few dots I used to mark down my last period appeared only on the first and second days of the month. I sighed with relief when the days told me not yet.

"No. I should start any day, though." I forced a grin at him. "Man, you are perceptive."

"It's probably just a touch of PMS then ..." He cringed at his own word choice. "Just stating facts. Nothing more!"

"You're probably right," I conceded.

"Honestly. I wasn't trying to make a joke or be mean. Just ... just trying to take care of my woman."

"I know, Paul. Don't overthink it, and I forgive you."

He turned away to grab a mug from the cabinet, and a grin pulled at the edges of my lips.

"Hey! There's my sunshine." A bit of the worry melted from his eyes, and he rolled his shoulders after filling the mug with hot water. "What kind?"

"Whatever is on top of the drawer. It's what needs to be used first."

I wiped the table as he dunked the tea bag into the hot water.

"Okay. Now, go sit down and have a chat with Mary." He took the wet rag from my hand and replaced it with a warm mug. "I'll dry the dishes before going over a few things from work."

"Thanks, Paul." I wanted to say more, but the words caught in my throat. I sipped my hot tea to dislodge the emotions.

"Go sit down with Gloria."

He guided me from the kitchen, and the sounds of Gloria's program greeted me as I entered the living room.

"You watch too much TV, kid," I teased.

Her little nose wrinkled, but she kept silent, her eyes glued to the dancing figures on the screen.

Three

I watched the days tick by on the calendar, waiting for my period to come, dreading the day it might be officially late and the "what if" it would bring with it while still hoping. That hope felt like a pin in my heart, threatening to pop my fragile bubble of control.

"Mama?" Gloria yelled from the doorway. "Mama? Are you COMING?"

I dabbed a bit of colour onto my pale lips before yelling back. "Be patient, baby!" The effort it took to brush my hair and fix it atop my tired head irked me. I'd planned to do my eye makeup. It had been weeks since I had, but I could hear Gloria stamping her booted feet in place.

"COMING?" she called again.

"COMING!" I sent back. Whoever thought it would be my four-year-old yelling for me to hurry? When had we changed roles?

"Breathe, drive to church, smile," I sighed to myself as I grabbed my jacket from the hooks by the wall. "Don't forget that last one, Debora." Holding that smile on was becoming harder and harder.

"It's probably just PMS," I repeated Paul's words to myself, as if the trite comment could cancel out my pain.

Gloria pulled the door open and a grey sky met us, drizzling down its own reversed smile.

Are you losing control too? I thought up at the clouds. The last few weeks of winter were always temperamental, and it looked like nature would be throwing rain at us instead of snow.

"MOM!" Gloria yelled, her small fists banging on the door of the car. "It won't open!"

Her whine grated on my nerves as I pressed my electric key to unlock the door.

"Mom, it's cold."

I groaned as I noticed a shine across the hood and doors of the car. "It looks like it's iced over, baby. Let me go grab the scraper."

"I'm cold," she muttered, her nose wrinkled in disgust as she shoved her bare hands into the small pockets of her jacket. "Stupid winter."

Her four-year-old sass made her sound like a teenager, and I rolled my eyes at her drama. The scraper was in the garage, and again I groaned as the door defied my upward tug.

"MOM! COME ON!"

"GLORIA, do you want to stay home? Because if you don't knock that off, you can march right back into the house and spend the rest of the day in your room." My frustration lent extra strength to my last tug, and I felt the ice across the bottom edge of the wide metal garage door giving way. It crackled as the crystals shattered.

I heaved the screeching metal door up and over my head as Gloria covered her ears, whining in protest.

"MOM!"

"I can't help it," I snapped back at her.

The ridge of ice along the ground crunched under my boot. I kicked at it in disgust while searching with my eyes for the scraper. Had Paul taken it? Why on earth hadn't I hung it up on the wall?

The garage was a cluttered mess of boxes and cast-off junk that Paul and I hadn't taken the time to throw out yet.

"I hate this place," I mumbled while rummaging in the left-hand corner of the room.

My mood was rapidly turning from gloomy to sour. Every shadow I looked into irked me. The piles of rubbish on the floor angered me. The fact I couldn't pull my car into the garage where it would be safe from the frost felt like a splinter in my eye.

Then do something about it, Debora.

You're so lazy. You should have cleaned this up ages ago.

You're useless.

I batted the inner voice away with my physical hand, as if swatting at the shadows could scare it off. The all too familiar cold fingers of darkness curled around me as a chill deeper than winter laughed behind my eyes.

"I should clean this up."

"MOM!" Gloria yelled from right behind me, and my heart skipped several beats as I shifted in surprise, trying not to fall flat on my nose on the cold cement floor.

"WHAT?" I screamed back at her.

"Scraper ..." Her frustrated face has gone pale. "You're scary," she whispered as she flung the plastic ice scraper at me. I hadn't even noticed her rummaging through the junk behind me.

"Where'd you find it?" I softened my voice as she retreated.

"There!" was all she replied, pointing a finger off to the right side of the garage.

Of course, the side I would have gone to last.

The next few minutes were a mess of grunts and flying ice shards as I chipped away at the passenger seat handle then the driver's seat handle.

"Are we late, Mom?" Gloria asked when I finally slammed the car door closed after myself.

"Yes," I stated, not wanting to hear her whine about it. "Still want to go to church?"

"Yes." She nodded as I watched her squirm in her car seat through my rearview mirror.

I turned the defrost up to high and wiped the condensation from the inner windshield with a gloved hand.

"Well, then, let's go."

I was relieved we weren't the only ones late as we pulled into the church parking lot. Every car boasted layers of frost and ice to varying degrees. I chuckled as I watched a figure so bundled I couldn't tell who it was pull in behind me, their windows frozen and wide open to the elements.

Ice crackled as the wheels of my car slowly crushed it. The mix of slippery and resistant felt strange as I manoeuvred the machine into a parking space.

"Let me out, Mommy!" Gloria cried as she spotted Mary Cooper and little James shuffling over the ice towards the church doors.

"Just let me park, please." The sound of her straining at her car seat straps and fumbling with the release made me turn and snap. "WAIT! You will not get out until I turn the car off and open your door."

I ignored the childishly hurtful words she whispered behind my back. *She's four, Debora. She doesn't know what she is really saying, and she doesn't mean it,* I told myself. Still, the muttered stupid and hate gave new footing for the ice fingers around my heart.

"I love you too, Gloria," I threw back at her, knowing full well she was too young to notice the irony of my words after her own.

Her nose wrinkled as she looked up at me once I had the side door open.

"Are you going to behave? I can still take us back home."

"Yes!" she said and jumped away from me as I released her from the safety harness.

"Slow down, Gloria!" I shouted as I picked up our bag before following her across the treacherous ice sheet. My boots resisted my directions as I slid behind her, and it forced me to balance with my arms held out to both sides.

"Watch your step, everyone!" someone yelled from behind me as I touched down on the well-salted sidewalk. I could see the white clumps of mineral clearly, sitting in the middle of gaps in the ice that still tried to cling to the cement slabs. But instead of the hard, smooth surface van the parking lot, the salt ensured the ice formed only thin, crunchy layers with larger bare patches.

"It's better once you get to the sidewalk," I yelled back to whoever could hear me.

I took my morning frustrations out on that thin layer of ice and stomped a path into the church, kicking any larger pieces off to the side.

"Gloria?" I called once inside the warm greeting hall.

I looked around and spied her coat lying on the floor at Mary Cooper's feet.

"She's already in the playroom, Debora. Man, that kid is fast this morning. What did you feed her for breakfast?"

Breakfast? I stopped for a second to think. Had we had breakfast this morning? My heart pounded with a moment's panic as I wracked my brain for memories that should have been there. Did I feed Gloria? Did I forget again? It took a moment, but finally, memories of cereal bowls and spilled milk surfaced.

"I got it!" Mary said as she stooped down to pick up the coat.

I sighed as Mary waved a hanger in between us and shrugged out of my own coat to hang it beside the big green one with the fake fur lining I guessed to be hers.

"Thanks. She's running me in circles today. I don't know how you do it with three and Jeff gone all week. No, I don't know how you do it ..." I let my words trail off as Mary smiled at me and shook her head.

"My kids aren't Gloria. She has more energy than if you doubled James." Mary's laugh rang through the air, the small rhythmic vibrations moving through the ice around my heart. I smiled at her and joined in.

"She is a little blessed handful, that's for sure. I never know what to think because I only have one. But I guess she really is like having two sometimes. All that sass! I have no idea where she gets it from. I don't think it's from me ... Paul is so laid back. It can't be from him. Maybe she got it from his mom. Grandma Annabel has a sharp tongue on her, though her energy is sure not what it used to be. What do you think, Mary? Do you think she gets it from me? Or Grandma Annabel? Do you know my side of the family at all? I can't remember ..."

The words just flowed out of me like fast-melting ice sheets. Mary nodded no and then yes she knew my side of the family. But when she opened her mouth to say something, I couldn't stop the flow, and my words stampeded over hers.

"You really would enjoy my Grandma Grace. She is such a lovely woman. Still does her own nails at eighty-four, hands as steady as a rock. I miss her ... They live so far away. Have you ever visited the west coast? Oh, it's so beautiful there, and Vancouver is so much warmer."

Again, Mary shook her head no.

"Oh, well, maybe one day you'll make it out that way to visit my old stomping ground. Though moving here with Paul has been good. Yes." I stopped and swallowed, my throat dry, and my tongue refusing to go on.

"We should go sit down now, Debora. I hear the leaders opening the Bible study."

"Oh, yes! Sorry for rambling on."

"It's fine. Why don't you come over tomorrow for coffee, and we can chat, just the two of us."

Her invitation was a spark landing on a tendril of ice. I felt a crack forming across one of the cold fingers that held me fast. It hurt. It warmed me for a second. I blinked back a tear and smiled.

"Okay!"

The offer of a visit was all I could think of as questions passed over the small table in front of me. I'd taken my turn reading a few verses from my open Bible but then kept silent. I didn't understand everything the other women were talking about. The story of Mary sitting at the feet of Jesus and Martha, her sister getting after her for not being in the kitchen helping, was an often repeated one. But the point eluded me. I didn't want to think about cooking and dishes and domestic duties. Like a restless child, I looked out the window. The sky had brightened a bit, but heavy clouds threatened from over the horizon, and the lighter grey canopy that still clung to the sky over our town refused to let all but a few shafts of sun through. Still, it sent the ice that crusted everything to glittering.

Cold, it wasn't always terrible, I thought. It could be beautiful too and bright.

"Debora?" Gail, who sat to my right, gently poked my shoulder.

"Oh!" I jumped. "Yes?"

"Would you like to pray to close today, dear?" The Bible study leader asked as Gail pointed towards her.

"Me?" Why'd she ask me to pray? I don't remember anyone ever asking me before. I never could remember the older woman's name. I searched my cold brain for it as she stared at me and blinked. Her eyes asked a question deeper than the one she'd just voiced. "No, thank you! No, I'm sorry. I never seem to know what to say when I try to pray ... Out loud, that is."

"You? Don't know what to say?" The whole table turned to Tina as she raised her hand to her lips, red flowing over her cheeks.

"Oh. I am sorry, Debora," she quickly muttered as our leader sent her a silent rebuke with her eyes.

I tried to swallow the lump in my throat, but it refused to leave as I croaked out, "Don't be sorry. That's funny. I talk a lot."

An awkward silence stretched out, and I chided myself for not bringing a bottle of water with me so I could wash my hesitancy away.

"No problem, Debora. Gail? Would you?" our leader asked.

What was her name? Joyce? Janet?

"Sure, Julie," Gail replied.

Gail glanced my way again as she folded her hands and rested them on the tabletop. I looked away, mimicking her in her pious posture.

"Dear Heavenly Father," she intoned. "Thank you for each woman able to make it out to our study today and for safety on these slick roads. Thank you for the insightful words of our leader. May the coffee in the fellowship hall be strong! Please be with us as we return to our busy weeks, and help us put into action the lessons we've learned. Amen."

A chorus of "amen" bubbled around me, and I added my own.

"Debora, what's wrong?" Gail leaned over and whispered as the other ladies pushed away from the table and exited the little room we had been occupying.

"Nothing. Why do you ask?" My voice warbled, my eyes hiding from her direct gaze.

"You sound terrible, and you were twitching through the whole study."

"What?" I felt my face flush as she lifted her eyebrows at me.

"Why are you so extra jittery today?"

I didn't have a reply other than, "I just need a warm drink. My throat is dry."

Jittery? Yes, I was jittery, but extra jittery? Really? I didn't feel like I'd been talking at all that morning.

"I mean, you usually are a chatterbox, but today you are jumpy and twitchy. Are you okay?"

Chatterbox? Jumpy? Twitchy? I blinked at her. Did she really expect me to tell her how I was feeling after talking to me like that? "I'm sorry if I was bothering you. I must have had too much coffee this morning. In fact, I should visit the restroom." I stopped another inquiry as I stood and said, "Really, I just need to pee."

I thought I felt her eyes watching me as I left the room and groaned when I saw the line for the restroom.

"Mommy!"

I heard Gloria calling from farther past the bathrooms.

"MOMMY!"

My heart rate spiked as she continued to call me with ever louder levels.

"I'll be just a few minutes, Gloria," I called over the rising noise of the ladies flooding the enclosed space.

I took my place in the line for the bathrooms and counted the ladies ahead of me. Four in the hall. That meant there were probably five waiting in line past the bathroom doors.

"MOMMY! I WANT TO GO HOME!"

"Oh, good Lord," I groaned as my heart compressed, the ice fingers thickening and tightening their grip.

I couldn't see her through the crowd but could imagine Gloria sticking her head out of the nursery door screaming for me.

You should never have come this morning.

As the cold continued to squeeze me, I felt exhaustion clawing its way back onto my shoulders.

"MOMMY!" Her scream was angry.

I left the line and pushed through the crowd of women making their way to the coffee room.

"Gloria! Knock it off!" I yelled back at her.

Everyone in the small space turned and looked at me as I grabbed her hand. She was standing right outside the wide open door while children and their mothers milled around. Her little face was stained red with tear tracks.

"Mama," she gasped up at me.

Everyone else looked away from my outburst, embarrassed by my lapse of control.

"Gloria, I need to use the bathroom."

"James hit me with a block."

"I'm sorry he did that." I was pulling her back down the hallway with me when she dug in her heels.

"I want to GO HOME!"

"Gloria! Be patient."

"NO!"

Something inside me snapped, and my vision tunnelled. I forgot about my full bladder as I picked her up and carried her to the coat rack.

"MAMA! PUT ME DOWN!"

"Stop it!"

People were trying to ignore us as our battle of wills exploded, but the entryway was too small and clogged.

Mary Cooper grabbed Gloria's coat when she saw us coming.

"Let me help, Debora," she said and took Gloria from my arms.

"Thank you." The words came out in a growl as I grabbed my coat.

"Call me tonight once you guys have settled," she whispered to me. "We still need coffee."

"Are we going to James' house? I don't want to go there. I don't like James anymore!"

"Oh, Gloria. That will make James so sad to hear." Mary tried to soothe her as she tucked each of her small arms into her sleeves.

"NO. He's mean."

"How about I have a talk with him tonight about what he did, and he'll say sorry when you come over in the morning? Would that be okay?"

"Maybe ..."

"Gloria, stop being ridiculous," I snapped over Mary's cooing. "I'll call you," I added as I stomped Gloria out the door.

"Calm down, Debora," someone whispered from behind us. But I never looked back to see who it was.

Once we reached home, I sat there in the car for a moment, my legs crossed, willing my bladder to hold for a dash to the house. I was humiliated by my failure to keep cool, and I told my body it better not make me wet myself in front of my child. Or perhaps that would be a fitting punishment. Did God work like that? I knew in my heart He didn't, but in my body's desperate state, the thoughts stuck like tar to my ice shield.

"I'm getting out," Gloria stated as she wiggled her way out of the harness.

You didn't strap her in properly. She could have died if you'd crashed.

"The door's locked, Gloria. You can't get in the house yet."

"Then open the door!"

How could a four-year-old's voice hold such disdain? Was it just my imagination? I was angry. Was that anger warping my perception?

My body wasn't ready to move yet when I heard her open the car door.

"Gloria! Just wait."

I pulled the keys from my car's ignition then slung my purse over my shoulder, whispering half prayers and half affirmations to myself as I prepared to move.

"You can make it, bladder."

It wasn't until I had the door open and was rushing towards the house that I noticed Paul's car pulled up close to the garage.

"What's he doing at home?" I wondered.

"GLORIA!" I called when I entered the house, almost tripping over her discarded boots and coat.

I shoved the keys I hadn't needed at the door into my coat pocket and ran for the bathroom, coat, boots, and all.

Four

While finishing my business, I found out why my emotional control had been slipping. I washed red from my fingers with cold soap suds. It felt right not to use hot water as an extra layer of ice formed over my heart. Its tendrils were expanding to form a shell trapping me with only a few spots for warmth to pass through, but I didn't want that warmth anymore.

You knew it wouldn't be this month.

It won't be next month either.

You'll just lose the next one, anyway. Stop killing your children.

All the tears froze as they tried to slip past my growing ice shield, doing their part to fill in the cracks.

"Paul is home," I said to myself and focused on finding him. My safe place.

Gloria must have been with him already, or I would've heard her romping through the house. It was then I caught his muffled voice coming from the kitchen and followed it down the hall.

He had his back to me while he sat at the table, his cell phone pressed to his ear. "I don't know what to do, Arthur. Something isn't right, and it's getting worse. Just the other day when I came home from work ... It's like ... She's forgetting meals, and Gloria had to feed herself from the cereal cupboard. She's scaring me."

My footsteps slowed, and I stopped just before entering the kitchen.

"No, her family's all out on the West Coast. We aren't really close to them either, her being an only child. She has tons of cousins, though. I just … I just don't know what to do."

I'd never heard Paul's voice sound so desperate. His words bounced around in my head and collided with my heart, sticking there, a frozen brand of guilt. *She's scaring me.* What did that mean? I turned and walked back up the hall, dragging my coat off, unblinking.

"Gloria? Where did you run off to?"

My voice sounded dull in my own ears as I looked into the living room and then double-checked the bathroom I'd just vacated. Had she, for sure, come inside? Yes, her coat and boots were lying on the floor in front of the door. I remembered almost tripping over them.

"Gloria? Please stop hiding. It isn't funny."

I didn't want to go back to the kitchen so first climbed the stairs to the second floor. The walls of the hall sloped with the roof, and I ducked my head past a curve before poking it into Gloria's bedroom. There she was, sitting in the middle of the floor, her clothes discarded to the side.

"Gloria, what are you doing?"

"My butt was wet," was all she said.

"What?"

I waited for her to elaborate, but she refused to look at me as she slipped a foot through the leg hole of a pair of bright blue leggings.

"I'm sorry you were wet. I don't like being wet either." She finally looked at me, her little eyes burning coals of hot sass, but something else lurked behind it—something that threatened to shatter my frozen heart.

"Don't yell, please," she whispered, her eyes moving past me, unwilling to settle on my face.

Fear. That look was fear. She was afraid of me, her own mother. I backed away, picking up her wet clothes and dropping them into the laundry bin by her door. I'd made it halfway down the stairs when Paul met me.

"Hey, Debora. How was Bible study?"

"Good. The roads were slick as anything, but we made it there and back in one piece."

"Where's Gloria?" he asked as he strained to look past me.

"In her room. Changing."

"Oh ... Hey, I have to work from home the rest of the day. The highway was pretty treacherous, so I came back home, but you'd just pulled out of the drive and must've missed seeing me."

"Oh."

"Debora. Are you okay?"

"I'm fine."

I watched him shift his feet on the steps as nerves got the better of him. "You don't seem okay," he whispered.

"I just started my period," I said and pushed past him.

He'd always been my safe place. He'd always kept the chill just far enough from my heart to breathe life-giving heat into it. But now, my ice shield held him at a distance, his words echoing in my mind.

She's scaring me.

As the words bounced off the cold walls around me, I couldn't shake the look Gloria had given me.

I didn't want much, just to be with him. Just to feel safe. But now, looking at him after I heard those words coming from his mouth … He wasn't safe. I wasn't safe. Gloria wasn't safe. Not with me.

I heard him calling Gloria as I walked to the kitchen. I wouldn't forget lunch today.

"Gloria, baby, are you okay?" He didn't trust me with our child anymore. I could tell by the catch in his voice.

You don't know that for sure. You can't read his mind.

Maybe that was true, but did I even trust *him* anymore? No.

"I can't come over tomorrow, Mary. Thanks so much for asking, but can I ask a favour?" Guilt crawled through my gut and played with the few bites of dinner I'd managed to eat. Or was it the cramps that were making me queasy? They'd started as I fixed Gloria lunch earlier in the day and were now a dull ache behind my pelvis as I sat on the hard dining chair, the telephone pressed to my ear.

"Would you be willing to watch Gloria for me tomorrow? I've gotten behind on some housework and need a few hours to power through it. You don't mind, do you? You know how it is trying to clean with kids snacking behind you as you vacuum."

Mary laughed and assured me that yes, she knew what it was like, and she'd love to watch Gloria for me. Paul agreed to drop her off early on his way to the office and smiled as I informed him I would be deep cleaning the house. I spent the rest of the evening avoiding him and his questions until he crawled into bed beside me.

"Gloria's asleep."

"Good. Thanks for reading to her tonight." I curled up away from him onto my side.

"I ah ... I spoke to Pastor Arthur today. Just ... Just before you came home, actually."

"Oh?"

"Do you ... do you think we need to go talk to someone? Like ... get counselling?"

I pulled my arms and legs tightly up and wrapped them around myself. His question felt like a needle poke I wasn't ready for. "I'm tired, Paul, and my gut hurts. Can we talk about it in the morning?"

"Sure. Um, goodnight." I felt the mattress shift as he slid down from a sitting position.

"I love you," he added before switching off his side lamp.

His words hit my ice shield and bounced off, disappearing into the darkness.

Five

I spent the night in a game of hide and seek with sleep, watching the shadows shift around me as the moon sent cold beams of light through our lacy curtains. They then disappeared behind gathering clouds. I made a plan of action while the clock counted my spent minutes.

Sleep must have finally come because I never heard Paul's alarm. Instead, I woke up when he called from the bottom of the stairs, informing me he was just about to make Gloria breakfast and asking if I wanted any.

"I'm coming," I answered after Paul called my name a second time.

My bedside clock flashed blue numbers as I rubbed my eyes free of the last grains of sleep. 7:30. I'd slept in.

Already behind on your day.

If you don't get a move on, this won't work.

Exhaustion had held on to my shoulder through the night, and its weight dragged on me as I dressed. I fumbled about with my jeans and almost fell, thankful for the cushioned bed that caught my rump as I slipped.

"Just great," I fumed as tears spilled. "How am I going to clean if I can't even stand straight?"

I pulled my house coat over my clothes. The plush material did nothing to warm me, and the frost that glazed the bedroom window told me winter was still holding tight.

Once downstairs, Paul pressed a hot cup of coffee into my hands.

"Feeling better?" he asked.

I grunted as a reply, and he smiled, planting a kiss on my forehead. I didn't react to his hug or his usual morning affection, but neither did I push him away. It was a cold acceptance.

"Tired?" he asked, as he pulled away from me.

"Yeah … And grumpy," I conceded.

"Well, that's normal." He emphasized the word "normal" as he smiled again and turned to pack his briefcase.

I stared at his back for a moment. Normal? Was my irritability really normal to him? Exhaustion gulped down my anxiety and by it gained weight. I sank onto a dining chair and sipped the coffee, not feeling the hot burn it left on my tongue.

Gloria looked up from her hash browns and sighed. "Going to James' house today?"

"Yes, you are," I answered quietly.

"Okay." She poked at her food and wrinkled her nose.

"Eat it," I gently encouraged. "You need the energy to play."

"Don't want to play. My tummy hurts." She took two bites as I watched then sat back in her chair. "I'm done."

I nodded as she jumped down from the chair. I didn't blame her. My tummy hurt too. But my plans didn't have room for her running around the house today.

After I drained my coffee, I packed a small bag for Gloria and waved as Paul ushered her out to his car. As they drove down the street, a fresh chill crept through my limbs. I had work to do, but would the imp of exhaustion let me finish in time?

I started with dusting and then moved on to vacuuming the living room, tossing Gloria's toys into the corner as I went. My steps were slow but steady, my resolve set firmly, though my body protested. I sat to drink some water before tackling the dishes in the sink. Should I eat lunch or skip it? Did it matter?

I looked around the house after the dishes were dried and stacked in the cupboards.

"Time for the garage! The house might not be perfect, but it's better than it's been in months. It'll have to do."

After pulling extra garbage bags from under the sink, I stepped outside, my unzipped coat flapping around me.

Keep going, were the words my inner voice repeated as my numb fingers sifted through the rubbish of the garage. I'd one garbage bag for trash and one for giveaway. Paul would thank me when this was done. Or would he be upset I threw something he wanted away? No matter, I told myself. It was for his own good—for their own good. I might have lost my ability to mother, I might have failed our relationship, but this was a gift I would leave them. Something done before …

After hauling the bags of garbage back to the trash can and fitting as much of it inside the bin as I could, I set to moving things around inside the building. The numbness in my hands ached, but I kept on. My stomach protested, but I ignored it. I stacked and organized until I made room to pull the car in. Paul wouldn't have to spend another morning scraping frost from his windshield after this. I was saving him time. I was helping, I told myself. He would thank me after.

He would ...

As I slid in behind the steering wheel of my little white car, the adrenaline behind my resolve gave out. I sat there in the cold and noticed for the first time that the sun was shining bright and deceptive. Spring was on its way. Spring meant new life. What would it mean for my family? Was I doing the right thing? Was this the right choice?

You're a burden.

The shell around my heart closed over completely, squeezing me. My breath caught as I started the car's engine and pulled into the garage.

They're afraid of you.

It took all my strength to get out of the car and pull down the garage door, plunging myself into darkness. The exhaust from the engine puffed around me in billowing clouds. The smell of burnt fuel grew as I climbed back into the car and closed the door.

You're tired.

I was tired—more tired than I ever thought possible. I lowered the back of my seat and reclined in the dark, giving into the weight on my shoulders that pressed me deep into the upholstery. My eyes closed as a throbbing in my temple began. I coughed and turned over towards the passenger side.

Was someone sitting beside me? It felt like there was. I opened my eyes to make sure I was alone. As the clouds thickened by the cold air pushed into the car, I felt something warm take my hand. It was painful as my stiff fingers began to thaw, but I was too tired to pull away.

I closed my eyes one more time and prayed, "I know I'm not a good Christian, God. But I'm done. Please ... Take me home. Wherever that is."

Abigail's Prayers: Five

She's gone.
I can't believe it.
God ... Why?
Just ... Why?

Scary Things

Gloria

One

My TUMMY FELT TIGHT, and I didn't know why. It made me wrinkle my nose at Mary as she took my hand to lead me inside. I liked Mary, and I liked James, but I didn't want to play today.

"You look tired, Gloria," Mary said as she patted my hand after the door closed. "Are you thirsty? Would you like to watch a show while you wake up?"

I nodded yes.

"James won't throw blocks, will he?" I asked her as I flipped off my boots. I really liked my boots. They were purple and had shiny flowers on the sides that when I poked, bounced back and forth. I liked running my hands over them and feeling the plastic pop. But today I left them alone.

"I promise to watch James and not let him throw any toys today," Mary assured me.

I walked to the living room, the floor grabbing at my socks as I walked. It made me giggle. I took a moment to stand still, pressing my feet down as hard as I could, then lifting one at a time. I laughed as my sock stuck and almost slid off as I pulled it away from the floor.

"What ya doing?" James asked from behind me.

"The floor's sticky. It's like walking on glue." I looked at James suspiciously and placed my hands on my hips as I asked, "Did you spill glue?"

He walked past me to the couch. "NO. Apple juice!"

We both laughed. As we did, I felt a heavy thing fall off my shoulders. James' eyes danced as he moved over to let me crawl up beside him onto the deep cushions.

"Mama forgot," he whispered.

"Forgot what?"

"You know ... this!" he moved his hands in wiping motions.

"Oh! My mama forgets too."

James shook his head as the laughter in his eyes jumped around like fireworks.

"What about mamas?" Mary asked as she came into the room.

She handed me a yellow cup with a sippy lid and James a blue one. I didn't use lids at home but didn't mind it when I was visiting James. I could take it anywhere in the house with me and not have to worry about spills as long as I didn't lose it in the toy box this time.

James shook his cup and laughed at the sloshing sound.

"Juice, Mama?"

"Nope, water. You can have juice with your lunch. Now, what's this about moms?"

"James said he spilled juice, and that's why the floor sticks to my socks," I told her.

"Spilled? Did he say he spilled? Ha! No, he decided he wanted to paint the floor with it right before bed yesterday. *Today*, he is going to mop the entire floor himself, aren't you, James?"

"Yes!" James didn't seem to mind.

"But first, I'm making James some toast for breakfast, Gloria. Are you hungry?" Mary asked me as she squatted down in front of the couch to look into my eyes. I shook my head.

"How's your mama doing today?"

I shrugged.

"She said she had a lot of work to do."

I nodded and took a sip of water. It tasted like plastic.

"How about a show before I get the mop and bucket out for James?"

"Train, Mom!" James shouted as he bounced in the seat beside me.

"You okay with that, Gloria?"

"Uh-huh," I said and leaned back against the cushions.

I spent most of the morning on the couch. The heavy thing that had fallen off my shoulders kept crawling back onto me. I hated it and would try to shake it off as soon as it crawled back on. My tummy hurt more when the weight was there, but slowly, I figured out that when I joined in the laughter, it would let go, and I would be free.

So I laughed.

I laughed when James mopped the hallway, spilling the water pail into the living room.

I laughed at Mary's shriek as the water sloshed against her feet.

I laughed as I got up to help lay bathroom towels all over the floor after Mary sopped up as much as she could with the mop.

"James water monster!" I yelled and tossed a wet towel over his head.

"NO, YOU!"

We slipped and slid as we chased each other across the slippery floor, tumbling and bumping into things until Mary said we needed a "time out;" but she smiled as she hauled us each over to our own dining room chair. "Come on, you two. No broken bones today please."

I watched James laugh so hard he started crying and then wiped his nose on his sleeve.

"EWW, James! Mary, James is snotty!"

"Oh my, oh my," Mary said as she pulled his shirt over her head and grabbed a clean one from a laundry basket hiding in a corner. "I guess it's a good thing I didn't get these put away."

"Now, you two," she continued. "What would you like for lunch?"

"Noodles!" James said, bouncing in the seat as he held onto the back of it.

"Careful, or you're going to push the chair over, James, and then I might have to laugh at you … Just a bit," Mary said.

"Yeah! Noodles. *Wet* noodles." I joined in the bouncing.

We giggled louder, and I felt my bottom sliding across the smooth wood of the chair. My shoulders shook as I swallowed my laughter and curled my fingers around the chair's edge, my grip turning my knuckles white.

"*Wet* noodles it is, then," Mary said as she shook her head at both of us. "With cheese."

"Yes, cheese!"

I could smell the bubbling cheese as Mary stirred the pot on the stove. "Not long," she assured James when he slid off the chair and trotted over to her to ask for the third time when the food would be done.

We were tired from running around and pulled our seats over to the dining room table. Soon blank white paper held colourful masterpieces. The sun I drew filled almost half the page to make sure the flowers had enough light to grow.

When the food was ready, Mary pushed our artwork to the side of the table and set down two steaming bowls. "Not yet! It's hot, James. Blow on it, okay?" Mary instructed as he lifted a spoonful in the air.

"What's this?" he asked as his nose wrinkled at a round green thing on his spoon.

"Peas."

"Peas?"

"Yes, peas."

"Peas and cheese aren't bad," I told him while blowing on my own food.

Mary grabbed the phone from the wall as she sat down. "Think your mama will be done with her work soon, Gloria?"

I shrugged at her question and felt the heavy thing crawl up my back and settle around my shoulders. After a few rings, she hung the phone back up and joined us with a hot bowl.

"She must be getting lots done to not hear the phone."

But I heard a drop in her voice and looked up across the table at her round face.

The thing on my shoulders squirmed and squeezed the side of my neck.

"Ouch!" I tried to push whatever it was off.

"What's up, Gloria?"

"My shoulder," I told Mary and pushed at the thing with a finger. "Can I go home?" I asked her as she got up and inspected my neck just under the collar of my shirt.

"Your mom's supposed to call me when she's finished with her chores, sweetheart. As soon as she does, you can go home. I don't see anything wrong with your shoulders. Are you done eating? Maybe they'll feel better after a rest. How about you go curl up on the couch? James is just about ready for his nap."

Mary's hands had been cold against my skin, and I felt the heavy thing shift and dodge away from her touch then slink down my arm onto the chair as she patted my back.

As I walked back to the living room, it felt like the thing was holding my ankles. I pulled it behind me as I walked, and my tummy gurgled as I crawled onto the couch. I was so tired. My shoulders relaxed even as the weight held my heels down on the couch. I knew something wasn't right, but I didn't know what. I hoped Mary would come to sit with me after James fell asleep. Her touch chased the weight away, and I wanted to hold her hand.

Two

"Your mom hasn't called yet, Gloria," Mary said as she pushed stray wisps of hair out of my face. A blanket was pulled up under my chin, and my fingers curled around its edge. Mary was sitting on the floor in front of me, the phone in her lap. "She's still not answering … Was your mommy okay when you left the house this morning?"

I nodded then said, "Maybe tired, maybe a little grumpy. My tummy hurt this morning, too."

"Does it still hurt?"

"Yeah."

There was a wet shimmer around the edges of Mary's eyes as she smoothed my hair back one last time.

"How're your shoulders?"

"Better." I smiled up at her. "Can I have a drink?"

"Sure thing."

Mary moved slowly as she pushed up from the floor with a grunt. Her big body didn't seem to want to leave the ground, but with a last heave, she stood and walked down the hallway. I pulled the blanket around my shoulders and curled my legs under it. Maybe if I tucked it in really well, that heavy thing wouldn't be able to grab hold of my ankles again.

I noticed the shadows had stretched across the room. It looked like they were running away from the light coming from the large window in front of me. The clouds were gone, and the sun melted the frost on the edge of the glass. I looked at it with sleepy eyes. But the light pushed the darkness from my mind, and I was happy just sitting and waiting.

"Hello, Paul?" Mary had walked back into the room and handed me a clean yellow sippy cup before turning and pacing while she talked. She lowered her voice but I could still hear. "Yes, it's Mary Cooper. I just wanted to ask if you had talked to Debora today after dropping Gloria off this morning. I can't get ahold of her at the house."

"No, Gloria's okay. Yes, she just woke up from a nap. She said her tummy wasn't feeling good, but she doesn't seem sick right now. Just tired. Was Debora okay when you left?"

The smile faded from Mary's face.

"No, we're fine here. I just ... Paul, it's probably nothing, but ... I have a terrible feeling in my gut. If I had the car, I would take the kids over and check on her."

I watched Mary nod even though my daddy wouldn't be able to see it, and I felt something trying to crawl up onto the couch beside me.

"Okay, yes. Uh-huh, I think that's a good idea. Sorry, Paul."

I pulled the blanket closer and used my hands to tuck it as tightly against my feet as I could. Something hard touched one of my large toes through the fabric. I gulped and felt yucky liquid rising into my throat from my gurgling tummy.

Then the hard thing was pulled away as Mary sat her large bottom down beside me. My shoulders relaxed, and I started to cry. A deep breath shook my shoulders and sent the tears spilling over my cheeks in several directions.

"Gloria!" Mary's arms wrapped around me as she carefully pulled me onto her lap. "Oh, sweetheart, did I scare you?"

I shook my head no and felt the shakes calm as her warm hug touched my heart.

Soft. That was Mary. All soft and safe.

"Thank you."

"For what, Gloria?"

"For squashing the Scary Thing."

"Scary Thing?" Mary's eyebrows lifted as she pulled me even closer.

"It followed me from home. But you sat on it, and I'm safe now."

"Didn't you know? That's why God made my bottom so big? It's perfect for squashing Scary Things." Mary smiled at me, but the corner of her eyes looked wet again. She folded my little hands inside of hers and closed her eyes. "Dear Jesus. Thank you for using my bottom to squash the Scary Thing. Please be with Gloria's mama while we wait for her daddy to go check on her."

My tummy settled as I sipped my juice, and Mary sat with me until she heard James banging on the wall of his room upstairs.

"James!" I called and squirmed out of the blanket and off Mary's lap to race for the stairs.

"Gloria still here?"

"Yes!" I answered him while Mary passed me.

"Coming, James. What shall we make for supper?" she asked while pulling him from his crib.

Mary carried the house phone in her pocket when we all went out to meet James' brother and sister at the bus stop. "The signal probably won't work at the end of the street there. But might as well, just in case, right, Gloria?"

"Yep," I replied, not really knowing what she meant. She kept it in her sweater pocket when we all trudged back into the house, kicking wet slush from our boots.

"Is it ever getting warm out there?" Joshua, James' older brother, said as he peeled his tuque off his sweaty head.

"Eww! Keep that away from me!" Harmony yelled as he threw it at her and bolted for the kitchen. "What's going on, Mom?" Harmony asked as she eyed the phone and helped me pull off my snow pants.

"Hopefully, nothing," Mary replied.

I heard her whispering to Harmony as snacks were made and set out on the kitchen table. "It's four, and I'm getting really worried. Paul should've called by now. Something's wrong. Harmony, Gloria might need to sleep on your bedroom floor tonight."

"Okay, Mom, I can get it ready just in case."

Sleeping over? I didn't *want* to sleep over. I didn't have any of my sleepover things. Mom hadn't told me I'd be staying.

"Mary? Is Daddy coming to get me?" I asked as James handed me the plate of sliced apples.

"He's supposed to be, Gloria. But he didn't say what time, so we just have to be patient, okay?"

I didn't feel okay. I didn't see it or hear it, but I felt the Scary Thing crawling around on the floor under my chair. My legs were tucked under me so it couldn't grab them while I was eating. I took a slice of apple and munched it, using the *crunch* sounding through my ears to help me ignore the tightness in my gut. When I reached for a second slice, I looked at it. White and crisp and juicy insides and bright red outside. A bit like me. Bright on the outside, but drippy inside. Or that's how I felt.

I looked around. Harmony kept glancing at her mom, but the boys poked and joked at each other. Then we all jumped as the phone in Mary's pocket rang loud and clear. My heart felt like someone was squeezing it, and I grabbed hold of the table.

"Hello?" Mary said.

Then she was silent as her face turned white. I cried again when I felt the Scary Thing sliding up the chair legs and grabbing hold of me.

Three

"Got your socks on, Gloria?" Dad called from the bottom of the stairs.

I did. But that was about it. I was looking at the piles of clothes I'd pulled from my dresser and thrown all over the floor. What should I wear to church? Mom always picked out my Sunday clothes.

"MOM!" I called. Then I froze, my hand over my mouth. My heart thumped as the shadows slid off the walls and crawled out from under my bed.

"Gloria?" Dad called from downstairs.

The shadows slithered across the floor and wrapped around my ankles, holding me in place.

"Mama..." I whispered, crouching down and hugging my knees. The colours of the clothing mixed as my eyes filled with tears. I couldn't see through them to pick what I needed, and my stomach gurgled around the toast I'd eaten for breakfast.

"Gloria?" Dad was right beside me then, his big warm hand on my back, his own tears threatening to rush down his cheeks.

"Mama needs to pick my clothes out today," I whispered to him.

"Baby, Mama can't pick your clothes."

"Can't she come down from heaven just for a visit?"

"That's not how going to heaven ... works." He pulled me into a hug.

I didn't look at him as my hand curled around his tie. The Scary Things were crawling with the shadows up my legs, on their way to finding a seat on my shoulders. I hated them, but I was used to it now. They'd stayed with me since that day when I went to James' house, and Mama had gotten sick with no one home to help her. Holding onto Dad's tie slowed the shadows down, so I gripped it and shuddered as the first Scary Thing curled a tail around my neck.

"Daddy?"

"Yes, Gloria?"

"What's Mama's favourite colour?"

"This one."

He grabbed something purple off the floor and helped me pull it over my head. Then he found tights from one of my drawers, and we did battle with my legs to get them on.

"Mama knows how to roll them up and slip them over my feet."

"I know. You can show me how she did it next time, okay?"

We'd never gone to church without Mom before. I wondered what it would be like.

"Can I still go to nursery? Or do you need me to sit with you?"

"What would you like to do, Gloria?"

"I don't know."

"Well, don't worry about it until we get there. You can decide then. But I'll be okay if you want to go to nursery."

The drive over to church was quiet. The streets were wet with melting snow, and the sun was bright. I still wore my hat and mitts but unzipped the front of my coat to let some cool air in.

I wondered whose hand I would hold after the service while Dad was talking with the men. Usually, I held on to Mom or ran around her legs when all the other kids started chasing each other. We often had cookies to bring and lay out on the counter after service. Mom and I loved baking cookies. She didn't like to eat them as much as me, but everyone at church loved them. Today, the seat beside me was empty, with no cookie tin to rattle away as we passed over bumps or made the turns.

"Will there be treats after church, Papa?" I asked his reflection in the rearview mirror.

"Probably," he said, his eyes dancing between the mirrors and looking straight ahead.

"We didn't bring any ... Do you think there'll be enough for all the people?"

"I am sure there will be, Gloria."

I didn't like the quiet as it stretched out between us, but I couldn't find anything else to ask. Mom's chatter usually filled the air as we drove, warm and constant. I missed it. The end of her sentences used to ring like little tinkling bells as she laughed at herself. I missed those bells.

As soon as we pulled into the parking lot and Dad opened the passenger's side door to let me out, people started crowding us.

"Paul, I'm so sorry about Debora. How are you doing?" one woman asked.

"If there is anything we can do to help, just let us know," a tall gentleman added.

There was a hum of voices as we walked into the building and over to the nursery door. Everyone was looking and pointing and asking questions. One older woman pulled Dad into a hug that lasted a whole minute. I tugged on his arm to get his attention, and when he finally looked down at me, his face was pale.

"Daddy?" I pointed at the nursery door, and he nodded yes while squeezing my hand.

"It's so brave of you to come to church today, so soon after ..." I heard someone say as I turned to wander through the people standing around us. Their adult bodies towered over me, closing me in a mountain range of eyes, arms, and legs. I pushed through the gaps between those legs and ducked under arms until the nursery door stood in front of me. Who would open it?

"Mama?" I glanced around the crowd. "No Mama."

The Scary Thing slid closer to my ear and whispered irritating sounds. It tickled, and I poked a finger inside, hoping it would stop the buzzing. It didn't help much. My nose wrinkled in aggravation, and I felt the shadows from my bedroom poking at my heart. I didn't like that at all.

"Hello, Gloria. Would you like to go inside?" It was Mary Cooper.

She stood behind me, looking down at my head. As the shadow of her arm fell across my shoulders, I felt the Scary Things shrink back. I smiled up at her and nodded yes.

She pushed the door open in front of me, and a wave of noise pushed the shadows from my insides. I bounced into the room, ready to play.

"Good morning!"

The words sang in the air as grandmas, mamas, and playmates greeted us. I turned back to the door, expecting to see Mom there waving to them all. She should have been there, but she wasn't. The bounce fell out of my steps, and I stood in the middle of the room, staring at the door. The shadows that had fled from my heart poked my tummy. It gurgled, and I crouched down in the centre of the room, watching and wishing for her face to appear in the doorway but realizing it wouldn't.

"Gloria. Are you okay?"

I nodded. "My tummy hurts."

"Do you need to go to the bathroom?" Mary asked in a whisper.

I shook my head no and sighed while looking from her to the door.

"Do you want to go out again, to find Dad?"

"No."

The whispers started again, and I scowled as I shrugged my shoulders, trying to rub them up against my ears.

"It's okay if you need to just sit here, Gloria. Let me know if you want to read a book with me, okay?"

Again, I nodded up at her, and she walked over to a vacant chair in the corner. Half of me wanted to go with her. Mary's lap was soft and warm. I loved it when she read stories, but my eyes were again fixed on the door.

"Mommy, why did you have to go away?" I whispered.

The drone of the Scary Thing on my shoulder blended with the chatter of kids around me. The nursery was full, and the noise tickled my opposite ear. Suddenly, it was all too much, and I grabbed a block from the floor beside me, throwing it at the nursery door window. Everyone stopped at the loud *crack* as the block hit the hard glass.

"Gloria!" One grandma sitting along the wall raised her voice behind me. But no one was fast enough to stop me from sending a second block towards the door.

"ENOUGH!" Mary picked me up. "Why did you do that, Gloria?"

"I hate that window!" I screamed.

I fought as Mary tried to calm me, my balled fists finding soft flesh and bone.

"Is everyone alright?" a man asked as he opened the door and examined the window.

"Ben, can you grab Paul Core, please? Gloria needs him."

The man looked at me and turned red. "Sure thing, Mary." And he was gone. A crack level with where his eyes had been now ran across the window.

My whole body was vibrating, I was breathing hard, and heat ran up my chest into my face.

"I hate it!"

I screamed again as my dad pushed his way into the room past a crowd of onlookers.

"Gloria? Church is starting. What's wrong?" he asked.

I couldn't answer him as my anger turned to a pain in my chest and water collected around my eyes. Pressure in my throat stopped my sobs from echoing around the room, stifling them to just a whisper as my little body shook.

"It's okay, baby. Let's go home." His voice caught on the words and grated on my ears like sandpaper on wood.

As he lifted me into his arms and walked through the crowd, Mary laid my coat over my back.

"Paul, this is normal," she said. "I'll bring over something for dinner tonight. Just go home and rest with her."

"Thanks, Mary."

Was my daddy crying too?

I spent the church hour curled up in a blanket, watching cartoons. Dad was watching something on his cell phone. He rubbed his eyes every once in a while.

I shivered and hugged the blanket closer. The shadows had dropped off me on the drive home. But they left behind emptiness, and the emptiness was cold. My dad had laid me down on the couch and sat beside me for a moment, his eyes closed, and the Scary Thing had slunk away and hid under the couch. I could breathe properly again, but my nose now dripped. I held a tissue under the blanket and dabbed the drops every once in a while.

"Feeling any better?" Dad asked when he saw me stir.

I nodded.

He fought back a yawn as he sat up straighter in his chair.

"Just about lunchtime. What shall we eat?"

"Popcorn?"

"Popcorn? For lunch?"

"Mama makes it for me when she's tired. With cheese and apples. I think you're tired, so we should make it."

"With cheeses and apples? Well, that sounds good. Sure. But I want peanut butter too. That okay?"

"Peanut butter?"

"Yeah, for on my apples."

I stuck my tongue out at him. "Ewwwww!"

"Don't knock it until you've tried it, kid." He winked at me as he got up and made his way down the hall.

It wasn't long before we were both sitting on the floor, a big steel bowl filled with popcorn in front of us. Dad had laid cheese and apple slices on top of the popcorn along one side. I grabbed fistfuls of the white puffs from the other end, unsure of what popcorn with apple juice on it would taste like. The whole open jar of peanut butter sat in between Dad's crossed legs, a butter knife plunged deep into its creaminess.

"Want to try one?" he asked as he used the knife to slather a chunk of apple with tan goop.

"No. I only like peanut butter on bread with jam. Strawberry jam, not the yellow stuff."

"Yellow stuff? You mean marmalade?"

"It's got chunks in it. They're yucky."

"I hear ya. I don't like it either. Strawberry is much better."

I tore a slice of cheese into two tiny pieces and nibbled at them.

"Papa, I'm sorry."

He slipped his arm around my shoulders and moved the steel bowl aside so he could draw me close.

"It's okay, Gloria. Sometimes I want to throw things too ... We just ... we need to try not to hurt other people, okay? Throwing things can hurt people."

"Okay."

Scary Things peeked out from under the couch at me.

"Am I allowed to go to church again?"

"Of course you are. If you want to, we can bring a colouring book, and you can try sitting with me in the service."

That didn't sound too bad, and that way I wouldn't keep looking through that window. I sighed and dropped a few uneaten bits of cheese back into the bowl.

"Hey! You need to eat those," Dad said with gentle annoyance.

"My tummy hurts." I tried to ignore the Scary Things as they edged closer from the corners and under the couch. But my eyes followed them, and I had to turn my head to keep them in view.

"What'cha looking at?" Dad asked.

"Scary Things." My answer was soft, and he leaned in closer to hear me better.

"Scary Things?"

"Yeah. They used to follow Mommy around the house, but now ... They like me. I don't like them, though. They make my tummy hurt."

"They followed Mommy?"

With a grunt, he moved all the food aside and pulled me up onto his lap, glancing down at the floor by the couch and then even bending forward with me tucked tightly against his chest.

"I don't see anything under there, Gloria."

"Mama couldn't see them either."

Dad's face turned white again. He stared at me. His eyes moved like they were trying to see past my skin. I shifted on his lap, uncomfortable sitting on his bony legs.

"We should pray, Gloria."

"Pray?"

"Yeah, the Scary Things won't like it when we pray."

"Really?"

"Really."

He folded my little hands inside of his huge ones, and I watched him while he closed his eyes.

"Dear Jesus. Thanks for taking ..." He stopped and coughed. "For taking care of us. You know, it's just the two of us now, and Gloria says she sees Scary Things."

I watched his face as a tear pulled away from beside his eye. It was strange. Tears were usually clear, weren't they? It almost looked like there was light inside of the drop as it fell. Just a small light ... But, yes, I saw it again as another tear followed the first.

At the same time, the Scary Thing pushing its way out from under the couch froze. When I blinked and turned towards it, it disappeared. I heard a scuttling noise and saw shadows slipping out of the living room and darting down the hallway. Warmth spread from my dad's hands into my fingers. I didn't understand most of the words he was saying as he prayed. But it was working.

"And Jesus, please keep those Scary Things away from Gloria."

He stopped and wiped drops of light from his face.

"It worked, Daddy," I told him, my eyes wide. "They all ran away."

"Good." His sigh was deep as he shifted underneath me.

"Did you know you have light inside of you, Daddy?"

"Light? Well, I guess, yes." He coughed again and ran his fingers through his hair before sliding me off his legs. "Jesus is the light of the world. When He lives inside of you, the light lives there too."

"Did Mama know that?" I asked.

"She did."

"Then why did the Scary Things follow her all the time?"

His eyes were red, and I could see flashes behind them as he thought about what to say.

"I think maybe she forgot, or she forgot how to let that light come out."

"Oh ..."

I glimpsed a Scary Thing out of the corner of my eye. It was watching us from the hallway. I wrinkled my nose at it.

"How do you let the light out, Daddy?"

"Talk to Jesus, baby, and when it's extra dark and scary, say His name out loud. Darkness hates it when we do that. It's scared of Jesus' name."

"Really?" My voice got loud as I got excited at the thought.

"Yes, really."

I looked at the Scary Thing in the hall, grinned, and shouted, "JESUS!" The grin spread wider as the scuttling noise sounded again. I jumped up and ran for the hall, yelling, "Jesus!" as I went, over and over again.

Four

Dad was tired and lay down on the couch for a nap after my run through the house. I sat in the crook of his knees to watch my cartoons. But it wasn't long before my eyes were wandering the room. The Scary Things had run away, and the shadows in the corners didn't look nearly as dark as before.

The chatter from the TV filled the emptiness of the house where Mom's voice should have been. I wasn't interested in the show anymore, but Dad's breathing, which sounded like it would soon turn into a snore, told me I needed to be quiet. When I stood, the cushions of the couch squished under my bare feet. Would I be able to step over Dad?

I grabbed the back of the couch, pulling myself up as high as I could before stepping over Dad's legs and standing on the couch arm. A grin spread across my face as I waited to see if he would wake up. Proud of myself, I crept over to the living room picture window. The ground outside was losing its blanket of snow, and brown grass peeked out from bare patches. The sidewalk was a dark grey. I knew that meant water, and water meant melted snow. There were puddles in the gutter across the street, and I could see drips falling from the roofs of our neighbours' houses.

I pressed my nose against the glass. The chill sent a shiver through my shoulders. When I pulled away, my nose print had made a peephole surrounded by the fog from my breath. The gap looked like a door to me, and I giggled as I traced a square around it, topping the shape with a triangle roof.

"Just like our house."

Glimpses of outside flashed at me through the cleared lines of my drawing. It felt so good to be free of the shadows, free of the Scary Things. I paused and remembered the feeling of it wrapping around my throat. I rubbed my neck and wrinkled my nose as colour flashed at me through the window.

I drew my hand across the glass to open up my view. Someone was standing on the sidewalk, looking up at the sky. She looked at my house, then at the neighbours across the street, then down the road. She wore a red cardigan rolled up to her elbows. Wasn't she cold? It was still winter. She looked at me through the glass and blinked, cocking her head to the side. She held a flattish container out in front of her. I knew that container.

"Church Grandma."

Then I jumped, anger flooding my heart as I saw something crawling along the ground within the shadows behind her. I started to shake all over. It was going to touch her! How dare it.

I ran for the door and twisted the large knob. My little hand could only pull it so far, and I had to grasp it a second time to turn it the whole way. My arms pulled like a funny pretzel before I felt the catch release and the door opened in front of me. A wind blew in through the gap. Goosebumps ran over my arms and up my neck.

"No time, Gloria. It will get her!"

Outside smelled like damp garden dirt. I ran down the cement steps before our door and paused on the walkway. Cold pierced through my tights into my toes and heels. I hadn't even thought about my shoes or a coat. Should I go back?

I glanced down the sidewalk. There was Church Grandma. She was walking again, her steps scraping on the cement slabs. The wind carried the sound of muttered words back to me.

"Hurry!" I told myself.

Church Grandma's shuffle seemed like it was much faster than it should be. She turned a corner as I raced after her, trying to let my feet touch the cement for only a burning second. I had to stop for a moment as I reached the corner and looked around to make sure she was still there to follow. I danced in place on the sidewalk, and the movement kept my heart pumping warm blood through my aching legs.

"Maybe I should go back."

I saw the red cardigan and silver hair already halfway down the next block.

I looked behind me from where I'd come.

"No, Gloria. Go!"

I had never felt a tug on my heart like this before. It wasn't fear, just a pull and a rumbling through my chest that told me I couldn't wait. If I could scare them out of my house, then I could scare them away from Church Grandma too.

"CHURCH GRANDMA!"

My hands balled into fists, and my throat scratched from the force as I pushed the words out of my mouth and into the air.

My scream caught her attention, and she stopped and turned towards me as I raced to her. I didn't stop running until I reached her shadow. It lay crooked across the sidewalk, and I jumped on it, landing beside her as she took a step away from me.

"JESUS! JESUS! JESUS!" I yelled at the ground as I stomped my cold numbing feet on the Scary Thing's tail.

It hissed as it ran from my attack, and I yelled at it a second time as it disappeared between two houses.

"Oh, my!" Church Grandma said as she stepped even farther away from me, her hand on her chest, her breath coming in large gasps. "Why ... Why are you swearing at me?"

I looked up into her face. It was blue. I could see goosebumps that mirrored my own across her arms.

"What's swearing? I was prayin'," I told her. "I stomped that Scary Thing *good*. Did you know they don't like it when we say Jesus' name out loud?"

"Really?" Her eyes flashed at me for a second longer before softening. "Well, then, I am so glad you prayed at me."

She paused, just looking. Shivers ran up through my back and into my jaw, sending my teeth chattering as I stood still. My feet were completely numb, and the burning had moved into my legs.

"Little girl, where's your mommy? Why are you outside with no coat or boots?"

"Why are you outside with no coat or boots?" I asked back.

"Oh! I was ...I was going somewhere. Where was I going?" Her eyes darted around the sidewalk, and her face twisted in concentration. I noticed the slippers on her feet as she spun in a circle. They made a shushing noise as they dragged across the cement.

"Church Grandma?"

She stopped looking in circles to stare into my eyes again.

"Who?" she asked.

Now I was getting frustrated, and stomped my foot, though I couldn't feel it much. "That's *you*."

"It is?"

"Yes, you're my Church Grandma. What's in there?" I pointed at the container she still held.

"Cookies. I was taking them somewhere."

"What kind?"

"You know what ... I can't remember." I spied a tear gathering in her eye.

"Let's look!" I jumped closer to her and reached, placing my hand on hers.

There was no warmth to share. It almost felt as if her fingers weren't there. Or maybe it was mine that were missing? But she smiled down at me and pried the lid off the container.

"Chocolate?" I asked as I spied dark chunks peeking from the round lumps.

"I think they're raisins. But maybe ... maybe we should try one just to make sure."

"Okay." I stuck my nose up over the edge of the plastic as I chose one. It didn't smell like chocolate, and the texture of the rounds was bumpy.

"NOT chocolate," I said as I took a sweet bite. "But still good."

"Well, I need to be going." I could see her shivering beneath the red of her cardigan. "If only … If only I could remember which way to go."

"It's okay, Grandma. Don't be scared." I curled my hand around her finger. "Come."

I wanted to go home. I needed to go home. The pull inside my heart had changed, and now I needed my dad. My legs hurt, and I knew he would be angry that I'd left the house. But there was Church Grandma, and I knew he wouldn't want her outside like this.

I was pulling her hand back the way I'd come when I heard a siren. It hurt my ears, and I covered them with numb fingers.

"Oh!" Church Grandma gasped as a white car with flashing lights on top of it pulled up close to the sidewalk. The man inside had only sounded the siren for a second, but it had sent my heartbeat jumping around in my chest. When he stepped from the car, his roundness reminded me of the brown police teddy bear from one of my cartoons. His deep brown eyes danced.

"Hello, ladies. Is one of you Beth Daily?"

"Beth? Yes, Beth Daily is my name. I knew it wasn't Church Grandma …" Beth muttered as the officer grabbed something out of the back seat of his car.

"I'm Officer Gregory. I've been looking for you, Beth. I'm so glad I found you." He smiled again as he wrapped a blanket around her shoulders.

"Looking for me?"

"Yes, Tina called the station. She was worried about you when you left the house."

"Oh ... Tina. Tina?" Her face screwed itself up again, and I could tell she couldn't remember that name.

Officer Gregory pushed a button on the radio buckled to his shoulder. I couldn't understand the words that sounded from it, but he spoke into it and nodded his head as the garbled sounds whispered something to him.

"Yup, I found her. She isn't alone. Got a little girl with her." There were more garbled words and an "Affirmative."

"Now, little one. Who are you?" He crouched down and felt my hands with his big ones. "Oh, so cold, and I have only one blanket."

"I'm Gloria."

"What's your last name, sweetheart?"

"Core. My house is down there." I pointed down and around the corner.

"Gloria Core? Is your daddy Paul Core?"

I nodded.

"Okay, Gloria, we take you home first. Is it okay if I pick you up?"

Again I nodded, and he unzipped his police coat before picking me up and wrapping it around us both.

"Ooof, those little feet and hands are sure cold. How come you're out here without your dad, Gloria?"

"GLORIA! Gloria! GLOOORIA!"

We all turned as the shouting started.

"Uh-oh ..." I whispered as I recognized my dad's voice.

"Gloria!" the calling continued.

"Over here, Paul!" Officer Gregory answered as my dad appeared at the end of the block, his head whipping back and forth as he searched for me.

When he saw us, his shoulders heaved in a deep sigh, and he slowed his pace from a run to a fast walk.

"Thank God," he breathed, still catching his breath as he reached us. "Gloria, what are you doing?"

I didn't want to leave the protection of the officer's warmth, but my dad held out my coat for me.

"She's got no shoes on, Paul, so here, let me hold her while you slip it on, and, Mrs. Daily, I'm sorry, we'll get you into the squad car. Tina should meet us any moment to help get you home."

Church Grandma just nodded as she clutched the open cookie container. She still looked confused.

"I was helping Church Grandma," I told Dad as he slipped my arms into my coat.

His cheeks were bright red from running and the cold wind. "You scared me, Gloria. You're not supposed to go outside alone."

"But the Scary Thing was following Church Grandma. She needed me."

Dad and Officer Gregory blinked at each other.

"Scary Things?" the officer asked.

"It's a long story," Dad replied.

"Are you okay, Paul?" Gregory placed a hand on my dad's shoulder after transferring me into his arms.

"I will be. I just … For a moment I thought I lost her too." I felt my dad's heart pounding in his chest as he held me close. He'd left his own coat open, and his warmth bled through mine and into my bare hands as I wrapped them around him.

"You can never run out like this again, Gloria," he told me.

"Your dad's right," Officer Gregory added. "Paul, they sell child-proof locks at the dollar store. I would pick some up soon."

"I was helping Church Grandma," I repeated.

"Come, Mrs. Daily. Let's just sit down in the squad car here to keep you warm."

"I was going somewhere, officer," Church Grandma persisted as Officer Gregory helped her into the back seat but left the door open.

"I'm going to have to come back and get a statement from you, Paul. Expect a knock at the door in a few hours."

My dad nodded as he turned. "Thanks, Gregory."

I watched as a second car with flashing lights but no siren pulled up, and a second officer let a tall woman with shinning black hair out of the back seat.

"Look, Daddy. It's Cookie Lady." I pointed as he kept walking but glanced back.

"Yes, that's Tina Hearth from church, Gloria."

"She gives out the cookies with the coffee."

"Yes, she does."

We watched as she squatted in front of Church Grandma and took her hand into her own.

"I was helping Church Grandma, really was," I whispered as we turned the corner. "She needed me."

My dad was silent as he shifted me to the side and ran his freed hand down his face.

"If someone needs your help again, Gloria, remember to take me with you."

"Okay."

I buried my face into his warmth and wriggled my toes.

"My feet hurt, Papa."

"I bet they do. I'll pull the heating pad out of the closet when we get home, and you can sit on it."

"Hot chocolate?"

"Sure, as long as you don't spill it."

"I won't."

Prayers and Pencil Crayons

Abigail

One

THE ROOM SMELLED LIKE leather and dust from the bookshelves that lined the wall behind Pastor Arthur. His eyes were soft yet serious as he leaned across his desk, hands laced together.

"We need someone to step in for Rose while we look for a long-term replacement, Abigail. Can you do it?"

I picked at the skin around my thumbnail. Desperation and question flashed in his eyes, but the softness sucked me in.

"Are you sure you want me?" I asked.

"I can't think of anyone better."

"I'll need to think about it and talk to Ben."

My heart was full of his praise as I left his office, my wheelchair carrying me almost soundlessly down the hall. But my mind spun with apprehension. Me, working in the church office? Sure, I loved helping out in the kitchen and with setting up small things like cookies and coffee for before and after Bible studies. But … What if I made a mistake? What if I wasn't good enough? What if … What if I hurt someone? That was my biggest fear. What if I did or said something wrong and had to watch someone walk away from our church—or worse, God—all because of me?

It's just for a few weeks.

But it's still so much responsibility.

You love these people.

But …

The more I thought about it, the more I felt a pull within me. As if someone had tied a thread around my heart and was urging me along with gentle tugs.

Several voices inside my mind clamoured to be heard. One sounded like my own voice, full of questions while also excited. A second trembled as it told me all the things that could and would go wrong. One sounded half asleep and told me it was too much work to add to my already full plate, and the last one whispered dark words.

They just want to use you.

He only asked for your help because no one else wants the responsibility.

You will fail, so why even try?

That evening I sat in my favourite recliner and listened to my inner confusion, sifting through the voices, looking for one that was missing. This turmoil wasn't new to me. Every change in my life dragged up their chorus. But I'd learned long ago how to find my way through the noise by looking for the one that often lingered at the back, and spoke in whispers.

I closed my eyes. "Dear Jesus, I wasn't expecting this. I don't know if I want to commit to even a few weeks of such a huge responsibility. Am I reading into it too much? They need someone … immediately. I'm afraid. Please, I need wisdom."

"Wisdom for what?"

When I opened my eyes, Glen, my stepson, was peering down at me from over the back of my recliner. I could see the blond peach fuzz on his chin and a single unsightly long hair growing out of his nose. I reached up over my head and made a show of trying to pluck it out.

"Excuse me! MOM?" He backed away as we both laughed.

"Serves you right for sticking your nose into someone else's prayers."

"Ha! What do you expect if you're doing it in the middle of the living room? Get a room if you want privacy."

"Oh, you!" I almost picked up a book from the side table next to me to throw at him, but he raised his hands in mock surrender and slid around my chair onto the couch.

"So, wisdom for what?"

"Don't be a Nosy Nellie. I haven't even told your dad yet."

"What? Don't you trust me?" Glen flashed a toothy grin I just couldn't resist.

I told him about Rose stepping back from the ministry. I told him how Pastor Arthur had approached me and asked for my help. Then I hesitated ... "But, I'm not sure if I should say yes."

"Well, why not? Like, you're perfect for this. And it's only for a few weeks, right? Come on, Mom. Why not just give it a try?"

"Well ..."

"You can always tell them it's not for you, if it's not for you."

"But what if—"

"What if what?"

I just looked at Glen, his curls spilling into his eyes, his face open and honest. He was right.

"Alright. Where's your dad?"

It still didn't feel quite real to be sitting behind Rose's desk in the small back room she'd used in the church office. Her chair had been moved to make space for my wheelchair and the desk shifted so I could turn around behind it with ease. Day four was almost over and I pulled myself closer to the desk, ready for some fun. The tips of my pencil crayons were sharp, and the light from the ceiling of the tiny office was bright. Blue, green, red, pink—they were all there. The graphite pencil I'd used to draw flowers and write my message on the once blank card was laid to the side, its nub now worn down.

"You are whole," I read the words I'd written in between the flowered edges. Then I prayed, "Thank you, God. With You I'm whole."

I picked up the light pink pencil first and started colouring the edges of a rose then changed to a darker shade before filling the centre with red. I loved doing this. I loved hiding these little treasures all over the church building. Even though they'd been popping up for weeks, no one knew who the artist was. I smiled as I moved on to the green leaves and then a blue blossom at the bottom. I usually made several of the same design, but people had started taking them home, so this time I planned to photocopy the original, save it for the future, and put out the copies. It was still surreal to be working in the church office, but it allowed me to easily replace the cards people took home. I'd already picked the perfect Bible verse to add to the inside of each one.

> *"Now may the God of peace himself sanctify you completely,*
> *and may your whole spirit and soul*
> *and body be kept blameless at the coming of our Lord Jesus Christ."*
> *- 1 Thessalonians 5:23 ESV -*

I'd looked up the verse in several versions and also really loved how The Message Bible worded it.

> *"May God himself,*
> *the God who makes everything holy and whole,*
> *make you holy and whole,*

*put you together—spirit, soul, and body—and keep you fit
for the coming of our Master, Jesus Christ."*
- 1 Thessalonians 5:23 MSG -

I hadn't decided on the one I would use yet. Maybe both? Yes, maybe I would try to fit both versions on one card. You could never go wrong with expanding your understanding of the scriptures, right? Wasn't that why God allowed so many translations of His word?

A knock on the already open door pulled my attention away from a blossom now blushing yellow.

"Hey, Abigail. Are you doing okay in here?" Gail leaned her head into the room and blinked at me under the bright light.

"Yes! I'm done checking in on all the Compassionate Ministries volunteers. Just finishing up one last thing before going home."

"Would you like some coffee while you finish?"

"No, thanks. I'd love to grab one of those date bars on the way out, though. Save one for me, okay?"

Gail chuckled as she nodded before disappearing into the church hall. She was a sweet woman, always checking on me. Maybe sometimes a bit too sweet and maybe she checked on me a bit too often, but she was still a sweet woman. I reached for a pencil sharpener. As the minutes slipped by, the little card came to life—a rainbow bouquet.

"Finished."

Now all I needed to do was photocopy it. I slipped the card into the kangaroo pocket of my hoodie and moved the small joystick on my wheelchair backwards. My ride was smooth, and I exited the small office and peered down the hallway. The photocopy machine was in a utility room a few doors down from me.

"The coast is clear, Abigail. Get a move on." I grinned as I snuck past the half-open doors.

I felt like a child sneaking around while a parent thinks they're napping. It was exhilarating. The utility room was vacant, and I manoeuvred my chair close to the photocopier. Everything was in order. Gail really was an efficient secretary. After I placed my artwork under the scanning lid, I selected colour and fifteen copies.

Start.

Lights flashed, and soon the machine spit out its duplicates, but I frowned at the half-blank pages. Of course my little card was much smaller than a full sheet. Why hadn't I thought of that? Could I turn the pages around and copy a second card on the blank portion? I tried it with one and smiled at my success. I wasn't so bad at this office stuff.

Unable to reach the fresh sheets on a shelf above the copier, I left the paper tray half empty, hoping Gail wouldn't be upset. Once back in my office, I stashed the pages on my desk and collected my purse. Time for home. My chair was gliding down the hall when Pastor Arthur burst from his office and collided with its backrest. His grunt of shock was deep.

"Pastor! I'm sorry."

"Abigail, tell Gail we need to get to Paul and Debora Core's house immediately."

The hairs on my arms stood on end as I looked into his strained face.

"What's wrong?"

"Debora …" He couldn't finish and instead chose to run the rest of the way down the hall, nearly knocking the coat tree over in his rush. "Pray!" he shouted back.

"GAIL!" I called. My heart fluttered in my chest as I watched the door slam behind him. "Gail, something's wrong."

"Yes?" she appeared in her doorway. "What?"

"I don't know."

She blinked at me as I related Pastor Arthur's instructions and described the incident, holding silent as her brows knitted together.

"Aren't you going to follow him?" I asked.

"Oh, yes. I'm on my way." She strolled to the door and carefully removed her coat from the polished wooden tree.

"We should really get a row of hooks." I heard her mutter as the door closed behind her.

A row of hooks would be easier for me, but why wasn't she in a hurry like Pastor Arthur had been? Should I go with them? Questions and indecision stalled my wheels. My fingers hovered over the joystick. Then the look on Arthur's face as he'd called back "pray" flashed into my mind. The word started playing on repeat in my brain.

Pray, pray, pray.

So I sat there in the church office hall, eyes closed, elbows resting on the armrests of my chair, fingers laced together across my middle, and I prayed.

"Dear Jesus, I don't know what's going on, but you do." I prayed for wisdom for Pastor Arthur. I prayed for safety for Paul and Debora. I prayed for peace of spirit in whatever was happening. When I finished, I sat in the quiet and waited, eyes still closed, hands still folded, a question mark in my heart, begging God to tell me what to do next.

My cell phone rang, the noise muffled by the mock leather sides of my purse. The number flashed on the load screen, Gail's name displayed above it.

"Hello," I answered.

"Abigail, they're taking Debora to hospital, but ... They think it's too late."

"What do you mean 'too late?'"

"Paul found her in the garage, in her car."

"What happened?" I snapped, my heart beating an ominous song.

"She closed all the doors and left the car running." We both fell silent. I could hear Gail's breathing coming in slow and controlled while I shuddered.

"Gloria, their little girl?"

"Paul said she's with Mary Cooper, has been all day."

I nodded, though she couldn't see it.

"Abigail, I'm going up to the hospital with Arthur and Paul. We don't know how long … I didn't actually see her. They had already loaded her up. Abigail, I think she is already gone."

"Gone?"

Had I heard a movement on the other end of the call? Was it Gail's turn to be nodding in silence for me?

"God …" I breathed, my eyes still closed.

"Can you call the prayer line? The name sheet's on my desk."

"Of course."

The call dropped with no goodbye, and I carefully turned my chair around and motored to Gail's office. I was hit by a wave of grief and self-doubt that stalled my fingers on the small joystick of my wheelchair.

Why did they ask me to step in last minute for Rose?

How can anything I do help in a situation like this?

Two

It was in the middle of calling the prayer line when I got the text, *"She's really gone."* I wanted to scream. How could this happen? I'd just seen her yesterday at Bible study.

"God, how is this possible? Debora? Bright and bubbly Debora?" He didn't answer my question as I spoke to the empty office.

I finished calling everyone with the updated news. I repeated the same lines again as each person reacted in gasps, tears, or pained silence. Hope is Here Church had lost people before. People aged, weakened, and then passed into the arms of Jesus. I recalled a few dear younger souls who had been called home after battles with illness. We'd all felt so hopeless as they slipped away. But this? Somehow this was different.

"God, how do I pray? What should I say? Is she with You?" That was the hard part. That ugly question. It hurt to ask it, but I still did.

As I drove home, the wheels of my chair locked into place in my modified van, I heard the whispers in my head. I pushed them away, refusing to think about anything but the steering wheel and the road in front of me.

I lived on the main floor of Echo Apartments, in one of the few units that sported a sliding door entryway. I parked the van in the spot marked with a wooden sign, my name printed in bold letters across its face. The owner of our building had made sure I got a parking space within an easy distance of the walkway to the apartment. The fact that we had a tiny enclosed outside space to ourselves? Another blessing. My husband, Ben, parked across the lot, closer to the street. He also drove a large van, but his was owned by the local phone and internet company he worked for. He never complained about the walk, even on the coldest of mornings. It was just a fact that I needed the closer spot, and he always said, "I can't complain about having the parking spot beside the street. I'm always the first one to get ploughed out after a winter storm." He was one of those people who could always see the good hiding in hard places or inconvenient circumstances. Glen was like that as well. I wondered what they would say this evening.

"Damn," was Ben's first reply after I'd pulled open the sliding door and powered over the gentle bump of the doorstop. "Damn, that's hard."

"Ben!" I warned, shaking my head at his word choice.

"What? There isn't any better word I can think of. How's Paul?"

"I only spoke to Gail. If they need me, they'll let me know."

"Just damn."

"Ben!"

He shook his head at me as tears gathered in his eyes. His soft heart waved from behind the shimmers of grief.

"Should I call Paul?" he asked.

My shoulders lifted in a helpless shrug.

"I'll text him. He can tell me if he's ready."

The rest of the evening dragged on as we watched the light fade through the glass of our sliding door. Glen walked through the door just before we pulled a bubbling lasagne from the oven.

"Man, am I hungry!" he said as he sniffed at the air. "Do we have garlic bread today?"

"Nope. Sorry."

"Oh, man!"

His backpack found a home beside the couch, and I smelled fry grease all over him as he walked past.

"Don't take too long washing up. The food's going on the table now," Ben warned him.

Glen lifted his hand in an okay sign before disappearing into his bedroom.

I left the hot lasagne on the stovetop and grabbed the bowl of salad waiting on the counter. The original card I'd made while in the office still rested in my hoodie. I fingered its edges before placing it on the table beside the salad. It felt good to rest my elbows on the hard, smooth surface in front of me. Ben plopped the lasagne down on the pair of trivets and placed his hand over mine.

"You okay?" he asked as Glen took his place across from us.

Glen had traded his work uniform for fuzzy pyjama pants with flames down the sides and an old relaxed t-shirt. We were not a family that kept the dinner table formal. Instead, it was a place to let your hair down and relax.

"What's wrong?" Glen asked as he loaded his plate.

I looked over at Ben, letting my eyes ask him to relay the horrible news. I didn't have it in me to repeat it again.

"Debora Core passed away today."

"What? She's not old, is she?"

I shook my head no.

"Got a little girl, too," Ben added.

"I'm sorry, Mom." Glen reached across the table and took my other hand.

With both of them holding me, I lost it. The tension and stress of the day flowed out of me in tears that soon turned to sobs until Ben pulled me into his shoulder.

"Eat, Glen," Ben said.

For a few moments, I just cried. When I was done, my heart and throat both raw, I looked up into Ben's face and asked, "I have this aching feeling in my chest that there's something I need to do. I don't know why. It's like something is pulling me." Even then I felt the tug in my heart. "Why, Ben? There is nothing I can do."

His arms tightened around me. "Don't know, babe."

"Got to pray about it, Mom," Glen said through a mouth full of lasagna. "You're good at that. Don't you always remind us we got to pray first? Always, about everything?"

"Pray and sleep on it, babe," Ben added.

I nodded again and thanked them both as they served me.

"Not sure how much I can eat," I confessed.

"You know we don't mind leftovers." Ben winked as I pushed my fork into a lettuce leaf.

I watched them both eat as I sat quietly, trying to sort out my feelings. I didn't know Debora well but still considered her and Paul friends. Their little family was in a completely different phase of life than Ben and I. I looked over at Glen, almost a grown man. I was so blessed.

Debora was a beautiful woman—one of those people who look twenty years younger than they really are. I thought back to the day they'd presented Gloria to the church for baby dedication, a proud moment for parents and church alike. I thought back to the many times we'd passed in the halls on Bible study days, the times we had both sung at the hospital together. Once, we'd visited at a church picnic. I'd listened while she rambled on about her life and how Gloria was growing.

I remember rolling my eyes when Ben came to check on me, and Debora hadn't let him get a word in. But still, my wheelchair kept me in the pavilion and away from the beach where most of the other women had gone, kids in tow. Debora had sat with me the whole picnic. She refused to leave me alone. Still, I hadn't pursued a deeper friendship with her. Our worlds seemed so different.

I felt a pull in my chest. What did it mean?

Later that evening, I called Hillary. I was making it a new ritual, checking in on her before either of us surrendered to our beds.

"How are you feeling tonight?" I asked her.

I could hear the creak of her chair as she shifted her position.

"Sore. I don't understand why the doctor wouldn't move my appointment up ... I can barely hold a pen the last few days."

"You just have to wait until Monday, Hillary. I know it's hard, but you can do this."

"Acetaminophen doesn't work, Abigail. Ibuprofen doesn't work. I need something stronger."

"I know, but you have to give Dr. Ivan time to make a plan. Do you want me to come with you on Monday?"

"No, no, I don't need a babysitter."

The noise of shifting fabrics and creaking furniture augmented our conversation.

"Okay, but I'll be calling you that evening. Take notes."

"If I can hold a pen. Sure."

I loved Hillary, but the whine in her voice was reminiscent of a spoiled child. Could she hear herself? Still, I knew keenly that battles with pain were difficult. I'd had my own tangles with it through the years. Pain changed people. I needed to show her grace.

"Hillary, you'll make it through this."

"I know."

As the tones of resignation slipped into her voice, I sent up a silent prayer for wisdom.

"We have a God who walks with us in our pain, Hillary. He understands."

"But does He? Does He really, Abigail?"

"Yes, He does." I felt calm assurance rising from my gut, a warmth that spread up and into my mind as I spoke. "He promised He would always be with us, Hillary."

I heard a grunt on the other end of the call before her "Yes" slipped through. "And was He with Debora?"

I wasn't ready for that question. My breath caught in my chest as I struggled to wrap my mind around words for an answer, but it felt like someone had smothered the letters in butter, and they slipped away as I tried to place them in order.

"Was He, Abigail?"

"I trust He was. I *choose* right now to trust that He was, and is," I managed, but my delivery was weak. It was too soon for this.

"I'm tired, Abigail. Thanks for calling."

"I'll pray for you tonight."

"Don't pray for me. Pray for Debora. Lord, I guess she doesn't need our prayers anymore. Pray for Paul."

It was a terrible way to end our conversation, but end it she did. It left my heart raw and searching for answers. I felt so small and helpless. The weight of reality had been slowly growing inside me all evening. I glanced over at the dining table. My little work of art was still displayed.

"You are whole."

Am I really, God? Am I really whole? It doesn't feel that way right now. Have I been spreading lies and false hope?

I felt that strange tug within me again, but the urge to rip the little card to pieces washed over me. I would have listened to it if I hadn't been sitting in my recliner, my wheelchair pushed in a corner as I enjoyed the deep, receiving cushions. So I just glared at the paper as it highlighted my doubt.

Hillary wasn't the only one who was tired. I felt the exhaustion brought on by emotional turmoil wash over me. I knew the difference between each kind of "tired" that existed. They had their own flavours and aches. I closed my eyes and sat with the feeling, knowing that accepting it was the first step to understanding it, and from understanding, I could move to mending.

I'd had a full day that started with a short shift at the dollar store, ringing through customers and driving up and down the aisles checking on shelf inventory. I'd made a list of everything that would need to be put out for the next shift and checked it with the inventory lists. Pulling it all down from the top shelves in the back was beyond me, but I knew how to make sure all the papers were in order so we knew what we had and when we needed to order more. The four hours had flown by. After lunch, I'd tackled the church office. Rose knew how to keep her space organised, but learning where everything was and communicating with person after person was energy draining. Then, the call had come.

The heartache, the tough questions I'd no answers for, the feeling of helplessness—it had all piled on top of each other, and if I was honest with myself, it had been more than just a full day. This first week of helping in the church office had been brimming with difficulty. Monday had been my first day organizing visits for Compassionate Ministries, and it had ended with me holding Hillary's hand at the hospital. I relived the panic of hearing her fall, the rush of making it to her side, and the shock of learning her secret. Really, it had been one of the heaviest weeks I'd ever experienced.

"When it rains it pours," I reminded myself.

Why was that? Why did trouble come in strings of disruptions?

"Why, God?"

My whispers hung in the air. He gave me no answer, and I felt the silence as a thick fog.

"Abigail." Ben's hand rested on my shoulder, and I opened my eyes to him squatting down beside me. "Sleep on it."

His repeated advice was like a fan, pushing the fog out of my face so I could take in a deep breath.

"You're right."

"You know it!" His grin was gentle and his kiss on my forehead soft.

"Push the chair back this way for me?"

My questioning prayers didn't stop as I pulled the bedcovers over my legs. As the warmth of the blankets pulled me down into sleep, the word "why" echoed through my heart along with a quiet "What now?"

Three

Ben's alarm woke me in the still-dark hours of the morning. As I rubbed the sleep from my eyes, the question "why" hung in the air before me.

"Are you getting up?" Ben asked as he sat on the edge of the bed and slid a leg into the pants he'd entrusted to the floor the night before.

"Not yet," I told him.

"Want an egg for breakfast?"

I nodded a yes and whispered a thank you as his sleep-shaky legs led him out into the short hall. A light flicked on and stabbed into the darkness of our room. As I shielded my eyes from the beams, I began my morning as I should have ended my yesterday.

Heavenly Father, my heart is heavy.

I'm facing a day filled with questions I've no answers for.

Is she with You?

What do we do now?

What do I do now?

Is this pull to action inside my heart from You,

or is it my need to fix this?

I can't fix it.

Jesus, please hold Debora close.

Hold Paul.

Oh, God, hold Gloria.

I reached for the glass of water that I kept ready on the bedside table. The need for replenishing was deep as tears escaped my sleep-dehydrated body.

Jesus, give me words.
Help me find Your hope.
Tell me what to do.

I held the water glass close and closed my eyes as I waited. The sounds of movement in the kitchen called to me.

"Focus, Abigail," I told myself.

A quiet space after a prayer was something I'd made a habit of years ago. I knew my God spoke with a still, small voice I could easily miss in the busyness and noise of life. Most often my wait was met with silence, but sometimes, a nudge, a feeling, or a word would push itself to the surface of my mind. So I waited, only stirring when my bladder told me it was time to move. It would take me a minute to shimmy myself over into my chair and then into the bathroom, then another minute to get situated so I could safely relieve myself.

"I'll meet you in the bathroom, God," I whispered.

I didn't hear God's answer while in the bathroom or in the hall when I paused in the quiet, snug in my wheelchair, trying to listen one last time.

"Abigail, I'm heading out," Ben called, and I motored into the kitchen and waved as he closed the sliding door. The sky was still dark, his face lit by the light above the lintel. That smile ignited a spark in my heart, and I was sorry I'd missed his morning kiss by taking my time getting up.

My fried egg lay in the skillet on the stove, still warm and waiting to be paired with some toast. As I gathered the separate elements of my breakfast onto a single plate and balanced it on my lap for the trip to the table, I heard Glen's alarm. I stifled a laugh as I caught the sound of skin hitting plastic, an attempt to turn off the incessant beeping.

"Delaying your morning will only make you late, Glen," I called to him. His only answer was a groan.

As I sat at the dining table, my little card stared at me. Ben had moved it to the side, up against the wall. I mouthed the words "You are whole" into the quiet.

"You're getting good at making those," Glen said as he lumbered into the chair beside me.

"Really?"

"Yep. I bet you could sell 'em."

"I enjoy giving them away too much for that."

"I'm just saying, Mom—money."

I shook my head and smiled as he pushed matted bangs from his eyes.

"You okay, Mom?"

"I will be."

"Have you prayed yet? I mean, really prayed? Like that power praying you do."

"Power praying?" I lifted my eyebrow at him and took a bite of toast.

"Yeah. You make praying look like an Olympic sport. Sometimes I can hear you while I'm watching TV and you're in your room."

"I don't believe you."

"Oh, yeah? You're amazing. I get past 'dear Jesus' and stall, not knowing what to say. You always know what to say when you pray."

I couldn't believe I was hearing what I was hearing. "I couldn't be that loud, honestly."

"Oh, yes, you are. Loud, I mean, and I still think you should sell those." He stabbed a finger past me towards the little card.

"Well, thank you, Glen. I love you."

"I love you too, Mom."

My heart was all aglow as he got up and walked to the cupboards in search of food. As he retreated, I took in just how tall he'd gotten. Why was I so blessed with the men in my life?

"Thank you, God, for that boy and his daddy."

I was sure I'd whispered but had to blush when Glen turned around and winked at me. "See, there you go again."

Glen opened the back doors of the van for me and made sure the ramp was free of ice before I was even halfway down the walkway to the parking lot. The sidewalk had been scraped and freshly salted. Small white crystals crunched as I rolled over them.

"I'll pray for you today, Mom, at lunch," he told me as I motored up the ramp and past him. "Even if it's just a 'Hey, God, be with Mom.'"

"Thank you, Glen. I'll pray for you too. You've tests coming up, right?"

"Yeah ..."

"You'll do fine. Just try to focus."

"I go to work after school again today, too," he said, changing the subject while fiddling with his coat zipper.

The few minutes it took to drop Glen off at high school was always an interesting start to the day. He was a bubble of humour and loved to fill the space between us with jokes and ridiculous stories of things he planned or what he hoped would happen throughout the morning. I sat back and listened to him talk about the new redhead in class.

"She sits a few desks in front of me, and WOW, her hair is like fire. It's even redder than yours, Mom! I think I'm gonna ask her out."

I laughed at his confident grin.

"Kent already asked her last week, and you should have heard the fire in her words when she said no."

"And you think you have a shot after that?"

"Yes! Well, maybe not. But it'll be worth it just to see that spark in her eyes."

"You be careful with my son's heart. It sounds like she has her hooks in you already."

"Oooh, yeah," he sang while pounding his chest with a fist.

"Good Lord. I hope the poor girl runs." We pulled up to the school, and if I could have raised a leg to kick him out of the passenger's seat and send him on his way down the sidewalk, I would have.

"Be good, Glen," I warned him as a full smile spread across my face.

"Promise!" He slammed the van door, flashing a smile one last time through the lightly frosted window and taking off at a run towards the school's double doors.

I filled the rest of my morning with manning a cash register and directing people to products, and as my shift ended, I waved goodbye to my boss and wondered if I should head home instead of going over to the church as planned. Did they really need me to come in? Yes, it was my first week. But really, should I even be doing this job? Who did I think I was?

No one. You are simply no one.

I rarely let such negative words slip into my heart, but I couldn't shake the feeling of helplessness that had gripped me since yesterday. Still, underneath those words, I felt a tug. The faces of my friends flashed into my mind. Rose, Pastor Arthur, Mary, Hillary, Beth, Tina, and lastly Debora. There were many others in the background as well, people I loved, people I interacted with in so many different ways, all important, no matter how much or how little I knew them.

I locked my wheelchair into place behind the steering wheel of the van and placed a hand over my heart as again that tug pulled, this time harder. "What is it that You want me to do, God?"

I sat there, my hands braced against the steering wheel, ready to grab the gas bar that was my key to forward motion in place of a gas pedal. But there was no clear answer I could think of, so I levered the van into drive and pulled out onto the street.

As I rolled into the church office, a wave of scent washed over me—coffee and caramel. The bubbling of the coffee machine from the table opposite the door was as cheery as any chime would have been. I noticed right away the circle of chairs set up in front of it. Really, I couldn't have missed them as I had to manoeuvre around the one on the end to pass into the hall. Gail stuck her head out of the utility room as I rolled by.

"Hello! Meeting in half an hour, Abigail. I'm glad you made it today."

I stopped and swivelled towards her before she could duck away.

"What happened yesterday? How's Paul? Are you alright?" I moved towards her as her lips puckered like she'd eaten something sour.

"I would rather not talk about it," she replied. "I'm sure it'll be part of today's meeting."

I couldn't help the lift of my eyebrows as she turned away and closed the door to me.

"What on earth?"

"She's upset," Pastor Arthur said from behind me. "Yesterday was hard."

"I'm so sorry, Pastor. Are you alright?"

"No, no, I'm not. Are you?"

"No," I admitted. "And I wasn't even there."

"I'm sure not knowing is hard too."

I nodded as he hid his hands in his pants pockets and turned to go back into his office.

"Half an hour, Abigail. But until then, I need to do some praying."

He didn't close his door, but I left him in silence, sensing something was way off. Was it just grief? I felt an underlying question to it all. What was going on?

I found the photocopies of my artwork in my desk and set to cutting them out and writing both versions of my chosen verse on the insides. Half an hour wasn't much time to get anything else done, but it felt good to do simple busy work. I was worried, and as I read out the words I wrote for others, they sank deep into my heart.

"May God himself, the God who makes everything holy and whole,
make you holy and whole,
put you together—spirit, soul, and body—and keep you fit
for the coming of our Master, Jesus Christ."
- 1 Thessalonians 5:23 MSG -

"God, what does it really mean? I thought I knew, but do I really?"

I noted the time as I heard doors opening down the hall and the murmur of people's voices.

It's time.

I felt the words in my spirit, and I paused before leaving my little end office.

"But time for what, God? Time for what?" I asked him.

I was surprised by the crowd gathering around the grouped chairs and nodded to several of the church's deacons and elders as well as Pastor Arthur and Gail. I did a double-take when Rose walked in. She claimed a chair, and I couldn't help but notice how pale she looked and the tremor in her thin fingers.

The room fell silent as Pastor Arthur called for prayer and asked for guidance. We all blinked at him and murmured amen as he unclasped his hands and rested them on his knees when he sat beside Rose.

"Well, friends, we are in the middle of tragedy. Most of you will know by now that yesterday Debora Core passed away."

The room was filled with nods and a few tears.

"What some of you don't know ..." Pastor Arthur cleared his throat as his voice caught. "What you don't know is that Debora took her own life."

I felt my own tears gathering.

"Paul found her in her car, in the garage, with the doors closed and the engine running. She was gone when he got there."

For a moment, silence reigned, broken only by the rustling of fabric or the shuffling of shoes against the floor.

"We need to stand with Paul as he grieves and support him as he now has to raise Gloria on his own."

Everyone murmured in consent, but Pastor Arthur again paused before continuing.

"I've assured Paul we'll help in any way possible with the funeral."

Again the room filled with nods and "Yes, absolutely," followed by "Of course."

"But." The deep catch in his voice stilled the room again. "An opposing opinion has been expressed to me."

What? We all looked around the room at each other. Rose took Arthur's hand and squeezed it.

"What do you mean?" one elder asked.

"Someone has expressed distaste for this arrangement. They believe that since Debora took her own life, she excommunicated herself from the church and God with her death."

The hairs on my arms rose, and more than one person in the room shouted "What?" while a few looked confused and as if they had just now realized that it might be true.

"That's ridiculous!" someone shouted.

"Is it?" Gail rebutted. "Is it really? 'Do you not know that you are God's temple and that God's Spirit dwells in you? If anyone destroys God's temple, God will destroy him. For God's temple is holy, and you are that temple. 1 Corinthians 3:16-17." She turned in her seat while she recited scripture, making sure everyone in the room was looking at her.

"Now hold on," a grey-haired elder exclaimed. "Make sure you're not taking scripture out of context, Gail."

"We are not here to fight," Pastor Arthur reminded us as someone handed Gail a Bible.

The room was filled with the sound of Gail flipping thin pages as she searched for the words to prove her point. "Here!" She lifted the page up for those closest to her to see.

"The heading says, 'Divisions in the Church,'" someone behind her said.

The hum of heated discussions rippled around the room as people turned to their neighbours and started their own one-on-one arguments. Gail tried to read the Bible passage aloud, but most of those gathered were having none of it, and I cringed as Pastor Arthur raised his voice in an attempt to calm the situation.

I felt a tug within me as I looked around at teary, sad, angry faces. What kind of things were each of these people hiding in their hearts as they shouted at each other?

Someone called "Calm down" and finally the hum began to settle, but Arthur was already sitting in his seat shaking his head, looking defeated. Frustration and pain rippled across his features.

"Listen to yourselves," I said above the whispers in the back of the room. "Our sister is dead, our brother is grieving, and all we can do is shout at each other? We're supposed to be a family."

Someone snorted, and someone else behind me muttered, "We fight like one."

"That's not funny," Pastor Arthur said in response. "So what now?"

I saw fear in some of my brothers and sisters as they shook their heads. In others, anger simmered, and in others, resignation froze. How had we fallen into disarray so fast?

One of the grey-haired elders stood. "We don't have time to argue. We vote, now, only on Paul's situation. If we need to open this can of worms and make a policy decision, we'll do it later." He nodded at Gail as she pursed her lips at him.

She nodded back.

"Just the board members?" someone else asked.

"Yes," Arthur said. "For the sake of peace, I think that's best."

As the church leaders moved down the hall to the room reserved for their meetings, my head spun with the words that started to again float around the room.

"Not right."

"I can't believe that."

"Gail's right."

"Think of Paul!"

"Aren't the living more important than the dead?"

I saw a church shaken to its core as one woman burst into tears and fled. Others followed her, and I felt a ripping inside of me as the cord around my heart tightened and didn't release.

"What just happened?" I asked as I looked at Rose sitting across the circle from me.

The sadness in her face broke me, and I cried ugly tears.

Four

Rose's arm wrapped around me from the side as she settled into one of the cold steel chairs that crowded the room. She perched there, an arm around me, face solemn, and let me cry.

As I leaned into her arm, I felt the papers in the front pocket of my hoodie crumple. I'd brought the cut-out cards with me, thinking that after the meeting, I'd have time to set them around the church.

I pulled one out and stared at it, thinking.

"What does it mean Rose, to be whole?" I asked.

Her eyes scanned the card, their edges crinkled with a soft smile as she read it. "I wondered who was laying those out."

"It started a few weeks ago," I admitted. "I'd been praying. I've been praying a lot these days. For myself. For the church. For you too, Rose." I looked up at her and felt the pull within me so strong I laid a hand on my chest. "I was feeling distant."

"I know that feeling." Rose let her arm slide away from me, but she shifted closer and let her elbow sit on the armrest of my wheelchair. "It's beautiful. Did you draw it?"

I nodded, still searching her face for an answer. Silence stretched across the room, and my heart thrummed with anticipation of her words.

Finally, she spoke. "I'm not sure Abigail. I don't ... I don't know if it's possible to truly be whole this side of heaven." She reached over a few chairs for a pew Bible. It looked like several of them had been placed around the room before the meeting. "Let's look it up."

She read to me, starting at 1 Thessalonians 5:1 with the header "The Day of the Lord." When she reached verse twelve she shifted so we could both view the words.

We ask you, brothers, to respect those who labour among you and are over you in the Lord and admonish you, and to esteem them very highly in love because of their work. Be at peace among yourselves. And we urge you, brothers, admonish the idle, encourage the fainthearted, help the weak, be patient with them all. See that no one repays anyone evil for evil, but always seek to do good to one another and to everyone. Rejoice always, pray without ceasing, give thanks in all circumstances; for this is the will of God in Christ Jesus for you. Do not quench the Spirit. Do not despise prophecies, but test everything; hold fast what is good. Abstain from every form of evil. Now may the God of peace himself sanctify you completely, and may your whole spirit and soul and body be kept blameless at the coming of our Lord Jesus Christ. He who calls you is faithful; he will surely do it. Brothers, pray for us. Greet all the brothers with a holy kiss. I put you under oath before the Lord to have this letter read to all the brothers. The grace of our Lord Jesus Christ be with you.
- 1 Thessalonians 5:12-28 ESV -

I'd read it before adding the verses I'd selected to the card I still held, but hearing her voice curve around the syllables as I sat silent, listening, pulled at something I'd missed.

"It's not about one person, but the church."

Rose nodded in agreement.

I mouthed a few of the words as I thought, *"And we urge you, brothers, admonish the idle, encourage the fainthearted, help the weak, be patient with them all."*

Rose shifted beside me, lost in her own thoughts as her eyes roved over the words.

"Have we lost something vital, Rose? Something we used to have or … at least used to have more of?"

"And what's that, Abigail?"

"Trust … Is it possible to do those things without it? We couldn't help Debora. She didn't trust us with her pain. There are others too—who don't trust us with their pain."

Pastor Arthur and the board members exited the hallway, cutting off Rose's response as we both straightened to watch them pass. Arthur found a seat by his wife while the rest shuffled out the glass office doors.

"Arthur?" Rose asked.

Arthur nodded to the last elder who closed the door when he turned to wave, his face sad and tired. "We'll be taking care of Paul."

Rose and I both let out breaths of relief, and I felt a tense knot in my chest ease.

"I hope we don't lose people over this," Arthur muttered.

"Do you think we might?" Rose pressed.

"Maybe …" Pastor Arthur leaned forward to look at me. "Maybe that's why God has given us such a gentle spirit to join our team."

They both looked at me, and I felt heat rise in my face.

"Abigail ... Rose and I have something to ask you."

Trust ... Trust ... Trust ...

The repetition of the word in my brain haunted me, even as I sat at the dinner table with Ben, picking at the floating vegetables in my bowl of stew like a reluctant five-year-old. We were alone as Glen was "hanging with the guys."

"What do you think, Ben?"

"About what?"

"All of it."

"Well, that's a lot to ask a guy about at once. Pick one thing, and we can tackle it first. Let me warm up the old noggin."

"The food."

"It's good. Could use a bit more salt, though." He smiled at me as he reached for the shaker in the middle of the table. "Next?"

"Why didn't they tell us? Why didn't Debora tell us?"

The creases around his eyes deepened. "Don't know, babe."

Rose had helped lay out my little cards all over the church building after our chat. We'd stuck them in many more places than I usually did. It'd been fun but also difficult as Rose had told me part of Debora's "why." "She's had miscarriages, one after the other for the last year. Paul thinks there was even more than she told him about."

"Her heart must have been in tatters," I gasped, unable to fathom repeated loss like that.

I pulled my mind out of the past and asked Ben, "Why do people think they need to hide their pain?"

He rubbed the back of his neck and then the five o'clock shadow on his chin that was lengthening to a seven o'clock shadow. "There could be lots of reasons people don't share stuff like that. It's personal. You don't just tell anyone and everyone."

"I guess." I couldn't help the disappointment from creeping into my voice. "But the fact is she didn't tell anyone ... Not one person." That string around my heart pulled again. It almost took my breath away, and when I was finally able to open my lungs for air, I shuddered.

"Well, you don't really know that. Maybe she told her family. They don't live here. Would be hard for any of them to help from far away. Maybe she told someone you don't know, here. You don't know all her friends, do ya?"

"I guess not." Memories of Debora's voice filled my mind. The ringing sound of her, the giggle that was so young it could have belonged to Gloria, the constant, sometimes incessant chatter. "It's just ... With Debora being, well, Debora, how could she not tell someone?"

"She sure was a chatterbox, wasn't she?" He chuckled from around a spoonful of beef and potato. "Does it matter why? Knowing doesn't change things."

"I think it matters. We can't change if we don't know what we're doing wrong."

"Now, wait, Abigail. You can't play the blame game. That's dangerous."

I nodded again and let it drop. "What about ... the other thing they asked me. Do you think I can do it? Do you think I *should* do it?"

Ben couldn't hide the glint that crept into his eye. "I think it's perfect for you. How much do they wanna pay you?"

"Ben!"

"What?"

I shook my head at him. "I won't be able to do it if none of the other women trust me."

"Well." He paused to stir his stew. "Then you're just going to have to make sure you're trustworthy."

Change was scary, and during this last week, my world had moved so fast. I was tired. My spirit ached. So, I spent most of Saturday in my recliner, making as many calls for Rose as I could while she took charge of organizing Debora's funeral. I leaned back, relishing the release it gave even while doing my best to help.

I'd never realized everything that went into organizing a funeral. There were so many things we wouldn't be able to help with, things Paul had to decide on his own. But we would be there in the background, ready to jump in when needed and take the small things off his plate.

After the phone calls were done, I had time to sit in silence and listen to my heart.

Trust ... How do you make sure you are trustworthy?

Ben's words had stuck to me like glue, and every time I thought about them, the pull on my heart would make itself known. A small voice within me resounded with the words *it's time. Time to do something*. But the other voices tried to drown it out.

You won't last six months.

You won't be able to keep up.

People won't respect someone like you.

You don't know enough about being a leader.

You shouldn't.

Who do you think you are?

"I know who I am," I told them, shifting against the cushions of my recliner.

Really? You mean the woman who has to ask for help to reach things from the top shelf?

"I'm Abigail. Wife, mother, daughter, friend, power pray-er." I said the last title with my eyes closed, wetness rimming their lids. Glen's remarks from yesterday morning lifted the corners of my lips despite my inner battle.

"I'll last six months because I'll have help learning. I'll keep up because I won't be rolling alone. God will help me do it." My spirit sent up the question, *"You will, right?"*

"I'm a child of God, and if I don't at least try, how will I find what He has waiting for me? I trust Him. Even if I'm only meant to do this for six months, I trust it will be a good six months."

If someone had been listening, they would have thought I was insane, talking to myself, but I didn't care. I'd learned years ago that I needed encouraging words, and when I was alone, I had to be the voice that spoke them, or the clouds would gather and lock me in doubt and fear.

"God. I need You."

I told Rose my decision on Sunday morning after the service. If I was going to see what God had for me in this new role, why not start when my church family needed each other the most?

Five

Rose and her daughter Amy had helped me set out a circle of chairs in the church office entryway again. The coffee was bubbling on the side table, and Amy sat on the floor in a corner, her nose glued to her cell phone screen. The eye rolls had been deep when I'd asked for help, but she'd done it, her mother blinking in astonishment.

"Are we ready?" Rose asked.

"Yes," I said as I joined the circle with my wheelchair.

Rose checked her watch.

"What's the water for?" Amy asked for a second time as she peered up at us from over the top of her phone. She'd growled at me in irritation as she splashed her "new jeans" while carrying it from the women's restroom. I gave her the same answer as I had when she asked then: "Stick around and find out."

As the second church service drew to a close, we could hear people filling the main foyer just outside the office doors. The afternoon service never gathered a big crowd, but the "goodbyes" and "see you laters" still created a buzz that hung in the air. We waited for the others, Rose trying to hide her yawn behind a hand, me praying the itch in my throat would go away.

Is this really the right way to start, God?

My hands trembled as I held them in front of me, my confidence dripping like a sheen of sweat down my back.

"Breathe, Abigail."

I met Rose's eyes as she looked at me, tired yet calm.

"It'll be a good start."

I nodded as the door opened, and Gail entered.

"Good afternoon, Rose, Abigail, Amy." I felt the chill in her demeanour and shrank back. Her left eyebrow rose as Amy waved a hand in the air without taking her eyes off the little screen in front of her. "I was wondering where you were."

"We had a few things to get ready before the meeting," Rose stated.

"Yes, I see that." Gail's gaze had fallen to the plastic basin of water waiting on the floor. "What's that for?"

"Hang around and find out." Amy's mocking tone drew a grunt from Gail as she looked at Rose, who shrugged her shoulders, defeated in the face of her daughter's angst.

Next, Mary and Tina entered together with Beth.

"Look! I brought cookies," Beth chimed, her smile a stark contrast to Tina's red-rimmed eyes.

Tina directed Beth to sit down while she took the goodies to the side table and opened the container's plastic lid. The room filled with the scent of dark sugar and oatmeal, and Amy left her corner to hunt one for herself.

"Only one please, Amy," Rose told her.

"Fiiinnne," Amy drawled as she dropped her second pick back into the container. "I'm not a child," she muttered to her mother's back.

"Are we all here?" Beth asked. "I'm sorry if we're late."

"Beth got a bit lost today, and we had to have a chat with a lovely officer," Tina added.

"Lost?" Rose asked, concern clear in her voice.

"Yes, we'll be getting a panic button and a tracking bracelet for Beth this week. I hope," Tina said. She drew a tissue out of her pocket and dabbed at her eyes before blowing her nose.

"Wandering is normal at this stage for Beth, Tina," Mary assured her. We all nodded in support. "She's so blessed to have you available to live with her for now. We are all grateful for you stepping up for her."

"I'm glad you made it safe, Beth. How was your day?" I asked as the other ladies chatted about the ordeal.

"Oh, it was lovely. I went for a walk with a little girl. But, you know ... I can't remember her name. We had fun, though, when the officer told me I could sit in the squad car. What a lovely man."

I made a note to get the full story later as Hillary joined us. "Good afternoon, everyone. My lord, the last snow drifts are melting fast out there today. Beth! I heard you ran away from Tina. Shame on you."

"I did no such thing," Beth said, offence seeping into her soft voice. "Why would I run away from Tina?"

Hillary just shook her head at her friend and let her have the win. For Hillary, not pursuing the matter more was her own personal victory.

I nodded to her. "How are you today?"

"Fine," was her only reply as she rubbed at her knuckles.

"Well, ladies, I'm sorry to interrupt, but we need to start," Rose said above the gentle hum of our conversation. "First, thank you all for being willing to come. I know this is difficult for all of us."

Tina produced a second tissue to dab at fresh tears. Her mascara ran, and Mary patted her hand as she shifted her chair closer.

"I can't believe she's gone." She blew her nose again. "I just … Can't believe it."

Tina's tears flowed unchecked as Mary pulled her into a hug.

"On Wednesday … In Bible study … I … I told her she talked too much."

"Oh, Tina." It was Rose's turn to lean over and offer a hand of comfort.

"I can't believe I said that!" Several minutes passed before Tina was calm enough for us to continue.

"I should've just bundled the kids up and walked over to check on her." I had to strain to hear Mary's words as they drifted to the floor. Her eyes looked like deep, empty wells.

"I should've spent more time with her," I told them all.

Hillary remained silent as she stared at the floor, nodding. I tried to read the conflicted feelings that crawled across Gail's face but failed.

"Haven't we all failed over the years, ladies?" Rose asked. "We shouldn't be blaming ourselves for this, but can we learn to do better?"

"Debora wasn't a good Christian. She was slipping." Gail's voice was hard and her eyes set. Any confusion from a moment ago had clearly been placed aside.

The hair on my arms rose at Gail's harsh words, but Rose shook her head at me. "Gail, there is no such thing as a 'Good Christian,' only a victorious one," she said.

Beth nodded. She had been looking back and forth between people the whole time. "We've lost someone, haven't we?" she asked.

"Yes, Beth. Debora Core died on Thursday," I told her.

"I don't remember who she is."

"It's okay," Hillary assured her. Her voice was gentle. "I'll remember her for you, Beth. You loved to laugh with her."

"Good Christian?" Beth repeated the phrase. "You're right, Rose. There is no such thing. None of us here are good, only God is, but He loves us."

I had to ask for a tissue myself when Beth pulled a little book out of her cardigan pocket. It fell open to a little card, flowers, and leaves encircling the words, "Do you feel loved?"

"Someone gave me this to help me remember," Beth continued. "Isn't it beautiful?"

Rose smiled at me from across the room, and Gail crossed her arms over her chest. She must have known who made it now.

"Who gave it to you, Beth?" I asked.

A shadow passed over her face. "My note says Gloria. But I can't remember who that is," she whispered then added, louder, "Only someone who loved me would want me to remember. Right?"

"Right," I agreed.

"Aren't we here to plan a funeral?" Gail complained. "We have work to do."

"Yes, we do. So let's move on," Rose smoothed over Gail's statement. "First, I would like you all to know that the church board has offered Abigail a part-time place on the church staff, and she has accepted."

The look Gail shot me was like a nail in my chest. Disappointment at her disapproval sent a tremor through my hands.

God, can I really do this? I prayed.

It's time.

I'd heard those words in my heart before. This time they wound around the string that tugged in a gentle rhythm, an encouragement.

"Congratulations!" the other ladies chimed, and Beth clapped for me.

"Thank you."

"She will be the new head of Compassionate Ministries and Women's Ministries and my full partner for planning Debora's funeral as she learns her new roles," Rose continued.

"This is taking forever," Gail muttered.

"Gail, if you do not wish to be here, you don't have to be." Rose's words closed Gail's mouth, but the storm clouds behind her eyes grew thick.

"I'm sorry to drag this out, Gail," I told her. "But I have one more thing I would like to do before getting down to details. If you wish to leave, I understand, but I know I will need your help."

This softened Gail's mood, and she nodded for me to continue.

"Do we trust each other?" I asked the room. "Debora didn't … she didn't trust us enough to ask for help. I had no idea. But, I have a confession." I forced the lump in my throat down with a swallow and splayed my trembling fingers out across my knees. "I wasn't pursuing trustworthiness. Trust has to be earned, and I didn't know her, not enough for her to trust me with her pain.

"Do you trust me?" I continued, my voice cracking with emotion. "This won't work unless you trust me and I, in turn, trust you."

Tina burst into tears again, and Mary curled her fingers around her friend's. Rose nodded, urging me to go on as I glanced at her for support.

"Are we in pain and not reaching out to each other? It's not easy ... but we can start. Here, for Debora. I'm going to need your help. I can't do this without you."

I reached down and unbuckled the safety belt that helped protect me from falling out of my chair. I wiggled forwards and, with the use of my hands, lifted each foot off the wheelchair footrest, then folded it up, making space to access the floor.

"Abigail, what are you doing?" Mary voiced the surprise, confusion, and protest of everyone but Rose.

"Don't hurt yourself!" Hillary gasped and half rose from her seat.

I held out a hand to stop her. "I'm okay."

Rose now had her cell phone out and read "John 13, Jesus Washes the Disciples' Feet."

As she read, I gingerly slid to the floor, pushing my legs out in front of me. It wasn't easy, but I did it. I reached backwards and grabbed the towel I'd wedged into my chair beside me, dragging myself over to the water basin. All eyes were on me while I huffed and eased it forward until it almost touched Gail's feet. The look on her face was utter shock, but she said nothing as I shifted myself backwards and then swivelled so I could take her feet into my hands.

"May I?" I asked.

She nodded and helped me remove her shoes and peel off her socks. It was awkward as I sat beside the water basin and guided her feet into the cool liquid. I thought she might cry as her skin touched the cool water but she clenched her teeth. I gently washed her feet then guided them back into the towel to pat them dry. I looked up into her confused face and smiled, hoping my sincerity would reach her.

I saw a wall there, behind those eyes that glittered like polished steel.

When I finished with Gail, I moved to Rose, then Tina, Mary, Hillary, and finally, I asked Beth if I could wash her feet. Rose finished reading as I dipped Beth's blue-veined and soft-skinned toes into the water. I knew she'd been losing bits of herself to creeping Alzheimer's, but for this moment, her eyes were bright and accepting. I prayed while I lifted a cupped hand of water to run over her ankles that she would please somehow remember this moment.

"Thank you, sister," she said when I gently towel-dried her feet.

Tina spoke from across the circle. "I don't understand. Why?"

"Feet washing. They used to do it a lot back in the 70s," Hillary told her.

"If I then, your Lord and Teacher, have washed your feet, you also ought to wash one another's feet," Rose quoted from the scripture she'd just read.

While I still sat on the floor, a wet towel in my hand, I looked up at all of them and said, "Debora is not the only one who has and is hiding something. I think we all do it."

Hillary looked away from me for a moment, and Tina's lips trembled.

"I should wash the feet of every woman in this church, but I don't think I could physically do that. So ..." I looked at Rose as I continued. "I chose to show the women who stepped up first to help me that there is trust here, and where it is weak, we will build it again, together."

I noticed Amy watching us from her corner, her eyes as big as saucers, her phone forgotten.

It had taken a few minutes to get me back into my chair. All in all, it was quite an undignified ending to such a moment, but it couldn't be helped. I felt free, and the rest of our meeting went smoothly as we delegated out jobs like who could bake cookies and make sandwiches for the reception after the funeral, where we should buy flowers from and how many, who would pick them up, and who would help decorate before the service. When we were finished, I was exhausted.

Tina was the last one to leave as she'd helped empty the coffee machine, and as we pulled on our coats and I grabbed my keys from my purse, she turned and looked at me.

"Abigail."

"Yes?"

"I'm not sure if you can do this job. But I hope I'm wrong. Thank you for being willing to try."

With that, she walked out the church doors, and I knew I'd have hard work ahead of me for the next six months. But I'd also not be doing it alone, not anymore.

Time Line

Early February

Week ONE

Wednesday

- Mary's story starts

Thursday

Friday

Saturday

Sunday

- Tina's story starts

Week TWO

Monday

- Harmony's story starts

Tuesday

Wednesday

Thursday

Friday

Saturday

Sunday

Week THREE

Monday

- Harmony's story ends

Tuesday

- Rose's story starts

Wednesday

Thursday

Friday

- Amy's story ends

Saturday

Sunday

Week FOUR

Monday

Tuesday

Wednesday

- Debora's story starts

Thursday

- Abigail's story starts

Friday

Saturday

Sunday
Week FIVE
Monday

- Beth's story ends

Hillary's story starts and ends
Tuesday
Wednesday

- Debora's story continues

Thursday

- Abigail's story continues

Friday
Saturday
Sunday

- Abigail's story ends

Early – Mid March

About the Author

Mary Grace van der Kroef is a poet, writer, and artist from Ontario, Canada. She enjoys the simple things in life, like a good cup of coffee and heart-to-heart talks with friends. She uses her writing to highlight those simple things while encouraging others and exploring her own inner world. She is a follower of Jesus Christ and writes from a Christian worldview. She believes every person, regardless of circumstance, is a creative being whose stories are important. She cherishes people's differences and believes diverse stories are imperative to understanding what it is to be human.

Thank you

So many people had a hand in me completing and publishing this, my first fiction book. All of my four sisters and my mother were my driving force to complete the manuscript. Thank you, I love you guys so much. Thank you to my husband for supporting me so I have the time and the means to write and publish. Thank you to my editors, you are all beautiful, knowledgeable people, and I am blessed to have been connected with you. To everyone who gave me a word of encouragement, you have no idea how important you are to me and others who create.

Thank you.

Honest reviews are one of the most important things for an indie author's success, and Mary is grateful for each person who takes the time to write a review or rate her books. If you enjoyed this book, please consider taking the time to review or rate it at your favourite retailer or review platform.